Whisper of Hope

J.B. MILLHOLLIN

Grey Place Books—Nashville, TN
ISBN: 978-0-578-55172-2
Library of Congress Control Number: 2019911683
Title: *Whisper of Hope*
Author:J.B. Millhollin
Digital distribution | 2019
Paperback Edition | 2019

New Book Authors Publishing

Previous novels by J.B. Millhollin

Brakus series;
Brackus(Book I)
Everything he touched(Book 11)
With Nothing to Lose(Book 111)
Out of Reach
Redirect
An Absence of Ethics
Forever Bound

Coming Soon...

To Hide from a Northern Wind Series:
Spencer Creek (Book I)
Wilson County (Book II)
Nashville Divided (Book III)
River of Tears (Book IV)

Once Again
Plausible Deception
The Reporter
From Time to Time
An Unacceptable Conclusion

The Kitchen of Thomas Series:
Life Altered (Book I)
Life on Hold (Book II)

Chapter 1

August, 2016
Nashville, Tennessee

Jack Whitmore, hands on hips, looked out his tenth-floor office window, to the street below. He figured it had to be a hundred degrees on the concrete. It was hot when he first arrived at his office building some three hours ago. But since then, the temperature had only gone up. That, coupled with the refection off the streets and surrounding buildings, had to have pushed the street-level temp to well over a hundred.

He couldn't help but notice the back-up of vehicles at every intersection as far as he could see. The traffic in Nashville was the worst he had seen since he moved into his current office some ten years ago. Before long, he figured he might need to move away from the hustle and bustle of the city and into one of the burbs.

His clients would, no doubt, follow him. Most of them had been with him for years. It was an established fact in his business that if you were happy with your financial advisor, you remained with him, no matter the circumstances, for as long as he continued making you money. He wondered how many new clients he had turned down just this week. Business had never been better—nor had his income. Which reminded him, he needed to talk to his own personal banker.

As he walked back to his desk, Jack checked the time, to make sure the bank, located in Aruba, would be open. He wasn't going to make the call if there was a chance his banker wasn't even in his office yet. He autodialed the number after determining the time in that time zone, and concluding his banker would indeed be at his desk, able to discuss business.

"Thomas, Jack Whitmore. How's the weather in the islands today?"

"Good, good Jack, how bout Nashville?"

"I'm thinking I would much rather be there, with you, than here. It's hot and humid. Good old August weather. How's business?"

As he was listening to the banker's response, Claudia, his secretary walked in.

"Hold on, Thomas. What?"

He put his hand over his phone, as she whispered, "I've been meaning to tell you how good you look this morning. Is that new cologne? New suit? You look really good."

"Yeah, thanks. Whatta you want?"

"Your appointment is here. How long you gonna be?"

"Not long. Give me five minutes."

"Okay." She smiled. "Where we eating lunch today? We goin' downstairs or down the street or…"

"Wait. Go. Get out. I'll talk to you when I'm done here."

The smiled quickly disappeared, as she said, "Okay, I'll wait for a few minutes and send him in."

Jack needed to complete the call, and didn't need anyone hearing any portion of the conversation. He waited until she pouted her way through the door, and had closed it behind her.

"Sorry about that. I won't bother you but a minute or two. How are your interest rates?"

"Depends on how long you want to invest, as you know. What are you thinking?"

"I've got some CD's with you that are coming due in about a month. Can you email me your current rates, along with your thoughts as to any possible change in the rates out about 30 days from now?"

"Sure, be glad to. By the way, Jack, we're still holding your monthly bank statements. Do you want us to continue that? I wouldn't recommend it. In fact, my superior has questioned me about it. He wants me to start sending them to you, either electronically or by mail."

"No, no, don't you dare do that. I don't want them coming here to the office or to my home. What's changed? Why can't you just hold them until I ask for them?"

"Change in practice. Do you want me to send them to your wife? Your name is the only one on the account. If, for some reason that doesn't work, we can send them to you in care of another email address if you wish."

Jack thought for a moment. "Okay, start sending them to Beth Jackson. Let me check her email address." He looked for a couple of moments before saying, "Thomas, let me call you back with her address. I don't have it right in front of me at the moment. I'll just call you in a few minutes with it. Oh, and by the way, as concerns future correspondence with me by mail or email, don't *ever* send *me* information concerning the accounts or the amounts I have with you. Even when you send the information concerning rates, just send all the information to the email address I give you later this morning."

He would send the information as a message through his phone—the burner no one but him knew anything about.

He could have sent him an email with her email address, but at this point in time, he wanted nothing in writing anywhere to indicate the offshore accounts were in existence.

Jack terminated the call a few minutes later.

He fluffed up his pillow, placed it behind his head, and leaned back. He would finish watching the evening news and then drive home.

Beth turned on her side, and propped her head up with a pillow as she said, "You wanna go again? I can, you know. Up to you."

"Not tonight."

She was quiet for a moment. Then she smiled as she said, "You putting on a little weight?" She took hold of a small love handle as she said, "I'm just thinkin' you're putting on a little weight, and it might just be slowing you down a little, in more ways than one."

He continued watching the news as he said, "Don't give me that crap. I haven't put on a pound and you know it. We've been together, what about two years now and during that time you've put on more than I have."

"You seem tired, and just a little grouchy. The day tire you out? Or is it that little bit of extra weight you've carrying around, making you tired at the end of the day?"

He quickly looked at her, and immediately noticed the twinkle in her eye, along with the smile she was trying unsuccessfully to hide. He wouldn't respond. He knew he had gained more than a little lately, and didn't need anyone noticing it for him.

He frowned and said, "Would you mind if we got serious for just a minute before I go?"

"I guess. What are we getting serious about?"

"You're gonna get some bank statements from an offshore bank. They'll come to you by email. Just print them off for me, and hold them."

She thought for a moment. "Why are they coming to me?"

"Because that's where I want them to come."

"I'm not sure I want them coming to me. What's going on, Jack? Are you trying to make sure your wife doesn't see them? If you are, I'm not sure I wanna be a part of that."

"So, you don't mind sneaking around and doing this, with me, here in bed, but you don't wanna hold on to a few emails for me? You know, that doesn't make much sense, don't you? I mean, you understand that's somewhat inconsistent, don't you?"

She thought for a moment, before she said, "Okay, yeah, whatever. You're right. I'll hold them for you until you need'em. I'm just not really comfortable with that, but I'll do it if that's what you want me to do."

He never looked at her as he said, "Thanks. When the news ends, I better get home. I told her I'd be there a little late, but in time for supper."

Jack arrived home at six-thirty. As he walked through the door connecting the garage to the kitchen, three-year-old Billy charged across the floor and into his father's waiting arms.

"Hi, Jack. Supper will be ready in about 20 minutes. You have time for about one drink if you wish."

He walked into the living room, with Billy in his arms, and saw the large pile of blocks in the middle of the floor. He sat down, and watched, as his son started to build a stack, doing the best he could to keep them steady as the pile grew higher.

His wife walked in the room and took a chair, watching the stack as it progressed.

"The Andersons want us to come over for supper Friday night. You wanna go?"

He thought for a moment, then said, "Oh, I don't think so."

"Is that it? You just 'don't think so'?"

He continued to help Billy, as he replied, "Yup, that's about it. I just don't think so."

"You wanna go out for supper Saturday night? We could go have a couple of drinks and a steak at that new steakhouse on the east side."

He looked up at her, and said, "Oh, I don't know. Let's see what Saturday brings."

"Let me know *before* then. I'll need to get a sitter for him."

"Okay."

He continued helping Billy with his stack, as she said, "You know we haven't been out for over a month. In fact, we haven't done much of anything in a long time. Do we have issues I don't know about? Should you and I have a talk about our relationship, Jack? If there's something we need to work out, please tell me."

He looked up at her, smiled and said, "No. We're fine." He hesitated before he said, "In fact, tell you what. Go ahead and get a sitter. Let's go out on Saturday."

She smiled, stood, and as she walked back to the kitchen, said, "Great. That sounds like fun."

He continued building the stack with Billy. Might be fun for her, but it would be like pulling teeth for him. He had had enough of her. They had been married five *long* years.

He, once again, considered those few matters he had left that needed his attention before he filed. He was almost ready. Earlier in the week, he had simply concluded he was not going to live in a house with a woman he no longer loved. He just needed a little more time and everything would be as it should be. Then and only then would he be ready to, once and for all, end a marriage he should have ended long ago.

Chapter 2

David Brenden sat across the desk from some woman with the first name of Joyce—maybe—maybe that was her first name. He was almost positive that was her name. David was pretty sure she had a last name to—he just couldn't remember what it was.

She was his last appointment of the day. His secretary, Gail, had unfortunately squeezed her in as his last appointment of what had been a very long day. Joyce had walked in the door 15 minutes late, which put her in his office at five-fifteen. The front door was normally locked by that time, and both he and his secretary gone home for the day.

She wanted her marriage dissolved, she wanted her husband to have no visitation with their children, she wanted this, she wanted that—blah, blah, blah. Whatever. He wondered if she cared what the man across the desk wanted. *He just wanted to go home, that's what he wanted.* He thought how simple his wants really were—he just wanted to go home, put his feet up, and have a beer.

The other complicating factor concerning that scenario, however, was that he had to stop at his mother's house and visit her before he went home.

"But sir, are you telling me I have to give him time with the children? He's a beater. He's beat me. He's beat the kids."

David knew how much seeing his mom would take out of him. It always did. He would be ready for way more than one beer once he finally reached home.

"Might I ask you what your retainer is, sir?"

"In matters of this nature, it's normally seventy-five hundred dollars."

She looked away. As she reengaged in conversation, she said, "So, I take by that you sometimes make exceptions? I don't got that kind of money. I could come up with some, but not that much."

"What reason would there be for an exception? Custody is an issue. Not only that, but you're also wanting to stop him from seeing the children altogether. Division of assets is an issue. Support and alimony are all normal issues of a dissolution of marriage. Your situation is not atypical. I would need that much to start, and probably more before it's all over with."

She stood, and said, "Let me see what I can do. I'll get back to you."

He stood, as he said, "Good day then."

He watched her as she left. If they wanted him, if they specifically wanted him, they always came up with the money. If they couldn't, and he extended credit, he was always left holding the bag—without exception.

After she had walked out of his office and closed the door behind her, Gail opened it, stuck her head in and said, "I'm out of here. You leaving or do you want me to lock you in?"

"No, I need to leave too. I need to see my mother. I'm already late."

As he drove across town, he stopped and bought her some fresh flowers, something he did at least once a week.

He knew it always brightened up her day—something she certainly needed in her condition.

He walked in to find his mother with plate in hand. The plate held what appeared to be a bologna sandwich and some chips. She was just sitting down as he walked in the kitchen.

"Hi, David" She saw the flowers in his hand, and said, "Oh my, those are absolutely beautiful."

She started to stand as she said, "Let me get you something to put them in."

He walked to her chair, and placed one hand on her shoulder, pushing her gently back down into her seat.

"Mom, I know where the vases are. I can handle this. Just go ahead and eat. Where's Martha? She already leave?"

As she sat, she said, "Oh, yes. She's only here until four. Of course, since I've declined a little, she's been staying longer. She doesn't fix me supper, at least not yet. I'm not sure how much longer I'll be able to fix anything for myself, but I'm going to continue to as long as I can."

As David put water, along with the flowers, in the vase, and placed it in the middle of the kitchen table, he said, "You know, Mom, you can't give up yet. They're making advancements in curing cancer every day. I don't like hearing that negative business from you, as you well know."

"You heard that doctor say there was little hope of me living beyond a couple of years. That's what I'm banking on—a couple of years. Now let's change the subject—let's lighten it up." She smiled. "How's that divorce of yours coming? That's a subject that should make you smile."

"Oh, sure. It just makes me tingle all over. The last hearing is tomorrow. The judge will rule then."

"Thank God you two had no children."

"I guess. The only issue that's really left is alimony. We basically agreed to a division of assets and debt, so I expect few surprises with those issues. But alimony is going to hurt for sure. Should have known better than to represent myself. I understand now why they don't recommend it."

She starred at him for a moment, then smiled before she said, "You know, with all you're going through, outwardly you don't show much of the wear and tear. You're still so handsome, you've stayed fit and trim—you certainly don't look like someone that's been under that kind of pressure."

He opened the refrigerator door, and grabbed a beer. He kept a few there for himself while visiting her, and he noticed they were all about gone. As he sat down across from her, he needed to remember to replenish his supply the next time he visited.

"Thanks, Mom. Obviously, looks can really be deceiving. I may look good on the outside, but I'm going through hell on the inside. I'm just so damn glad this is almost over."

She took a bite of her sandwich, then hesitated for a moment, before she said, "Not to change the subject but what about your brother? Have you seen Griffin lately?"

He would need to choose his words carefully.

"No. I haven't seen him in a couple of weeks. Has he been here?"

"Last time I saw him was about a month ago. Is he working?"

"He was at the time, but I have no idea what he's doing now. I got him a job helping some carpenters that are good clients of mine. The boss called and apologized about a week ago. He told me they weren't sure how much longer they were going to be able to keep him. They fired him shortly after that, but I guess he's found employment with another business. I haven't talked to him since he was fired."

She looked away, as she said, "When he was here, he was so nervous. He twitched and fidgeted the whole time he was here. He needs help so badly. I wish there was something I could do—*we* could do. I know he's gotta *want* to get the help he needs, but what a shame. What a loss. So much to offer and he's just a mess. Breaks my heart."

"Until he reaches bottom—until he wants to dry out himself, he's gonna continue to be a lost soul. I've tried. I've done all I can. I've recommended treatment a thousand times, but it just goes in one ear and out the other. I just hope he's not dealing. If they catch him dealing, he's done. Of course, if they do, maybe in prison, he can dry out. Hate to say that, but getting caught could be the best thing that ever happened to him. I'm just afraid he'll overdose."

"Don't say that, David. Let's move on. Since you walked in the door, we've now touched on every negative aspect of our lives. Surely we can find something a little more uplifting." She smiled. "Like our current world affairs."

David couldn't help but laugh, as she started to rip apart one world leader after another.

On his way home, he grimaced as he thought about tomorrow. The only positive element of the hearing was that he would never need to come in contact with her again. Their dissolution had been contentious, in spite of the fact they had so little in the way of assets. Alimony was *the* issue from day one, and tomorrow that matter would finally be settled. He only hoped the judge would place some conditions on his payments to her, and also establish a termination date.

David was still getting used to his new home. He walked up the steps and took his mail out of the mailbox. He walked through the front door, and looked around. She had taken *their* home. That was one of the assets she wanted, and he really didn't give a shit one way or the other. He was renting his new home and it was about half the size of the one she got.

As he turned on the nightly news, and pulled out a beer from the refrigerator, he couldn't help but think about the conversation he had with his mother about his brother. Griffin was truly lost. David was afraid his situation had reached the point of no return.

He would continue to assist any way he could, but it appeared to him, his brother had reached the point where any chance at a normal life was nearly hopeless. He would give most anything to return to the relationship they enjoyed as children. But at this point, he figured it probably didn't matter *what* he wanted, or for that matter, what he tried to do to help. He was just afraid Griffin had most likely reached the point of no return.

Chapter 3

"Okay, so how do you wanna handle the day? I mean, I know you have that hearing with your wife at one, but then what? You have appointments most of the morning, and I assume you'll go eat somewhere at noon, but what time do you expect the hearing to end? What do you wanna do with the remainder of your day after the hearing?"

Both David and Gail sat in the quiet of his office, each with a cup of coffee, just prior to the start of the morning madness. His first appointment wasn't until nine, and it was now a little after eight.

"I really don't think the hearing will last long. The judge already has all the information he needs to rule. We've basically agreed on most issues, except alimony, and all he needed to do was review the specific factors involving that one issue. I would think, if I don't end up lying in wait and strangling her, I'd be back here no later than two-thirty or three. Do you have anything set up for this afternoon at all?"

"You have a new client coming in at three. She has kids and they got a little money. We have no information about her, so the appointment might take a while. Do you want that one to be your one and only this afternoon?"

"Yes, unless someone calls that I really need to see. Use your own discretion. Other than that, just set up appointments on Monday for others that might call. I have a feeling I might be ready to bite someone's head off after the hearing, and I would rather it be yours than a bunch of new clients. Let me just take care of the one you have already penciled in and maybe I'll be in a better frame of mind come Monday morning."

Gail put her pen down, and leaned back in her chair. "What are you expecting today? Your comments worry me a little. Whatta you think the judge might do?"

"I'm hoping he sets alimony around two thousand a month for maybe five years, but I'm afraid it could be higher than that and for a longer period of time. She works, she just got a job, but I make a lot more than she does, so I'm thinking, because of our long-term marriage, and the disparity in income I'm gonna get stuck pretty good. If I do, I just hope he puts some type of restrictions on it, so I don't have to pay her as long as I fricken live."

"What type of restrictions? I don't understand."

"I hope he terminates it after a few years, or he could terminate it if and when she remarries. It's going to be problematic if he lets it run much longer than that. That would be a financial disaster for me."

She stood. "Do you mind handling the office by yourself after the hearing? I think I'll go home at noon, and just see you on Monday morning. I'd rather not be here when you come back from the hearing."

He smiled. "Come on now. I'm never that bad around here, even when I'm really upset."

She said nothing.

"Am I? Have there been times I've really been that hard to get along with after court? Now tell me the truth."

"Well, there've been times when I knew better than to bother you. And the hearing this afternoon is personal— really, really personal." She smiled. "I'll be here, you know that, but I really hope it comes out better than you're anticipating, both for your sake, *and* mine. By the way, once the divorce is over, I got someone I want you to meet. Great girl, and she too, is recently divorced."

He rolled his eyes. "I'm done, at least for a while. I'm not seeing anyone for any reason. It's gonna take a hell of long time to get over the woman I was married to for 14 years. Don't go there, no matter who she is. If I reach the point where I wanna start dating again, you'll be the first to know, but until I give you the word, don't even think about lining me up." He stood. "Now, I gotta go."

She turned to walk out of his office, and as she did, she said, "Okey-dokey, but it's your loss."

Everyone was seated, waiting for the judge to take his place. He had informed the court attendant he needed to make one additional phone call concerning another matter, and then he would open court.

David sat quietly, but as he turned to see if there were others in the courtroom, he noticed only one man, near the back, that apparently had an interest in the proceedings. He was an old friend, but one he hadn't seen in a while. As he heard the judge enter the courtroom, and turned to face the bench, he wondered why he was there—it certainly wasn't to support him. Might she be seeing him? More importantly, was she seeing him prior to their separation?

"Well, folks I've had time to review the files, along with all the testimony given in this matter, and I have come to a conclusion concerning termination of this marriage. Before I go any further, even though the record has been closed, are there any corrections or changes you believe I need to know about?"

David said, "No, Your Honor, not that I know of."

The attorney representing her responded in a like manner.

"Fine, fine. Well, first of all, I'm going to accept your own recommendations concerning division of assets and liabilities. I will incorporate that division in the decree. Now, as concerns the issue of maintenance, I would first point out that this has been a fairly long-term marriage. Fourteen years is long-term."

He studied his paperwork for a moment before he continued. "In addition, I think it's important to note that Mrs. Brenden does now have a job, but certainly it doesn't provide the income Mr. Brenden is making, so I do believe that some type of transitional alimony is necessary."

Once again, he studied his notes before continuing.

"I believe the sum of three thousand per month is appropriate, same which should commence the first of next month."

David took a deep breath. How could he possibly afford that, along with all his own expenses?

"I'm going to leave that in effect for a period of ten years or until Mrs. Brenden remarries, cohabits or dies, whichever occurs first. Now, I realize this may be somewhat higher than Mr. Brenden wanted to pay, or felt was appropriate, but *I* feel it is an entirely appropriate amount. Mr. Brenden if you don't, you can certainly appeal my ruling. Now, does anyone have any questions?"

Neither party responded.

"Good, good, then we are adjourned for today."

David sat in stunned silence. He heard some movement to his right, and as he turned in her direction, he noticed his friend was already standing by her side.

David stood, and walked out the back door of the courtroom, acknowledging neither of them, nor her attorney.

"Your mother' s on the phone. You wanna take it or call her back?"

"Do I have anyone else coming in this afternoon? I'm not showing any more appointments today. Is that correct?"

"Yes, you're done for the day. You wanna talk to her?"

"Yes."

He connected to line one, and said, "Hi Mom, how are you?"

"I think the more appropriate question is, how are you?"

"Doing fine. The day's about over. That, for me, is a good thing."

"Now come on, David. You know what I'm talking about. How did it go? You all finished up?"

He smiled. "The marriage is over, yes. Unfortunately, that was the best part of the proceedings. The rest wasn't so good."

"What'd he do?"

"Three thousand per month."

"Holy shit."

Again, David couldn't help but smile. "My sentiments exactly, Mom."

"Is there anything you can do? That's a lot higher than you were hoping for."

"Yes, it was and no, there's nothing I can do. I could, theoretically, appeal, but I figured, before the hearing started, he would set it between two and three thousand. That's pretty much what the record had established. So, while I don't like it being at the high end of the range, I don't think it's enough of a mistake for the supreme court to change it. Besides, it would take forever to get a decision which I believe would most likely not be favorable for me anyway. No, I'll live with it and hope it eventually goes away before the end of the period for which it was established."

"How long do you have to pay?"

"Ten years."

"Can it end early?"

"Yes. If she remarries, or decides to cohabitate, or dies, it would end. And to be honest the remarriage issue might be a possibility. I noticed an old friend of ours in the courtroom watching what was going on with interest—and he wasn't there for me. So who knows? As for now, I have a new three hundred sixty-thousand-dollar obligation. I can only hope she moves in with someone, or marries someone during that time, or…"

"Yup, or she dies."

"Correct, Mom, that's correct."

"You going to be okay financially?"

"Yes, I'll be fine. It's going to hurt, no doubt about that, but I'll just forget about vacations, along with breakfast—and sometimes dinner, until it's paid. Not taking vacations and missing a few meals will be well worth getting rid of her. I don't like being financially strapped like that, but believe me Mom, it's worth it. Now, how is everything with you?"

They talked for another fifteen minutes concerning her health and what had happened during the day. Later as he sat alone in his office, Gail having gone home, he leaned back in his chair, thinking about the end of his marriage. It wasn't going to be easy—paying her off would be a strain.

But he meant every word he said to his mother earlier in the afternoon. Getting rid of her, and all the emotional strain involved in their relationship near its conclusion, was worth every penny he would ever have to pay her. It was definitely time for him to move on, move in another direction—and this time, without a marriage which had been devoid of love for much longer than he cared to admit.

Chapter 4

They sat across from each other next to the back wall of a small bar located in Antioch, just south of downtown Nashville.

They had met here before, but for a different purpose. Many times, Griffin Brenden would buy what he needed from either Mr. Chase, or his associates, at this very bar. Today the parties were the same: their purpose for meeting was not.

"How'd the job go today?"

"Good, good, Mr. Chase. We almost got it done. The crew worked as quickly and as hard as they could, you know, so we could finish up today. It was a major fix and I knew you wanted it done quickly and right the first time, so we did a good job for you. Should be completed maybe tomorrow. That work out okay for you?"

"Sure, Griff, that works fine. You and your crew do good work. You're not usin any of that stuff you buy from me while on the job though, are you? I know we've discussed it before, but I catch you usin while on the job, you know, you're done. I been through this with you a number of times, but those two things don't go together. I don't mind selling to you, but neither you nor none of your crew's gonna use while working for me."

Griff hurriedly perused the room, then leaned forward, and whispered, "No, no I understand what…"

"Wait a minute. Speak up. There's no one near us. Talk louder."

"Sorry, boss. I understand what you're sayin and I guarantee you no one is using while on the job. By the way, I may need something before I leave, if you got some with ya."

"We can take care of that when we're done talking about whatever it is you called this little meeting for. Now what'd you wanna discuss?"

"Well, I been a thinkin. I think I may wanna go out on my own. Maybe start a little construction business of my own. Only a couple of guys and me. But I need some money to get goin. What would you think about loanin me a little so I could go into business by myself?"

Chase smiled. "You mean so you could become a competitor of mine? Do you think that really makes good business sense for me to do something like that?"

"Boss, you *know* how much business there is in Nashville. We would never even be in the same end of town. I wouldn't provide any competition to you at all. In fact, I would promise to not even bid a job you want. There's enough work for both of us, for sure."

Chase leaned back, and took a long, slow, drink of his beer, while never taking his eyes off Griff.

Once he set his beer down, he said, "Okay, I'll tell you what. Right now I'm thinkin' you're into me for a few bucks, but nothing you couldn't pay me out of a few of your paychecks. You get that paid off, and figure out how much you need, and we'll talk. The interest rates gonna be damn high, but we can discuss that too."

Griff smiled. "I'll put some figures together and let you know when I'm ready to discuss it further. Now, let's talk drugs. You got some stuff on you? I don't have any cash on me, so charge it to me and take it out of what you owe me at the end of the week."

Chase reached for his briefcase. "Sure. Whatever you wanna do."

As Griff drove home after the meeting, his phone rang.

"Hey, bro, what's up?"

"Hi, Griff. Where are you? You off work? You wanna go get a beer somewhere?"

"Better take a rain check. I just got out of a meeting, and Kristy is waiting supper for me. What about next week?"

David hesitated. "Well, okay. You know it's been a while since I've seen you. I talked to mom the other day, and she said she hadn't seen you in a while either. Anything going on? You okay?"

"Yup, everything's fine. Just really busy. Tell you what. I'll give you a call on Monday, and we'll get together after work."

"Sure, that's fine. Just don't forget. I got it marked on my calendar. Don't forget, Griff. I miss you."

Griff laughed. "Yeah, I miss you too. By the way, how *is* mom?"

"Not too bad really. She's hangin in there. I saw her a few days ago, and she's still maintaining her spirits. I can see a bit of regression, but she's hangin in. When you gonna stop by and see her? Like I say, she said it's been quite a while."

"I'll try to stop by and see her tomorrow night. Maybe after work. I would have stopped tonight, but I had that meeting."

"What's that all about? What kind of meeting?"

"Business, strictly business. I'll tell you all about it, if it works out."

"What kind of business? What are you getting…"?

"It's legitimate, David. I know what you're thinkin, but don't go there. It's a business meeting concerning a legal business activity, and has nothing to do with drugs, which I don't do anymore anyway. Don't concern yourself with it. I'll tell you all about it when we get together next week. Better go. I'm almost home."

"Okay. Don't forget about Monday. I'm looking forward to it. I'll touch base with you during the day and we'll figure out where we wanna meet."

Griff terminated the call. Fifteen minutes later he drove into a parking lot of a small duplex on Nashville's west side.

He walked in his unit, and shut the door behind him, as he yelled, "You home yet?"

Kristy said, "Sure am."

He walked in the bedroom, where she had just removed her blouse and bra leaving her clad only in the thong she wore to work.

"What are you doing home so early? You never get home during the summer until eight or nine."

He started to remove his shirt, as he said, "I had that meeting with Chase, and he wanted to meet at five, so that's when we met."

As she grabbed an old ragged tee-shirt from the floor where she had dropped it the night before, Kristy said, "How'd the meeting go? He gonna loan you what you need?"

He turned to face her, gave her that boyish grin, and said, "Yup. I just need to repay what I owe him, and figure out how much I need. I thought later tonight, you and I could figure out how much I should ask him for." He stopped putting on a clean pair of jeans, looked her up one side and down the other, smiled, and said "You know, even as old as you are, you still got a smoking hot body."

She frowned back at him as she said, "Thanks, I think. You know, I'm not that old. I'm certainly not as old as you are. Not having kids probably helped me a little. Now, back to the subject. How you gonna get him paid off?"

He kicked off his jeans, walked toward her, and pulled her close. "We'll get him paid off, don't you worry. Somehow, we'll get him paid."

He kissed her. She pushed him away, as she said, "Not now. Did you get some stuff from him?"

He smiled, as he said, "I sure did. What's for supper?"

"You gotta have him paid off before he loans you any more money? How you gonna get that done?"

"I'm not sure. We can discuss it, but I thought about asking David for it."

"You already owe him. Besides, you know he just finished up his divorce. I have no doubt he's more than broke after that. You have any other ideas?"

He put both his arms around her. "We'll figure it out. Now, you wanna use up some of this stuff I got, or just let it remain in the bag, unused and useless."

"Sure. I've needed it since noon. Supper can wait."

He grinned as he said, "Music to my ears, baby. Just what I was hoping you'd say."

Chapter 5

Hope Whitmore had gone shopping for the first time in weeks. She had received a call from Ann, her closest confidant since grade school, wanting to meet her at Macy's around 10:00 a.m. They had met, shopped for hours, and then split up while Ann went to purchase that 'dress she absolutely had to have.'

Hope now waited for her return, just having finished one cup of coffee and ready for a refill.

She could tell she wasn't the shopper she used to be. At 35, she wasn't in the physical condition she was when she was 20, and today for the first time, she gave in to her lack of physical endurance, telling Ann to go ahead and get the dress on her own—she would just meet her at Starbucks.

She thought about Billy. She needed to buy him something for his birthday which was coming up in a few days. He would turn four and since this was their only child, with no more planned, this would be the first and last time for her to enjoy all those fun birthday activities with a child of this age.

Hope reviewed all she had planned. She wondered if her husband, Jack, would even be there. She had detailed everything they would be doing, and Jack said he would be there, but she knew his word concerning most everything was accurate about half the time. She figured the percentage would not change much with this event—there was about a 50-50 chance he would make an appearance.

As she continued to consider all that was planned, Ann walked into view. She motioned she was going to get in line to get a cup of coffee.

A few minutes later she arrived at the table, and as she sat, she said, "You know you never grow old. You remain as striking today as you were the day you were married. To be honest, that really pisses me off. It appears to me I just keep getting older by the hour, and then there's you. Have you changed in dress size since I met you? Are you still the same size today you were twenty years ago? No, no, on second thought, don't answer. I don't wanna know."

Hope laughed and said, "I wish. Although I can tell you raising a four-year-old doesn't hurt one's dress size—I run after him constantly."

"Everything ready for the party? You all ready to go?"

"Yes. You're coming right?"

"Wouldn't miss it."

"Billy thinks of you as his second mother, so I just want to make sure you don't have any conflicting plans. Wouldn't be the same without you."

She smiled. "Have I told you lately how much I love you? Ever since Tom died, you've been right there every time I needed you. I'm closer to you than any member of my own family." She reached out and placed her hand over Hope's hand. "I just want you to know how much I care for you, for your family." She hesitated. Well, except maybe for Jack." She pulled her hand away. "Jury's still out on him."

Hope smiled, but said nothing.

"Still having trouble with him?"

"No, not so much anymore."

"Don't lie to me, Hope. What's going on now?"

She looked up at Ann and said, "I don't know. I really don't know. I'm not sure this time if it's another woman, or it's just me, or it's his job—a lack of business. Since I married him, at some point, it's been one of the three that's been a problem, but I'm just not sure this time."

"Well, you know it's not his job. At least from what you tell me, he's making more money than he's ever made. One thing about him, he's good at what he does. Just prior to Tom's death, he set us up with a few investments that have been just short of incredible. I really wouldn't think his recommendations concerning our investments would be much different than what he recommended to any of his other clients."

"No I don't think it's his job. He pays so little attention to me. It's like I'm an afterthought, day after day. I've approached him about it a couple of times, but he just waives it off, and says there's not a problem, but there is. There is definitely a problem."

"Another woman?"

"I'm thinking maybe so, but I can't tell. I know one thing. We have no life in the bedroom. We maybe have sex once every two weeks, which is a marked departure from how it used to be. I've approached him about that, but again, he says it's not me—that he's 'just really busy and has a lot on his mind right now'."

"What about Billy? He paying any attention to him?"

"As little as he has to. He plays with him some at home after work, but spends little time with him on the weekends. He's always going to work 'for just a bit', on Saturday mornings, and then he's gone all day. I basically live my life, and he lives his. She turned away as she said, "I'm really not sure when it's going to end and he's going to turn back into the man I married."

"Maybe it's time for a change, Hope."

"I've thought about that, but I just don't want to go through that if there's any chance our relationship might revert back to the way it was. I still love him. And he's Billy's father. I feel the daily contact with his father, even though minimal, is really important."

"How long you going to wait for things to turn around?"

"I don't know. I've never been in this exact position before." She smiled. "And I can't find any rules on the internet for me to follow. I just don't know what to do."

"You got a lotta life left in you, Hope. You would make someone a wonderful wife. Obviously, your current husband hasn't noticed that yet, even though you've been married way long enough for him to figure that out. Looking at it as objectively as I can, sounds to me like it's time to get out."

"Did I ever tell you I've been down this road before with him?"

Ann stared at her, but said nothing.

"I didn't think I had. I really didn't want anyone to know. I filed and told no one. That time the problem was his work, and I knew for a fact it was. But the change in our marriage was substantial. We hadn't had Billy yet. He drank all the time, then came home mean. He promised me he would change and asked me to dismiss it. I dismissed it about a week later. We've been okay until the last few months. Now it's back to the way it was—not so much mean, but just two people occupying the same house as if we're just both paying a part of the rent—our marriage is nonexistent."

"You never told me about the first time you filed. I knew nothing about it."

"No need to."

"Well, that just solidifies my thoughts about you getting this marriage terminated, and moving on. I got a good attorney for you. He specializes in this type of law, he's fair, and he's good at what he does."

"Give me a little time. I'll do what I can to push him into telling me what's going on. If nothing changes in the next few weeks, I'll call you and get his name. Right now, I wanna try, once more, to determine what's going on—what the problem is *this* time. If that doesn't work, I'll call you. I guess I could at least discuss my legal position with a lawyer, even if I don't go ahead and file."

Ann leaned forward and placed her hand over Hope's hand, as she said, "You know, it may not be something as specific as a single issue. Maybe it's just him—maybe he's just a fricken asshole."

Hope smiled. "I'll get it figured out, and if there's nothing can be done, I'll follow your advice. Give me a few weeks. Believe me, I get it. I'm not going to live the rest of my life this way. Just give me a little more time."

Chapter 6

Last night, David Brenden had tried to reach his brother, Griff, for hours. He repeatedly redialed his cellphone, with no success, until well after 10:00 p.m. and until he was just too tired to punch in the number.

This morning, he walked in his office, sat down, and had just started reviewing the files Gail had left on his desk before she left work yesterday. She hadn't arrived yet. She wouldn't walk through the office front door until sometime after 8:00 a.m. He had an hour to himself, and while there was much to review, he knew what needed to be done. He closed the file on his desk and picked up his phone. The first thing he would do, before he did *anything* else, was try to reach his brother—again.

He spent most of the hour alternating between reviewing files and redialing his number. On the eighth try, after leaving a message that would have burned Satan's ears, Griff answered.

"Hey, bro. Awful early for you to be makin' phone calls isn't it?"

"Not important ones. Missed you last night."

Griff hesitated. "Was I…supposed to be…where…where was I supposed to be last night?"

"With me. Remember? We made plans to meet and talk. I tried to reach you for two hours. What happened? Where were you?"

"Oops. You're right. I just forgot. I'm so sorry. Let's set something up again. What about tonight?"

"Where were you last night?"

"I was...let's see…I was home I think—all night. I think I just forgot."

"You didn't answer your phone. Did you forget to do that too?"

"You know, I just got tired of hearing it ring. I turned it off."

David hesitated.

"Let's meet tonight. I'll meet you at that bar down on second street where we normally meet—I can't remember the name of it, but you know which one I mean. I'll be there this time, I promise."

"Can't tonight. What about Friday? Same place."

"Sure, sure that's good for me. Friday's good for me."

"See you then."

He terminated the call, knowing there was no way in hell Griff would remember to meet him. David would go, he would be where he was supposed to be at the correct time, but there was no way Griff would show up.

"Damn it."

"I'm sorry. Is that the kind of greeting I get for showing up a little early at my job in order to do all the things you have for me to do today? I don't know what anyone else would think, but I'm thinkin, under the circumstances, that's not an appropriate salutation."

He quickly looked up, and noticed Gail standing in his doorway.

"Oops, sorry. Didn't know you were standing there. How long you been there?"

"Just long enough to hear you swear at me."

David frowned, and said, "Yeah, whatever. You know that wasn't directed at you. It was however, directed at that stupid brother of mine."

"Uh-oh. That doesn't sound good."

"I'm sure he's using again. I thought putting him through that treatment center would do the job. It was the second time for him. I really thought this time he'd be okay. But, I have no doubt he's using again. He's gonna kill himself if he doesn't stop."

He looked away deep in thought. "It's so frustrating—I don't really know what else to do for him. We were to get together last night, and I thought I'd have a chance to get a grip on how bad it is, but I never could reach him. That's something he does when he is using. He forgets, he doesn't do what he says he'll do, and he sniffs a lot—all factors I've noticed the last few times I've talked to him."

"I'm so sorry, David. I know how important Griff is to you. I wish I could help."

"In the end, there's nothing any of us can do. If he doesn't want to do anything about the problem, *no* one can help him."

He continued to look out the window, as he considered the future welfare of his brother. When he reengaged in conversation, he said, "Enough of this. It's my problem. Actually, it's *his* problem. You and I need to concentrate on the problems of our clients that we *can* have some input in solving. You looked at the schedule today? Anything interesting going on, or just another day full of people wanting to dump their spouses?"

Gail laughed, and said, "Nope. Same as yesterday, which is the same as tomorrow. I think you pretty well wrapped it all up in one tidy little sentence. They start about nine and run until around three-thirty."

"Let's get started then. You have anything for me to sign?"

"I do. I'll bring everything in."

His day was unremarkable. He had no hearings scheduled in court, and, as a result, it was appointment after appointment with every client, male or female, young or old, rich or poor, all wanting the same thing—a permanent separation from their spouse. But, his most interesting appointment came as the day was finally coming to a conclusion.

David stood as she walked in this office. He extended his hand to an attractive, middle-aged woman dressed to kill, and said, "Hi Hope, I'm David Brenden."

She shook his hand as she said, "Nice meeting you, Mr. Brenden."

"Please call me David. Have a chair."

They both sat, as he continued to quickly review the information she had provided Gail.

David looked up and said, "Sounds like you have a few marital issues. First of all, tell me about yourself and your marriage. Has he filed to have the marriage dissolved yet?"

"No. And really, I'm not sure I'm ready to do that either. I'm here basically to ask a few questions and nothing more."

"Okay. Why don't you ask your questions and maybe along the way, I'll ask a few of my own if I need additional information before I give you an answer. Go ahead."

"First of all, does it matter who files—or who files first?"

"No. Racing to the clerk's office to file first is not important. The issues, no matter who files, will still remain the same."

"What's the situation with custody? What factors do the courts consider concerning that? Does my husband have as good a chance for custody as I do?"

"All things being equal, yes he does. Now, there are many factors that come into play concerning custody. Any one of them could tip the scales in favor of you or him."

"Those factors you mention—if I have nothing that might create a problem, and he maybe does, might I get primary custody, with him having limited rights of visitation?"

"Most likely, but no matter what, he's going to have the right of visitation with the child, unless he is a horrible man in some respect or another. You can't take his child away from him, unless he has literally done something awful."

"Well, that's not the case, so I imagine he'll at least get visitation, and that's fine. I don't wanna take our boy from him, but I also don't want a shared arrangement where he gets him half the time. That's something I just don't want to happen."

"I understand. But I would need to get into specifics before I could advise you any further in that respect. Moving on from that issue, are there assets that will need to be divided between the two of you?"

"Yes. But I am not going to push that part of it. Maybe we can even agree on dividing those, along with the debt. But my primary concern is the child."

"I understand. However, you know, *everything* is an issue. If you don't make sure the division of assets is fair, and you find out later he treated you unfairly, you'll most likely regret how you resolved everything. How old is your son?"

"Just turned four. In fact we had his party about two weeks ago, and his dad never even showed up. That was the final straw and why I made this appointment with you."

"Are there other women involved?"

"I don't know. Nothing I can prove right now, but yes, there could be."

"Are there a number of assets to divide?"

"Maybe, I don't know. He handles all the finances, and payment of all the bills—things of that nature. I handle the household, and our son."

"How long you been married?"

"A little over ten years."

"Never any other woman that you know of?"

"No, not that I am aware of anyway."

"What about you, Hope? You been involved with any other man during the marriage?"

"No."

"How old are you?"

"Thirty-five."

"Where's your home?"

"Brentwood."

"Probably a nice home then?"

"Yes, it is. What happens if I just move out and take Billy with me without filing? Can I do that?"

"Yes. Or you could try to get your husband to leave the house without filing. That might likely prove difficult, but you could at least try, if you really think it would help. Let me ask you this, do you still love him?"

She looked away. After considering her response, she turned toward David and softly said, "No, I don't."

"Have you tried a marriage counselor?"

"Yes. A few years back we tried one and everything was okay for a while. But it wasn't long before we were right back where we started."

"Well, it appears to me, based on your answers here today, you can move out, he can move out, you can both move out, but in the final analysis, it isn't going to do either of you any good. You do as you wish, but if the love is gone, which you have told me it is, normally the marriage is over."

She remained quiet. It was clear she was deep in thought concerning what she was about to say.

Finally, she said, "I'm not going to file. I'm just not going to start this. If it's going to happen, I'm going to let him do it." She stood. "If I need someone to help me, I'll make an appointment. I'm hoping it all works out some way, but if I do need someone to help me through this, I'll be back."

David stood, smiled and said, "I understand. Hopefully everything will all work out for you."

She nodded, turned and walked out.

David sat down as he watched her walk out his office door.

He quickly concluded it wasn't a matter of *if* she would be back, but only a matter of *when*. He had no doubt he would see her again, and most likely, very, very soon.

Chapter 7

"Last night was fun."

"Yes it was."

Jack Whitmore was about to go to lunch, but he had just called Beth to discuss coming events with his lover before the afternoon's activities engulfed him.

"We need to discuss a matter involving both of us. Can you talk? Are you too busy to talk?"

Beth said softly, "No, go ahead. It's slowed down here. Earlier today, it was crazy. Women were everywhere. We were selling clothes like none of them had anything left to wear, but it's calmed down now."

"I just want you to know it's gonna be a while before I can see you."

She didn't respond.

"But it'll be worth the wait, believe me it'll be worth the wait."

She hesitated. "You finally going to file?"

"Yes. The paperwork probably won't actually be filed until late next week, but while I'm waiting, and while it's pending, I can't take a chance someone is following me, especially to your house. She isn't aware I have this phone I'm now calling you on. So, I'll continue to use it to call you and remain in touch—fill you in on what's going on. But I'm not going to be able to see you. That's the downside."

She hesitated for a moment before she said, "Explain the upside."

"We'll talk about marriage as soon as the divorce is final."

"*You are kidding.* You really wanna get married?"

"Hell, yes. But, while all this is going on, you don't know me, *period*. In fact, you have no idea who I am, what I do, or that I even exist. I've got a few things in both of our names, like lock boxes in banks outside Nashville, that she knows nothing about, and we need to keep it that way. If anyone asks if you know me, you just need to tell them no. Absolutely no one knows about you and I, and we need to keep it that way. One of the major reasons for that is that I think I'll ask for custody of Billy."

"Wow, that's ambitious for sure. But I'd love to be his mother, realizing of course, he'll still have Hope too."

"I'm just going to wait and see how it all plays out."

"I'm assuming with these different assets you have my name on, you're not going to tell her anything about them."

"No. She came into the marriage with nothing, and whatever we have now, we have because I earned it. She's never worked one single day during our marriage. She's never done a damn thing to increase our net worth. I have money in the islands, in Switzerland, and in lock boxes. All of those accounts have only your name and my name on them."

She hesitated.

"You still there."

"I'm here."

"Something wrong? Did I say something wrong?"

"You really think that's fair—to her, I mean?"

"I do or I wouldn't be doing it this way."

Again her response was only silence.

"I don't get it. Do you *not* think that's the thing to do?"

Beth said, "You know, to be honest, I don't. She's the mother of your child. She did put up with you during those years you've told me about, in the beginning, when things weren't so good. It just doesn't seem fair that you leave her out in the cold."

"Wait a minute, I didn't say that was what I was doing. I'll offer her the cabin at Lake Tahoe, which is free and clear. I'll give her the house here, and some cash. She'll probably also get some alimony. Support for Billy is up in the air, based on what my position concerning custody might be. She'll get more than she's entitled to, but it will still leave you and I a nice nest-egg to start our lives with. She'll be fine Beth, she'll be fine."

"Okay, if you say so. I'm still not sure I entirely agree, but certainly it's all up to you. Your wife, your money, your life. I'm going to miss you. Hopefully we'll be able to talk every day, if that works for you."

"It should. I better go. I need to discuss everything with my secretary. I'll talk to you later tonight."

Just before closing the office for the day, he asked Claudia to come in.

As she took a seat, he said, "There's something you need to know. I'm filing for divorce most likely near the end of next week."

"Actually, that's no surprise to me. I knew you were having issues, and I figured it was just a matter of time. I'm sorry."

"The reason I'm telling you this in advance of filing, is that there may be people coming in asking about me, about my business, about my relationship with people. Don't answer any questions about me in any respect no matter who it is or what they ask, until you tell me what's going on. Do you understand?"

"Okay…like who? What might they ask me about? Who are you thinking these 'people' might be?"

"Could be attorneys representing her, could be private investigators, could even be someone masquerading as a new potential client. Just be careful. I don't want anything going out of this office, business or otherwise, unless I know about it. You just really need to be on your toes about who's walking in the front door and asking questions until this is all over."

"How long's that gonna be?"

"I'm thinking maybe up to six months. I'll let you know how things are going."

She thought about the conversation for a moment, then said, "Is that all?"

He smiled. "That's all, Claudia. You can go. In fact, you can leave for the day if you're ready to head home."

She stood. "I am. Again, I'm sorry for all your family will be going through. I really like Ms. Hope, and Billy."

"I understand. These types of family issues are never very pretty, and I'm sure this one won't be either. I'll see you Monday."

Later that evening, after supper, after Hope had put Billy down for the night, Jack felt the timing was now appropriate.

He turned toward her as she lay quietly on the couch, mindlessly watching whatever was on the TV screen, and said, "We need to talk."

"Okay. What about?"

"You know 'what about'. It's time to end the marriage, Hope. It's just time we each went our own way. Our relationship has been nothing but a joke for months now, and I don't want to live this way any longer."

She looked away, but for only a moment, before she turned toward him and said, "I agree."

"I'll get out. I can get a hotel room for tonight, and then figure out later where I'm going to live while this is all pending."

"That's fine."

"Do you think you and I can discuss settling all this and resolve our issues without having a judge decide everything?"

"I really have no idea. I guess it depends on what you feel is right—what you feel the right division of property and debt between us might be."

"We can discuss that—maybe next week sometime. I've talked to an attorney and he'll file the paperwork sometime during the week. I hope we can settle things up without going to court."

"So do I, Jack."

"I'm sorry, Hope, I really am."

She looked away, as she said, "Can you please go? I would rather be alone."

Jack stood, picked up a bag of his necessities which he previously packed, and already had lying by the side of his chair, out of her sight. Once he reached the doorway, he turned and looked at her. Then, without saying another word, he opened the door, and walked out.

Chapter 8

Both men sat on a bench next to the tennis court, neither with enough strength to stand and walk to the judge's basement and shower.

Finally, David said, "First time you beat me in a hell of a long time. I don't remember you beating me since grade school."

Judge Henry Armstrong remained quiet as he continued to catch his breath.

Finally, he said, "That sir, is bullshit to the max. I, if you remember correctly, beat you in 2014, 6-4, 6-4, and 7-5. It was like, in June. After it was over, you sulked around the court like your mama just spanked you for somethin you hadn't done."

He had been his friend, in fact his *first* friend, when David's family had moved to Nashville during his freshman year in high school. They remained as close as brothers through the years. That was in spite of David's frustration with the judges' thick southern drawl and slow way of talking, which many times caused David to wait forever, while the judge made his way through a sentence—even though David knew full well, long before he finished, how it was going to end.

"You *know* why you remember that so well don't you?"

The judge failed to respond.

"Because it was the only time, before today, in all the matches we've played, you've beaten me, that's why. And, by the way, today, most likely will be the last time you'll beat me."

"Ya know, Mr. Williams, that's just a mite cruel. I must say, sir, that's just a little bit much. I'm thinkin, after today, I may go on to beat you like an old coon dog. I may just beat your ass from now on, time after time after time, now that I've found the secret."

David stood, put his hands on his hips, stared down at his competitor and said, "Secret my ass. If you call luck your secret weapon, you're full of more shit than I thought you were, and really, *sir*, I didn't think that was possible."

The judge looked up, smiled and said, "Let's go shower and fix a drink."

David returned the smile and said, "Good plan. Get up, let's go."

They sat on his back patio, looking over a peaceful 80 acres which he judge now called home.

"You tired of playing tennis? Maybe we should change to some other sport."

"If you wanna change the game because I beat your ass every time we play, hell, I don't care. I'll play whatever you wanna play. I have no doubt I'll beat you at whatever game you name. Now, sir, just name your game."

The judge said, "Let's try something in the pool next time. I think I could beat you at something if it were water related."

"Hell, you can barely swim. Whatever you want. You're the…judge."

"I didn't say I wanted to play in the deep end."

"Whatever."

They sat quietly, both nursing a beer, until Henry said, "How you gettin along?"

"Oh, I'm a little tired. I was tired before I played today, and I'm assuming that's why you beat me."

Henry smiled, took a long swig of beer, and said, "Now, you know what I mean. You been single what, about a month now? How's everything going? You changed your mind about the divorce or still feel it was best for both of you?"

David took a drink, and continued to stare at the wide-open countryside in front of him. Finally he said, "You know from past experience in your own family practice, it's never easy watching a long-term marriage come to an end, no matter the circumstances. It's tough. So many mixed feelings." He turned to face the judge, and said "But, I have had such peace since the marriage ended, I know, at least for me it was definitely the right thing to do. I have no idea where I'll go from here. Obviously, I'm hoping that somewhere along the way, I can meet someone, maybe even have a child, and live the dream, 'happily ever after'. But who knows. I'm just content where I'm at right now."

"She with someone else?"

"That's what I've been told—apparently an old friend of ours. I really don't care. I wish them all the best. It didn't work for us—maybe it'll work for them."

Henry said, "I've been lucky for sure. Susan and I have a good relationship, and both kids seem to be at least a shade of normal. I'm not sure we could ask for any more than that."

"You're the luckiest man I know. You got a great wife, a couple of great kids, and the cushiest job I ever saw. You only lack athletic ability to make your life perfect. Unfortunately, you'll never be worth a shit in that area, but you're the luckiest man I ever saw without considering that particular problem."

Henry smiled, as he said, "You're right. I feel very fortunate. You been going out with anyone, or just playing it low key?"

"I haven't even looked at another woman. To tell you the truth, it feels pretty good, at least for right now, to be responsible only for myself. The marriage turned into nothing but tension the last year or so, and it just feels good not to have to wake up every day under that kind of pressure, I think I'll sit back and enjoy that for a while— maybe forever, who knows."

"I haven't had a chance to visit with you long enough since the hearing to find out exactly what happened. Did the judge drain you financially?"

"Oh, you know how those judges are—they're all a bunch of pricks. Yeah, he hammered me pretty good. He set alimony just high enough to hurt, but not high enough to justify an appeal. I'll be fine. It's gonna mean going without meat for about ten years, but who knows—she might marry this jerk she's dating and it'll all come to an end." He turned toward Henry and smiled. "Or she could just die, and it would end then."

Henry hesitated for a moment, then smiled and said, "You know, both Susan and I know women that would suit you—women that would love to meet you, go out with you. We could…"

"Don't even think about it. I don't want to even think about another woman, or certainly date a woman anywhere, anytime, until I have a chance to recover from this marriage. Thanks, but please don't either of you go there."

"Okay, okay, I understand. Just saying."

Henry stood, as he said, "You want another beer?"

"Whatta *you* think?"

The judge smiled, and walked through the open glass doors leading into his walk-in basement. A few minutes later he returned with two beers, and again took his seat next to David.

"How's the practice? You busy?"

"Yup. As busy as I've ever been."

"You gonna take in a partner, or just travel that road by yourself?"

"By myself. I don't have time to train anyone, and really don't want someone in the office that I need to continually oversee, at least not for now."

Both remained quiet until David said, "By the way, there's a woman that came in to see me once a few weeks ago, and I see by the calendar she's coming in again later this week. She was pretty tightlipped about her situation, but she was inquiring about a divorce. She told me very little at the time, but I assume now he has either filed or she wants to. Her name is Hope Whitmore. You ever hear of her? I think she mentioned maybe her husband's name is Jack Whitmore."

Henry smiled. "Pretty good looker, isn't she? Got a figure to match too. Or did you notice? Did you notice either of those things when she came in?"

"Hard not to. But that doesn't matter at this point. You heard of her husband?"

"Jack Whitmore? Oh yeah, I've heard of Jack. He's one of the hottest money managers in town. He's also the most expensive. He invests money for people, and manages their accounts. The guy, at least from what I hear, is really good. He's also really wealthy."

"She doesn't seem much interested in the money. They have a child, and she's concerned mostly about him. When she told me who her husband was, she acted like I should know him. I had no idea who he was, since I have no money and therefore am never in need of the type of service he offers."

"Just so you know, you've most likely got a hot one there, my friend."

"Hot one how—hot client, hot woman?"

"Both. She'll be easy to look at while you represent her, and, in addition, representing her should result in a nice fee, especially if it's contested."

"At this point, it's all about the fee, buddy, all about the fee."

Henry laughed. "We'll see about that."

As he drove home later in the day, he thought about Henry's remarks. What a bunch of bullshit. David had no interest whatsoever in Hope Whitmore as a woman. His interest in her was in how much revenue she could generate for the office and nothing else.

Still, the judge did have a point. If one didn't consider her as a money producing commodity, she was an attractive woman. But there were many of those around— attractive and single. He might consider that issue later, much later. For now, he needed the revenue she could provide, and that factor and that factor alone, would be the only issue upon which he would focus.

Chapter 9

etty Brenden had just finished an abbreviated breakfast, and had now moved to her living room. It was almost time for her favorite game show to begin, and she hated to miss even the first few minutes. Each day she would situate herself in her favorite chair at least five minutes before the show began.

Martha, walked in the room from the kitchen, and said, "You comfortable? I see you have your pillow. Here let me fluff it up for you before you start watching that show so I won't have to bother you after it begins."

When Betty spoke, her intent was never, ever misunderstood, and today's discourse with her caretaker proved to be no exception, as she tersely responded, "I'm fine."

Martha stopped in her tracks, and said, "Now, Ms. Betty, don't get short with me. You know I'm just a tryin to make you comfortable. That's all I'm doin. Just trying to help."

"Well, help in some *other* way. My pillow's fine. Sit down. Relax. Watch some of this with me. It's a great show."

Martha considered her offer, then slowly sat down, as she said, "You know I have things I should be doing, Ms. Betty. You sure you want me here watching TV with you when I should be cleaning up."

Betty looked over the top of her glasses, as she said, "Now why would I have asked you to sit if I didn't mean it. If I felt you should be somewhere else doing something else, I'd sure as hell tell you. Besides, it only lasts half an hour. You got time later in the day to clean up."

Martha watched until the first commercial break, then stood and said, "I got too much to do. You mind if I go do the things I'm supposed to be doing?"

"No, no go ahead. I don't care. Just stop bothering me. I'd really just like to watch and listen to the *show*, rather than you *and* the show."

Martha walked over to her chair, and said, "Lean up."

As Betty leaned forward, Martha fluffed her pillow as she said, "Okay, I'm done. *Now*, I'll be off."

The commercial ended, and Betty said nothing as the show resumed.

Martha stopped in the doorway, thought for a moment, then turned around and said, "Ms. Betty, you look a little peaked today. You feelin all right?"

Betty never acknowledged her.

Martha cleared her throat, and once again, said, "Ms. Betty, you okay today? Should I be worrying about you?"

Betty slowly turned toward Martha and said, "Hell yes, you should worry about me. You should worry about me *every single day*. I'm dying. For god's sake, you know that. You know I don't have much time left. And yes— today is worse than yesterday. But for now, move your ass to the other room, do your job there. Worry about me like you should, but quit talkin' to me so I can watch this show, which, by the way, is one of the few pleasures I still have left."

About an hour later, as Martha was walking through the room, Betty said, "Can you give me a hand?"

"Sure. Whatta ya need?"

"I need to go to the bathroom. I just need some help getting up and maybe some help on the way. I'm a little shaky this morning."

"Hmm." Martha helped her stand, and on the way to the bathroom, said, "This is a first. You've never needed me to help you stand before."

"Just a little dizzy, that's all. I'm sure it'll pass."

"How was your visit with the doctor last time you saw him. You never mentioned much about it."

Betty said nothing, until they reached the bathroom, when she smiled and said, "Martha, let's just say the days of hoping I get better are long over. It's basically all downhill from here on."

"You telling your boys that's what the doctor is saying, or just keeping it to yourself?"

She stopped, and without turning around, whispered, "What good would it do to tell them? Now go to work. I can handle this from here on. Thanks for the help."

Later that morning, Betty's phone rang.

"Hi, Mom."

"Morning, Griff. How's everything today?"

"Oh, it's fine. Just getting settled in. I need to come see you, but haven't had time. You know how it is."

She hesitated. "Yes, I understand—but I really would like to spend some time with you when you can break free."

"I'm coming to see you, but I'm just not sure when. I should have some time within the next few days, but I did want to at least talk to you before then. I think it's been a while since we visited."

"How's everything going?"

"You mean, am I using again, is that what you mean?"

She hesitated. "That might be part of it, yes. And now, since *you* brought it up, *are you using again*?"

Griff laughed. "No, I'm not. I'm fine. Listen, Mom, I need to get back to work. I'll stop by sometime soon."

She hesitated. "Don't you have a few more minutes— just to visit?"

"I'm sorry, I really don't. I gotta go."

"I understand. See you soon, Griff."

The longer she thought about her conversation with her youngest son, the more upset she became. She touched David's number and he answered immediately.

"You talked to Griff lately?"

"Good morning to you too, Mom".

"I'm sorry. Yes, yes, good morning. Now, have you talked to Griff lately? I just got off the phone with him."

"It's been a few days. Why, what's the problem."

"You know what the problem is and always has been. I just talked to him and I think he's using again. Do you know for sure whether or not he's back on that stuff?"

"No, not for sure. But I, like you, sense that he is. I've talked to him a few times on the phone, and the last time we talked I felt he was probably in trouble again."

"Whatta we gonna do?"

He hesitated. "Well, really there's not much we can do. We've seen him through treatment twice, and apparently neither time did the trick. At some point, you know, the guy has to want to help himself. I haven't seen any indication of that at all. Until that happens, I really think we're wasting our time…and our money."

"I just feel so bad for him and for all those around him."

"Unfortunately, most of those around him anymore, are doing the same thing he's doing. Your voice sounds a little weak today. You doing okay?"

"Yes, yes I'm doing fine. I'm just worried about your brother."

"I know. So am I. I'll continue to try and stay in touch with him. I'll keep you informed."

After she had terminated the call, Martha sat down by Betty and said, "Have you told either one of them about your latest doctor's report? Don't you think they're entitled to know?"

"No, they're not. That's my business, and who I tell is my business. They already know it's not good—and they know it's not going to get any better."

"But, don't you think…"

Betty put up her hand to stop the conversation, as she said, "You know, they both have substantial issues of their own. Griff has a definite problem with drugs, which he apparently can't shake, and David just went through a divorce. At this point, neither of them need updates concerning the status of my disease. They already know how bad it is—they don't need to know how much worse it's becoming."

She turned away, as she said softly, "Good God, this whole family is falling apart. And unfortunately, there's not a damn thing I can do about it, but watch it happen."

Chapter 10

She eagerly awaited his arrival, peering out the window through a gap in the curtains, waiting for him to drive in her driveway. So many times, Griff's promise to appear would end only in disappointment. He would make arrangements to stop by, and then, without further contact, simply fail to appear, or call at the last minute to tell her he wasn't coming.

But not this time! She had waited over two hours for him to arrive, and she quickly moved away from the window when she saw his car drive into view. She stood and walked toward the door, as he walked in.

"Hi Mom, how ya doin?"

She embraced him, and said, "Doing good, Griff. In fact, right now, I'm doing *really* good. I'm so glad to see you."

She leaned back while leaving her arms securely wrapped around his waist, as she said, "How long can you stay? Can I get you a cup of coffee or something?"

"No, no I can't stay long. But I just wanted to see how you were feeling. It's been awhile."

"Yes, it has." She grabbed his hand, and started walking toward the living room. "Come along, let's sit in here." She quickly turned toward him, and said, "You do have time to sit a *minute,* don't you?"

"Yes, I do, but that's about it."

They walked in the living room, and Betty sat down on the couch, Griff sitting near her.

"Where's your helper? Is she here today?"

"She had something she needed to do this morning. I just told her to go do it, and I'd see her this afternoon. That happens often. It's no big deal. I'm not to the point where I need her every minute of every day anyway. How's everything for you? Are you and Kristy still with each other?"

"We are, yes. We're both good. We just live day to day. She works at that fast food place I told you about." He hesitated and looked away for a moment. "I can't really remember the name of the place." He smiled and said, "It'll come to me sometime today. I'm still working construction. We're both doin good."

"Still not married?"

"Nope, still not married."

She hesitated, considering a response to his answer, but then thought better of it, and changed the subject as she said, "Everything else going okay? How's that little problem we've discussed before?"

"I'm feeling good. And as to the drug issue you so subtlety refer to as 'that little problem,' I'm doing okay. Oh, sometimes, when things are tough, I feel like I might regress, but I'm doing good. Now let's discuss you. How's your 'little problem'?"

She smiled. "Okay, yes, we both have a problem. I get it. I'm doing fine. About as expected I guess."

He hesitated for a moment before he said, "Mom, I need a little help."

"Okay. What kind of help?"

"Well, I need to pay off a debt I owe, and then borrow what I need to start a construction crew of my own. I think if I can get it going with my initial seed money, I can just expand from there. We could have our own business—do it all ourselves instead of working for a wage."

"Wow, that sounds great. That sounds like you have it all figured out."

"We do, *except* for the money to pay that original debt off."

She leaned back, hesitated for a second, then said, "Is that why you're here today? You need money?"

"No, no of course not. I'm here to see you—to see how you're doing. The money is secondary to all of that."

"You know, Griff, I don't have much money, never have. And right now it's taking all I have to keep that woman here. I have no insurance coverage for her so it's coming out of my own pocket. In fact, I was going to ask you if you had any to spare."

"You're kidding. You were going to ask me the same question?" He laughed. "We're quite a pair aren't we? Both of us broke, for completely different reasons. I guess that answers my question right quick. Okay let's move on. Tell me how you're getting along, with a little more detail, rather than in generalities."

Griff, his purpose for visiting his mother having quickly vanished, only stayed another 15 minutes, before he said he had used his morning break to come see her, and he needed to return to work. He promised to stop by sometime this coming weekend, and spend a little more time with her, but after this visit, she seriously doubted that would happen.

She quickly touched David's phone number.

"Hi, Mom. Great to hear from you. You seldom call me at work."

"I'll be brief. Have you talked to Griff yet?"

David said, "No. Why? Should I contact him? What's going on?"

"He just left here. I think he's on his way to see you and I wanna forewarn you. He hit me up for a loan. I told him I didn't have enough money to last until I died, let alone give him any. I asked him if he was going back to work, and he said he was, but he needed to see you for a minute first. I just imagine you'll see him shortly and I wanted to tell you what he wanted before he got there."

She heard his secretary whisper, "Just so you know, Griff's waiting out here to see you. I didn't know how long you would be, but I wanted you to know he's here."

David hesitated for a moment, then said, "He's out front now. He wanted money from you?"

"Yes. That's why he's there to see you. He'll tell you about it, but I wanted you to know before he got there so you could be ready for him. You know what he wants it for and so do I, regardless of what he tells you."

"Send him in, Gail. Thanks, Mom. He's walking back to my office now. You might as well listen in, I'll just put the phone on speaker. Don't say anything. You can listen in on our conversation."

"Okay."

She heard him walk through the door, as David said, "Hey Griff. Haven't seen you forever, despite my own efforts to the contrary. What's going on?"

She heard Griff as he sat down, and said, "I know, I know and I'm sorry. I'll try to do better."

"This a social visit or business?"

"Well, I really did wanna see you just because you're my brother, and I haven't seen you in a while. But to be perfectly honest, it's a little of both."

"Okay, can you explain?"

"I'm wanting to start my own business. To do that, I need to pay off an existing loan. I'm looking for the money to do that."

She heard David hesitate before he responded. "You surely aren't thinking *I* can loan it to you, are you? If you are, I'm sorry man, but I am absolutely broke. I just went through that divorce, and I'm cleaned out. I was going to talk to you about that—the divorce—and what it's done to me financially, when I saw you, but I haven't…seen you…since you don't show up when we're supposed to meet."

"I know. I'm sorry. And I understand. I was just hoping you could help, but I understand the timing is bad."

"I can't promise you anything, but give me a few months to recover and maybe we can talk then."

Betty listened while they discussed both of their personal lives and all that had happened since the last time they talked. It only took a few minutes, and she heard Griff tell David he needed to move on.

"Well, Mom, that didn't take long. Clearly, all he wanted was money. He wasn't much interested in my personal or professional life."

Betty said, "That's how he was with me too. I'm really worried about him."

"So am I, but dammit, we can only do so much."

They talked for a few more minutes before she said she would call him later and terminated the call.

As soon as she terminated that call, she punched in Griff's number.

"Hi. Is there a problem?"

"No, no not at all. I was a little worried about you, and your money issue. Did you have a chance to talk to David?"

"I did. Sounds pretty promising too. He's a little short now, but we're going to work it all out in the very near future. In fact, I'm certain enough about it, that I'm not going any further to try to find the financing—he's assured me he'll take care of it. So, yes, it was a good meeting."

They only visited a few more moments before he terminated the call. She knew he had lied to her—without doubt not the first time, and most likely not the last. He was following the same pattern he had in the past—following the same road that had ended in disaster so many other times. This time, like all of those prior occasions, she once again had no solution—nothing that would even begin to stop him from following the same path that had led to so much pain and sorrow for the whole family in the recent past.

Chapter 11

It had been nearly three months since David's marriage had been terminated. As concerned his personal life, he had never been more at ease. But his professional life was a disaster. He needed another secretary, a bigger office and an associate or two—he was simply finding it difficult to keep up—to handle the number of people that found their way through his office door.

"Morning, Gail. Have you looked at my calendar for the day—actually for the week? Good god, you must have been mad at me while you were setting all those people up for appointments. I notice you even set a couple of them up when I have to be in court on Wednesday. You're going to have to call them and reschedule."

"Sorry. There were a couple of days that weren't so good, what with all that was going on here, and what was going on at home."

"You got trouble at home?"

"With three kids, there's always trouble. But last week presented more challenges than most."

"You know, if problems come up at home, you can always leave work and go handle whatever it is that needs to be handled. I'll get by. Certainly, that's way more important than being here."

"At the time, you were heading to court, and there were two appointments sitting in the office waiting to see you when you returned. Going home was not an option."

"Sorry. Hope it all turned out okay."

"It did." She hesitated. "But when you and I have a moment, can we discuss my salary. I'm not sure it's where it should be. Would that be possible?"

David looked away. When he reengaged, he said, "Sure, we can discuss it. But keep in mind I just went through a divorce, and I'm a little light on cash right now. I'll be glad to discuss it, and see what I can do to keep you happy. I certainly don't want to lose you over money. By the way, not to change the subject, but I see that Whitmore woman is coming in again. She get served?"

"Yep."

"Figured."

An hour later, Hope Whitmore walked in his office, and threw the paperwork on his desk.

"He wants full custody."

David looked at the paperwork, which, apparently at some point after she was served, she had wadded into a ball. Even now, she was clearly angered to the point of tears.

He started smoothing out the paperwork on his desktop, and as he did he said softly, "You know, wadding all these papers up does make things a little more difficult. I'm sure you were upset, but…"

"I'm sorry." She looked at him defiantly, and said, "Guess I wasn't thinking of you when I read those for the first time."

He figured, at this moment, it might be best to keep still and continue smoothing paperwork. She was clearly in no mood to be scolded.

Once he was able to read the words and sentences, David determined her husband had, in fact, requested full custody of Billy.

"Did you see the court order attached to the back of the papers? There's a hearing set for next week, next Wednesday, to establish temporary custody with him. Did you know any of this was going to happen? Did he forewarn you about this or discuss that particular issue with you at all?"

"No, absolutely not."

"Do you have Billy physically with you now?"

"Yes, he's at a sitter's house, and Jack has no idea where he is."

"Don't let him go with Jack. Keep him with you until the judge rules. If he wants to see him, let him come to the house. If he asks to take him, you can tell him he can see him in your home, but he isn't taking him until after we get a ruling. Did you see where he's also asking the court to divide the property you both own, set alimony, and set child support?"

"Yes." She was still clearly angered about the custody issue.

David leaned back, and said, "I wonder if we should be discussing anything other than custody right now. Would you feel more comfortable just discussing the custody hearing, rather than discussing all the other issues that the petition raises?"

She looked away, then started to cry.

He pulled out a box of tissues, and pushed them across the desk. As he did, he said, "You know, you can sit. You don't have to continue standing."

"I will when I'm good and ready." She reached for one of the tissues, and dabbed at her eyes. "I can't believe he's doing this to me. I thought I knew him better. I would have never expected him to pull this. I'm still not sure if he's using Billy as a pawn to get his way concerning other issue, or he really wants him."

"That might take a while to determine. In the meantime, we have a hearing coming up next Wednesday. Now, at this point, what are your thoughts?"

"I don't mind if he has visitation, and in fact, I'm really not concerned, within reason of course, how much visitation he has. But for him to have custody even half the time, is absurd."

"Why do you say that?"

She sat down for the first time since she entered his office.

"He works all the time. He's never home. I have no idea why he wants him when he won't have time to be with him, to see him, or play with him…or…"

"Do you have friends that can testify for you—you know, people that can testify concerning how good a mother you are? Are there people you know that might testify against him? What about family? Is there anyone around here that's a member of your family that could testify for you? I really don't want to establish a precedent at this hearing, concerning him having temporary custody until the final hearing, so *this* hearing is pretty important."

"I have friends that could testify as to how good a parent I am. I have no family near here, and very little anywhere else. There's hardly anyone that we know mutually, that can testify for him, because they just don't know him. He's never around."

"I need about three or four of your friends that can be in court on Wednesday to testify for you. What can you, personally Billy, say about Jack, in terms of his parenting ability?"

"Really not much, because he's never home—he's never with either of us. He does very little with Billy other than occasionally play with him—that's it, nothing else."

"Well, I guarantee you he'll have a plan all prepared to submit to the court, as to why he should have custody . I know the other attorney. He's good at what he does, and he handles many custody cases. So we need to be ready."

"Should I have my friends come see you and discuss their testimony?"

"No. Have them call in, and I'll discuss it with them on the phone. If I think I can use them, I'll tell them to be there on Wednesday."

"What about the rest of the shit in the petition? What should I be doing concerning all the other issues?"

"Make me a list of everything you own, along with an estimate of value. Also, make a list of all the debts you're aware of, and the amount you believe the remaining balance on each obligation might be."

"You know, nothing matters to me, but custody." She turned away and whispered, "Nothing matters, but full custody."

"I understand. However, we can't let these other issues go by the board. We need to prepare for *all* of them. I don't want you saying later you wished you had been more diligent concerning all those other issues as *well* as custody."

She moved forward in her chair, and looked directly in his eyes, as she said, "Listen, Mr. Brenden, because I don't wanna tell you again. That child is all that matters to me. I want him with me, with full custody, at all cost. Period. Nothing less will do."

"I understand how you feel, but I would be derelict in my duty to you, if I let all the other issues slide by, so while you can keep telling me that issue is important to you, at the same time I'm going to keep telling you we need to look at the whole picture. Now, don't forget, you and I are on the same side here. We're both working toward the same goal. I'm just not going to let you forget everything other than custody and then tell me later *we*, not *you*, but *we*, made a slight mistake—*we* should have looked at the whole picture. Just so you understand where I'm coming from."

She stared at him for a moment, then said, "Do you need me for anything else today?"

"Not really. We can talk about a retainer the next time you come in. I don't come cheap by the way. Just so you know."

"I know that. I'll give you a check the next time I come in. When do you wanna see me again?"

"Monday."

"I'll set up a time with your secretary as I leave." She stood. "Thanks for hearing me out. I…I can get a little excited as you can tell. I'll see you Monday."

He watched her walk out the door. She was full of fire for sure. He would need to handle her with kid's gloves, but he had done that before—with others. They were in for a fight, the petition made that clear. But a nice retainer would make it all worthwhile. He had traveled down this custody road many times, and been highly successful. Hopefully, this time would prove to be no exception.

Chapter 12

Betty reconsidered her conversation with Griff many times since she had turned him down. She felt guilty. She figured she had more than enough money to handle whatever he needed to pay off the debt he mentioned. But she had no doubt where some, if not all of it, would end up—either being snorted or injected, and she just wasn't going to play a role in his addiction.

"David, did you talk to Griff after he talked to you the other day?"

"No, I didn't. He never called me back, and I never called him. No reason to. He knew where I stood when he left the office. He also knew monetarily it wasn't going to get much better for me in the near future.

"I feel so guilty. I should have helped him."

"Forget it. We've helped him time after time. Look what we got in return. I believe he's worse off now than he's ever been. He'll work it out if he really needs the money. I just hope it's not for drugs this time."

"He never did tell you what he was going to do if you couldn't loan him the money, did he?"

"I didn't ask, Mom, and no, he didn't tell me. Now stop worrying about him. He'll be fine. He's a big boy now. He'll figure it all out."

"Oh, I suppose. He put both of us in a very awkward position." She hesitated. "But, then again, what's new. That's not the first time he's done that to one of us."

"How you feeling today?"

"Ya know, not too bad. Other than my concern for Griff, I feel pretty good."

"Great. Now forget about him, and just enjoy the day."

"Oh, I will. What do you have planned for today?"

"Well, I just got a ruling concerning a temporary custody issue that one of my clients isn't going to like. I need to call her and tell her about it before I do anything else. I've been avoiding it all morning."

"Did you lose the case?"

"No, not really. Not yet, anyway. But the impact the ruling will have concerning final disposition could be substantial. It'll all work out, but my client isn't going to be happy. Now, don't start worrying about me. I'm fine. It's one case, it's one client. The only reason I even mention it is it's fresh on my mind, and I was in the middle of trying to determine how to tell her. I better go so I can figure this out. Love you. I'll call you later this week."

Throughout the rest of the morning, Betty visited with Martha, and even helped her with some of the cleaning. Martha would tell her to 'just stop'—that *she* was hired to do that kind of work, and that she felt guilty having Betty do any of it. Once lunch was over, Betty took her place on the couch, and turned on the TV. Her show was about to begin, and she had told Martha not to even think about vacuuming the living room while it was on.

She heard the phone ring, but, during this time of day, it was no more to her than a distraction—she couldn't care less who might be on the phone while her show was on.

"Betty."

"*Betty.*"

She turned, looked up at Martha and said, "What the hell do you want? I've told you a thousand times to leave me be while I'm watching this show. Now, go do something constructive and leave me alone."

"There's some guy on the phone wants to talk to you. Name's, Howard Keating. I tried to tell him you'd call him back later, but he says you two go way back, and if I tell you who it is, you'll talk to him. Whatta you wanna do?"

She remained silent, continuing to stare at Martha. Finally, she said, "You sure that's who he said he was?"

"Yes. It's not a difficult name to remember."

She looked away, as she said, "Get his number, and tell him I'll call him back."

Martha disappeared.

When she returned a few minutes later, she said, "He told me to tell you he'd be waiting by the phone until you called. He really wants to visit with you. Said it had been a while since the two of you talked. Who is this guy?"

"No one, no one at all."

"Yes, he is. Now, I'm not going to stop pesterin you, until you tell me who this guy is."

Betty turned to watch what was left of her show, but noticed Martha was still waiting for a response. She took a deep breath, then turned off the TV.

She looked out the window, and said, "We dated in high school. In fact, I never dated anyone else all through high school. He was a year older than I was, and when he left for college, we both promised neither of us would date anyone else." She turned toward Martha and smiled. "But you know how that goes. One thing led to another, life got in the way, and soon, he was married and I had two boys."

By then, Martha had taken a chair. "What happened then? You ever see him again?"

"No. Over the years I've thought about him many times, but I just didn't feel comfortable contacting him. Even now, I don't know whether I should call him back."

Martha stood, and walked to the table, where she had placed Betty's phone.

She walked to the couch, held out the phone, and a small slip of paper with his phone number. "Call him."

Betty looked at the phone and finally up at Martha.

"Hurry up. I wanna know what he has to say."

She took the phone, tapped in his number, and said nothing, when he said, "Hello."

Again, he said, "Hello."

Finally he said, "Is this you, Betty? Please answer if it is."

"Yes, it's me, Howard. How are you? Been a long time."

"Yes it has, it certainly has."

"How you been."

"You know, it's been too long. I'd like to see you if you'd see me. Do you mind if I stop by?"

She hesitated. So many thoughts ran through her mind. His wife, her own illness, and so many lost years, stood in the way. Finally she said, "What about your wife? What would she think about you stopping by?"

"She's been gone for almost a year. She died of a stroke a year ago."

"I didn't know. I'm so sorry. That must have been a terrible loss for you."

"It was. We were close. You know Betty, I thought a long time before I called you. I was so nervous, I…but I'd really like to see you, just to catch up, if you have the time."

She thought for a moment. "When?"

"Whenever you have time."

"This afternoon?"

"What time?"

"About two?"

"I'll see you then. Looking forward to catching up."

She terminated the call, looked up at Martha and said, "Holy shit, what have I just done."

A few minutes before two, just after she had changed clothes and fixed her hair, she heard someone knocking softly on the door. Martha smiled as she walked past Betty and toward the door.

Betty stood as he walked in the room.

He walked toward her, hand extended, and she remembered—he was still good looking, maybe a few pounds heavier, but handsome as ever.

He told her to sit, and he sat next to her. Martha got them both a cup of coffee.

"I was so sorry to hear about the passing of your wife, Howard. You were married a long time."

He looked away, as he said, "Yes, we were. We were close. She died unexpectedly. It was a difficult time for me."

"Did you have children?"

"No. She was unable. What about you? Children?"

"Two boys. One is a lawyer, the other's in construction."

He took her hand. "You look well. The years have been good to you."

She looked him straight in the eyes and said, "I have cancer."

Without hesitation, without letting go of her hand, he said, "So do many others."

His response caught her completely off guard. She could feel herself blush.

She said, "What happened? What happened to us?"

"Oh, I don't know—time, events, everything just seemed to snowball and before you know it, it's 50 years later. What's the difference? The past is no longer relevant. I don't know what happened, and it's too late to think about it, or become fixated on it at this point in time. I'm here, you're here, and for now, that's all that matters. How bout you telling me a little bit about your last half a century, and I'll tell you bout mine."

He stayed through the rest of the afternoon, and through two pots of coffee. When he left, they made plans for supper the day after tomorrow, at a small restaurant not far from Betty's home.

He had just walked out the door, when Martha sat down next to Betty and said, "What happened? I could hear the two of you talking, but couldn't understand specifically what you were saying. Good Lord he stayed forever. I haven't seen you smile like that since I started work here. Now tell me all about him, about the two of you. And don't you dare stop just because it's time for me to go home. I'm not going nowhere, Ms. Betty, until I hear the whole story bout the two of you. No sir, I'm not movin. Now you start talkin."

Chapter 13

"Y ou ready for tonight?"

David had been so intently reviewing his file for the hearing he had later this morning, he hadn't heard Gail walk down the hallway. He looked up at her and said, "Hell no. I think I'm going to pass. Call her up, and tell her I had something come up. Tell her my father died or something like that. Just tell her anything so I don't have to go."

"Nope. You told me you'd go out with her, I made all the arrangements, and you're going. This will be the first time you've gone out with anyone since you finished up your divorce, and tonight, you're going to enjoy yourself. You need to pick her up at seven."

"Shit."

"Come on, now, David. Loosen up a little. She's a nice person. I've known her a long time. She too, is recently divorced. You'll have a good time. But to have a good time, you need a little better attitude going in. Now, relax. You're not marrying her. You're going out for supper, and that's it."

"Yeah, yeah I know. What the hell's her name again? Gertrude, or Glenda or… something like that, right?"

"It's Gloria. Write it on the back of your hand if you can't remember—in small letters of course. Now come on, you need to change your approach before you pick her up."

He rolled his eyes, looked at her and said, "Oh, I will—I'll be fine don't you worry about that. I just got a lot on my mind right at this moment. When is Hope Whitmore coming in?"

"One."

"Okay, thanks. Her trial is coming up before long, and we need to get ready to go. You marked off a couple of hours for her, didn't you?"

"Yes. You only have one appointment after her. It isn't until three."

She was just a few minutes late, as she always was. He stood as she walked in the room.

As she sat down, she said, "So, are we all ready to go? We're still on the schedule for two weeks from today right?"

He sat down and said, "Yes, that's when it's scheduled. But we need to discuss that."

"Did all my witnesses call you?"

"Yes. I had them schedule appointments for next week, and they already indicated they would be available for trial."

"Has he made an offer yet? If he hasn't, should we?"

"He made an offer. I just got it this morning. Rather than call you and discuss it on the phone, I figured we could discuss it when you came in."

She sat up, and moved forward in her chair. "What's his offer?"

"Well, you're not going to like it. He wants the child half the time. If you'll agree to that, he'll try to come to an agreement with you concerning property, and drop his demand for full custody."

She continued to stare at him, but said nothing. Finally, she sat back, and said, "That's just bullshit. I'm not going to agree to that."

"Didn't figure you would. If you don't, you realize he'll be requesting full custody at the time of trial don't you?"

"Yes, yes I understand that. I also figure him getting full custody is most likely not going to happen."

"He's had Billy half the time since that last hearing. How has that worked out?"

"I haven't told you enough times? You need to hear it again? It hasn't worked out well. Not at all."

"Specifically, what's the problem?"

Mocking him, she said, "*Specifically,* the problem is he has him *half the time.* But he never sees him when he has him. He's always with a sitter. That's just plain *bullshit.*"

"I understand. And to be perfectly honest, I've never had a judge do what he did. I've never had a judge handle a temporary hearing by limiting testimony to only the two parties, and rejecting testimony from witnesses. Hopefully, being able to call our witnesses this time will help."

"I sure as hell hope so. This arrangement is driving me nuts."

"You know, there are also some other issues we need to discuss concerning the case, specifically property and debt. His attorney has provided me with all the information they say they have concerning assets, but it really makes no sense to me. I mean, it's way short of what I feel the two of you should have accumulated. I think he's hiding assets."

"Probably is. Now, what are your thoughts about this custody issue? Do I need more witnesses?"

"Hold on. Let's go through this property issue first."

"Nope. We're going to discuss this custody issue before we get into that. Now, do I need more witnesses? What are your thoughts about that?"

"I don't believe so. I think we have all we need to make our point."

"I don't wanna end up without sufficient testimony concerning that issue. I have plenty of other people I can call."

"Look, there's no sense in overkill. These three can all testify as to your abilities as a parent, and that's all we need. We should be fine. But what about this property issue? I think he's lying to us."

"What's he offering?"

"Well, he'll give you the house here, and…"

"That's big of him. It's already got a huge mortgage on it. I'll have to sell it and buy something I can afford that's much smaller."

"I understand. Just let me throw out the rest of the offer before we discuss the individual elements, okay?"

"Go on."

"He'll give you the house at Lake Tahoe…"

"Oh sure. What am I gonna do with two…This is just…" She looked at him, then remembered what he had said about discussing "the rest of the offer", and said, "Oops, sorry. Go on."

"He'll give you half of what he shows in cash on his financial statement, and let the court set child support and alimony."

"Not interested."

"You know, Hope, I really think he's lying about his assets. He's got them hidden somewhere, and I think we need to figure that out before we go any further."

"How do we do that?"

"We need to ask for a continuance, and then start…"

"Nope. We are *not* continuing this trial, under any circumstances. We are going to either settle this or try it, one way or the other, and finish this all up within the next two weeks."

He looked at her, trying to determine if there was any sense in discussing a continuance any further.

Hope said, "You know, Jack contacted me about your efforts in trying to determine if he has money he's hiding. He's assured me he isn't hiding anything, and to be honest, I believe him. In fact, he's really angry concerning your efforts to determine if he's lying."

"You know, I really don't care what he thinks, or what he says to you. In fact, you shouldn't be talking to him at all. You need to go through me if you wanna talk to him about something."

She moved forward in her chair, and said, "Here's what I think we should do. I have a feeling if we back off this property business, he'll back off his request for custody."

"What are you saying?"

"*I want you to back off*. Stop looking for other assets. Maybe that will change his approach to custody. I do *not* care about the property. I want my son."

"So you are telling me to do nothing about trying to determine what his other assets are? You're going to go to trial with only the information we now have? That's wrong, that's just wrong. If we're going to do that, I'm going to have you sign a statement saying that's what you've ordered me to do—to stop doing my job. You know, if he doesn't cave in on the custody issue by the time of trial, you could lose out all the way around. You know that don't you."

"I'm willing to take that chance."

"Are you then willing to accept his property proposal because to be honest, based on what I've seen, and what he says the two of you have in assets, it's fair. Again, I have no doubt he's hiding assets, but this is all up to you."

"No, let's wait until trial. Let's leave everything as is, and see what happens on the day of the trial."

"You know, there's no turning back if I back off. There's no 'do over.' We are locked in from here on. The judge isn't going to grant a continuance the day before we try the case."

"I understand and I'm willing to accept the consequences. I'm just hoping if I have you back off, and accept his proposal the day of the trial, he'll change his request for custody."

David studied her for a moment, then said, "Okay. Up to you. We'll just sit back and see what happens, but I really believe you're making a huge mistake."

"It won't be my first, David, nor my last."

The next morning, he arrived at the office after Gail had already opened the front door. He walked right past her without saying a word.

As he started to review his files for the day, she walked in. "Well, how was last night?"

He leaned back, and said, "Do not *ever* set me up with one of your friends again. I had a tough afternoon with Hope the way it was, and then I had to face Greta."

"You know, that could have been part of the problem— that is, if you really called her Greta, when her name was Gloria."

"No, no, I called her Gloria. I misspoke. What the hell does she do? How does she make a living?"

"She works. She has a job. Why?"

"When I let her off at her home, she wanted me to come inside. And she wasn't subtle about what was going to happen. Holy cow, all we had were a couple of drinks and an abbreviated supper and she wanted go to bed with me. Is she a street walker in her spare time? Hell, I wasn't going to go home with her a couple of hours after I met her. As far as I knew, some dude by the name of Bubba could come walking through the door, and shoot me. Do *not* set me up again."

"I think you're overreacting just a little. She called me after she got home. She wants to go out with you again."

"Well, that's not happening under any circumstances. Now go to work. I have things to do."

She said nothing, but she did disappear from his doorway.

He sat back as he considered the prior day. He had a difficult afternoon with Hope, and then had to fight off the overly aggressive Gloria for two hours.

He turned his chair around, leaned back and looked out his window. In a way, it was a sad evening for him. Before he met Gloria, to hear Gail discuss her, he thought she might be someone he could spend some time with, and maybe just enjoy her company.

That certainly didn't work out. He wondered if he would ever enjoy time with another woman as he had Janice, especially right after they were married. Those were good days. Their favorite song, their favorite restaurant, lying next to each other in bed after they had made love—he wondered if he would ever enjoy those feelings, those moments, with anyone again…

David quickly spun around, grabbed Hope Whitmore's file, and started making notes for the trial. It was time to move into reality mode. Time to get ready to confront the issues her case presented, even though, at this moment, he wasn't entirely certain what those issues might eventually be at the time of trial.

Chapter 14

She leaned down and kissed him on the check. "You need to be good for your daddy. Do what he tells you to do."

Billy looked down for a moment, and when he looked up at her, he had tears in his eyes, as he said, "I don't wanna go. I wanna stay here with you."

"Now Billy, your dad loves you and wants you with him since he can't be with you here. You'll have fun. You'll have a good time with him. I'll see you when you return home in a few days."

"Can't you go too?"

She smiled. "No, that's not possible. You don't need me there anyway. You're a big boy now. You'll be fine. Your dad can't wait to see you. He should be here any…"

She heard a car drive up the driveway.

"There, he's here now."

The knock on the door came too quickly. She opened it to find Jack standing there.

He looked down at Billy and said, "Hey there, partner. You ready to go."

She said nothing to Jack. She got down on her knees, pulled his jacket collar up around his neck, and said, "You have a good time. I'll see you in a few days."

Jack took his hand, and together they walked toward his car. She shut the door, leaned against it, and cried.

Hope sat alone, on a small bench inside Opryland Mall just off Briley Parkway. Even though this wasn't the first time Jack had visitation, the pain never lessoned. She simply couldn't forget the image of her son crying, and his last-minute plea, asking her to allow him to remain at home.

She removed a tissue from her coat pocket and wiped away the tears. This was not the way it was supposed to be. This was not the way the divorce was supposed to end. She had not planned on this turn of events when she considered her separation and eventual divorce from Jack. Everything was backward—property division, custody, support— nothing was working out the way she had planned.

"Hope. Hey, I thought we were to meet in front of that one dress shop we like. What are you doing here? I've been looking all over for you. You have your phone with you? I've called you a dozen times."

Hope looked up to find a disgusted Ann walking toward her.

"I'm sorry, you're right. I was thinking for some reason we were meeting here. My fault. I had my phone on mute. Again, I'm sorry."

Ann sat down beside her and said, "You alright? What's wrong? Why are you crying?"

"Oh, I just sent Billy off to be with his father for a few days…again. I guess I should be happy he wants to be with his son, instead of having a husband who could care less about his children, but Billy didn't wanna go, and…"

Ann put her arm around her and said, "Hang in there. Isn't the trial coming up next week? This will all be over then, one way or the other. You don't have much time left.

"Yes. It starts Tuesday. I should be getting ready for it as we speak. I have no idea why I'm here."

"You wanna go get a cup of coffee?"

"No. I need to go home. I need to get all my thoughts organized. I'm meeting with my attorney tomorrow morning."

"How's it going? Are you happy with David? He came highly recommended."

"Yes, he's fine. I have to admit, I haven't really let him do what he's wanted to do. I've probably made a huge mistake in limiting what he really wanted to do. But I just figured, in the end, I'm the one that will benefit or suffer from the decisions I've made—and I'm paying his bill, so I guess I don't feel too badly about that. Yes, I think David is a good attorney. I also like him as a person. It's just all such a mess…"

Ann pulled a tissue from her pocket, and said, "Here. You've destroyed that one. Use this. What are his thoughts about custody?"

"He thinks Jack has a pretty good chance of getting Billy half the time. He doesn't think there's a chance in hell he'll get full custody, but even half the time, to me, is unacceptable. I don't know what I'll do if Jack gets that much visitation on a permanent basis."

"Can I come watch? Can I be there for you when this all starts?"

"Yes. He told me it's an open hearing. Anyone can be there."

Ann was quiet for a few moments before she said, "You going to be okay? What if Jack *does* get him for half the time? Can you handle it?"

Hope looked at her, smiled, held up her tissue and said, "If that happens you better buy stock in the company that sells these things, cause I'm gonna go through one hell of a lot of them."

Hope had waited as long as she could. Since she had arrived home, she had done nothing but sit in her living room and cry. She needed to know how he was.

She tapped Jack's personal cell phone number.

"How's Billy doing?"

"Fine, he's doing fine. Is that the only reason you called?"

"Yes. I was concerned. He left here crying, and I just wanted to make sure he was okay."

"He's doing fine. He's with a sitter, and I'll pick him up in about an hour. I just talked to her, and she said he was playing with his blocks and doing well. Now, is there anything else?"

She hesitated. "Well, no I guess not. I was just…"

"Gotta go. See you in court."

He terminated the call, leaving her on the line, listening to nothing. She held the phone for only a moment before she tapped a different number.

Once she got by his secretary, she said, "David, this is Hope. You heard anything?"

She could hear his chair squeak, as he leaned back.

"No, I've heard nothing. They've made no more offers, we haven't accepted the offer they previously made, and that's where we stand."

"Have you talked to his attorney lately?"

"No."

"Should we call them? Should we start the process of trying to settle all over again?"

"No. His attorney made it clear that was the only offer they would make. So unless you want me to make an offer of our own…"

"No, no I don't wanna do that. Let's just see what happens. I'll see you tomorrow."

She terminated the call. It was getting dark. She had turned on none of the lights in the room. Hope walked to the window, thinking of Billy, wondering if he was really doing as well as Jack said he was.

She pulled another tissue from the box, sat down on the couch, looked out the window and cried. She could only hope that David could pull a rabbit out of a hat at the time of trial. Because, based on her assessment of the case at this point in time, she was really concerned this was not going to end with a favorable result. Unfortunately, her assessment ended with Jack getting just what he wanted—a conclusion which would also be consistent with most every other issue Jack had ever been involved with, for as long as she had known him.

Chapter 15

David was waiting for his first and only appointment of the day.

Hope Whitmore had a 9:00 a.m. appointment and would be the only client he would see today, as he continued to prepare for her trial. While looking through his materials, he once again considered the fact he had never tried a complete case before Judge DeWitt. He was the judge that had ruled on temporary custody, and the result had not been favorable.

Judge DeWitt had only just been appointed to the bench. David was really concerned the judge's ruling concerning temporary matters, could, in fact, affect the final result when they fully tried the case in a few days. Perhaps a short phone call concerning this new judge, would provide him with additional information which might prove helpful.

"Morning, Henry. I wasn't sure you'd be up yet. I know you judges all have an incredibly cushy schedule. Many of my colleagues tell me most of you don't even get out of bed until after ten every morning. I hope I didn't wake you."

"Yup, that's true. In fact ten is early for me. Now cut the bullshit. Whatta ya want?"

David laughed, and said, "What's on for today? How's your schedule look?"

"Busy. I have no time for you if that's what you want."

"Actually, I just need a few seconds. What can you tell me about your newly appointed comrade, Judge Dewitt? What do you know about him ? I've never tried a case in his court. He handled the hearing concerning temporary matters, but as you know, this is a different situation altogether."

"Before we discuss that, I understand from a couple of mutual friends, you had your first date since the divorce. How'd that go? You get along alright?"

His tone of conversation told David he already knew how it turned out—he was just trying to rub it in.

"Went fine. Now tell me about the judge."

"Oh really. Glad to hear that. Tell me a little about it."

"Come on, you smart ass, you already know how it turned out. Now move on."

Henry laughed, and said, "Just hang in there, Dave. You'll find someone that's interested in you, just hang in. Now, about Judge DeWitt—he's a good man. He's a little, should I say, light in brain power, and probably won't dig too far into the issues, but he's fair and upfront. You'll always know where you stand. You trying something in his court?"

"Yeah. I got that Whitmore dissolution coming up. I just wondered what he was like in the courtroom."

"To be honest, and obviously just between the two of us, he's got no depth whatsoever. You'll have to lay everything out for him, because the ruling he makes will be based strictly upon what you present. He has no creativity and no insight. Is that up front enough for you? By the way, I never said any of that."

"I get it. We never had this conversation. You wanna meet somewhere for a beer late this afternoon?"

"Can't. We're going out tonight, and I told her I'd be home early. Good luck with the judge. Let me know how it all turns out."

She walked in his office, sat down, smiled and said, "Morning, David. Have we heard anything from his attorney?"

"Not a word."

The smile disappeared. She looked away and said nothing, clearly deep in thought. When she finally reengaged, she said, "I made a mistake didn't I? My thoughts, my ideas on how this might all be resolved were wrong. Sorry. I should have listened to you."

"Forget it. We all have our own approach to issues of this nature. Yours had as good a chance of success as mine. But now, we're going to need to face the consequences of what we've done. We have very little to go on concerning matters of property. In fact, we're pretty much at their mercy. Whatever he says you two have accumulated, we're going to have to accept. We have nothing upon which to question his figures."

"So, you're saying we should just accept his plan concerning division of our assets and let it go at that?"

"I don't think we have a choice. Obviously, the custody issue is still up in the air, but Tuesday morning before we begin, I'll discuss these issues with the opposing attorney and we'll see what we can iron out before the hearing starts."

She nodded her approval. "He has Billy for another couple of days." She started to cry. "Sorry. Everything becomes a little more difficult to handle when he's not with me. Apparently, I better get used to it, but it's just hard."

"Let's go through the procedure. I know we've been through it a couple of times, but let's go through it briefly, once more."

"Okay."

"He filed the petition, so he'll put his case on first. Assuming he continues to maintain his position that he should have custody, he'll testify, then put on witnesses who will all say he's a good father, and would be a good custodial parent."

"You can cross-examine them, based on the notes I've provided you concerning those people we already know will testify, right?"

"That's right, but as I told you, don't expect much to come of that, just as cross-examining our witnesses by the opposing attorney won't gain him much. The people that are testifying for both sides are basically good people, and it's going to be difficult to impeach any of them. The strength of our case will be with you and theirs with him."

"How are you going to approach your cross-examination of Jack?"

"You haven't given me much to go on. He has a temper issue, which I will point out through you, and I'll also question him about that. He's sometimes lax on the attention he pays to Billy, especially when his work conflicts with his time with your son. I think that is an important issue to emphasis."

"What about the judge? He didn't do us any favors at the temporary hearing, that's for sure. Do we know any more about him than we did?"

"He's fairly new to the position. I understand everything needs to be pretty well laid out for him—that he's perhaps not a deep thinker, to put it politely, so we'll do what we can to lay it out for him. He's a bit of an unknown at this point, not having been a judge that long."

"That doesn't help much does it?"

"No. Now, I assume there's no need to, once again, go through all those rules you need to follow when you testify.

"Just touching upon them briefly, you might recall I told you to speak up, and don't argue with the other attorney under any circumstances. Do not attempt to answer a question if you don't fully understand the question. Now, the judge may have a question or two for you too. Don't worry about it, just answer whatever question he might ask."

"Can I take a break if I don't understand the question, and talk to you about the answer first?"

He smiled as he said, "You mean like a 'time out'?"

"Yes."

"No. Just answer it the best you can, but make sure you know what the question is before you answer. Ask whoever asked the question to rephrase it."

"How long will this take?"

"Until we're done."

"Will the judge rule right away?"

"Probably."

"Okay. I guess I don't have any more questions."

"I'll meet you at the courthouse about eight. You have my home number. Call me at home, if something comes up."

It was past time to lock the door, and call it quits for the day. David continued to review Hope's file, but his eyes were tired, and he was ready to go home, put his feet up and have a beer, or two, or three.

"Alright if I head home?"

Gail had also remained after working hours. She had previously told David she would work late to clean up a few issues she was concerned about.

"Sure, go ahead. Don't lock the door. I'm just a few minutes away from leaving."

"Whatta ya think?"

"About the trial?"

"Yeah."

"I think she's sorry she tied my hands concerning those property issues. She made a hell of a mistake, and Tuesday she pays for it. Too bad, but I told her so. She's bull-headed as hell."

"What about custody?"

"Oh, I think she'll get the kid half the time, maybe all the time, who knows. But, here again, she hasn't given me much to work with concerning reasons he isn't a fit parent. We'll just have to see how the evidence comes in, I guess."

"Just so you know, I'll be in early Monday and Tuesday of next week. I've got a lot to catch up on."

"I'll probably be here before you are, at least on Tuesday morning. I'll want to go over everything one more time before I leave for the courthouse."

"See you Monday morning."

Chapter 16

Jack Whitmore was having trouble concentrating on anything. Tomorrow was a big day—a big day in many ways. Tomorrow his marriage would finally be dissolved. Tomorrow all the financial maneuvering he had needed to do to insure Hope wouldn't know what they actually had in assetts, would finally end, and he could spend all the time he wanted with the woman he planned on eventually marrying.

He felt perhaps one last call to his attorney, Ted Carnie, just to confirm everything was in order, might be appropriate.

"Ted, Jack Whitmore. We all ready to go tomorrow?"

"Yes, yes, we're ready. I haven't talked to her attorney, but at least from our standpoint, everything is ready. As I told you, the only thing I am somewhat concerned about is this new judge. I don't know much about him. But it's a mutual problem because they don't know much about him either. He did us a favor concerning the temporary hearing but, beyond that, I know nothing about him. Nothing any of us can do about it anyway, but other than that, yes we're ready. I'll meet you, as we discussed, around eight at the courthouse."

"Thanks, Ted."

He touched a second number on his phone.

"Hi, Carrie, how's Billy doing?"

"Good, he's doing fine. When are you coming by to pick him up?"

"Well, that's why I called. I thought I might be there by six, but something's come up. Can you keep him overnight?"

She hesitated. "He's been asking for you."

"Yeah, I figured. That seems to be a daily occurrence, as you know, but he'll be fine. I have a few matters that I need to handle before tomorrow morning. I'll make it worth your while if you can keep him overnight, I really will."

He held his breath. He didn't want to deal with a child in the middle of everything that was happening. He also had other plans for later in the evening, of which Billy was not to be a participant.

Again, she hesitated. She finally took a deep breath, and said, "When can you pick him up?"

"After my day in court has concluded—maybe around five. Does that work for you?

"Yes, that's fine. But you need to pick him up then, and no later."

"I will. Thank you so much. See you tomorrow."

He quickly touched another number, and waited for her to answer.

As soon as she answered he said, "Hi, baby. You just get home?"

"I did. It was a long fricken day. Just poured myself a drink, and got out of my clothes."

"Don't put anything else on, I'm coming to see you."

"But...I don't understand? Isn't the trial tomorrow? What are you doing?"

"Yes it is, but they've done nothing to follow me, or check on assets or anything else for the last two months, and I hardly think they're going to start now. I'll be over in about 30 minutes—and I don't want you to be wearing anything. See you then."

He heard her start to say something as he terminated the call, but he terminated it anyway. Didn't matter to him what she was about to say—he had already said all that could possibly be of importance during their abbreviated conversation. She could add nothing of relevance.

"Hey Claudia, can you come in a minute?"

As she walked through the door, he said, "You know I'll be gone all day tomorrow, right?"

"I do. What about the following day? You have a few appointments scheduled. Are you thinking you may be gone then too?"

"I think it would be a good idea to move them. Better be safe than scramble around explaining to them what happened. Just give them a call tomorrow and tell them I had something come up and set them up with a new time. I really don't think this will go three days, but I have little doubt it'll take two."

"How's it all looking?

"Good. Now why don't you take off, and I'll touch base with you sometime tomorrow. I'll be here a few more minutes, and then I'm leaving too."

"See you in a few days."

He only knocked once and she opened the door. He walked in, and just as she started to say something, he put both arms around her, pulled her close and kissed her. She had nothing on but a light-weight bathrobe, and as he kissed her, he moved one hand inside the front opening of her robe, and placed it over her breast.

As he did, she pushed him back, and said, "Hold on their, Jack. What's going on? I don't understand. We're away from each other for months because of the divorce and on the *eve of the day it's to be tried*, you're over here with not a concern in the world about being seen with me. Explain!"

He walked away and dropped down on the couch, as he said, "They have done absolutely nothing to investigate me, or my money, or my woman—nothing. I don't figure they're going to start the night before trial. It's just like she gave up when I asked for custody."

She sat down by him. "By the way, where's Billy? I thought you had him while the case was being tried."

"Sitters got him. I called her and asked her to keep him tonight and all day tomorrow. She said she would. I'll pick him up after the hearing tomorrow. I assume no one has been in contact with you concerning me?"

"No. I haven't heard from a sole. I don't understand. What is she doing? What is her attorney doing?"

"Nothing, absolutely nothing at all. Like I said, it was like she just quit when I said I wanted full custody. I don't understand it, but I'm also not complaining."

"You don't really want full custody, do you? It was my understanding you never wanted *any* custody, let alone full custody."

"When my attorney gave me an idea how much I would have to pay her in support if she got the kid full time, I changed my mind. I'll be glad to keep him if it means that I'll have to pay her as much as my attorney said I was going to have to pay her if *she* gets full custody. No, I don't want him full time, but money is money, Beth, and you know me and my money."

"Very true, I certainly *do* know you. And I know there's nothing much more important to you in life than your money."

He leaned over, pulled her close, kissed her, and whispered, "Now could you slip out of that dreary old bathrobe? I haven't been with you for two months."

She pushed him away and said, "You know, if you get full custody of Billy, you'll break her heart. You know that don't you?"

"If I do, I figure we can work out some kind of deal after the trial. I'll worry about it then. I just don't want to be obligated to pay all that support. My attorney told me if I did get custody, it might result in a slight reduction in the amount of alimony I have to pay too. He wasn't sure that would be the case, but there is a possibility that will happen. As I say, maybe she and I can work something out between us after the trial. But for now, I want custody of him, and that's the way it'll stay until the trial ends. No compromise. You haven't received a subpoena have you? I know you haven't mentioned it."

"I haven't heard from anyone concerning the case since it started."

"You mind if I stay here tonight?"

"No, I don't care, as long as *you* don't think it'll hurt your case."

"I think we're fine. Do you have all those interest statements I had them email to you? Did you print them out? I'd like to see them and review them tonight."

"I have them. I printed them out and I'll dig them out later. You wanna go out for something to eat, or order in?"

"Order in," he said, as he grabbed her robe, pulled her close, and started to caress her upper thigh.

She put her hand on his, and stopped its upper movement.

"Tell me again, what's gonna happen when this all ends? What happens to you and I when your marriage is over?"

He smiled. "Like I've told you a hundred times before, we're getting married. We're gonna give it a little time for everything to simmer down, and then we'll get married. I meant it when I said it months ago, and I mean it now."

She thought for a moment, then placed her hand over his, and slowly moved his hand up her thigh. When he had finally reached its intended distention, he kissed her.

She placed her hand between his legs and started to gently caress him. He opened his eyes and said, "This is insane." He stood as he said, "Come on, let's go. I've waited two months for this. I'm not going to wrestle with trying to take off my clothes on a damn couch."

She smiled, stood, dropped her robe and said, "Lead the way…Jack."

Chapter 17

Just as David reached the courthouse steps, his phone buzzed. It was Griff. David didn't have time for him. As he continued to stare at the caller's name, he reconsidered. He needed to *make* time.

"Hi, Griff. What's up?"

"Hey bro, not much. Where you at?"

"Just walking up the steps at the courthouse. I start a contested custody case today."

"You're busy then. I won't bother you."

"No, no I'm not involved yet. Just let me get through security. I'll call you right back."

Once he passed through security and reached the conference room where he was to meet Hope, as he kept an eye out for her, he returned Griff's call.

"Sorry 'bout that. What's going on?"

"Just workin. We been on the job now for 'bout a week. Almost got the project done. I've got two or three others lined up once we get this one done. It's going well."

"Mom told me you got your loan, and hired a crew. How'd you come up with the money?"

"Kristy talked to her parents and they agreed to loan it to us. Couldn't believe it. They're really good people. They did, however, make it clear—in fact, very clear—that this was it. There would be no more where that came from, and that's fine. I understand that. I'll make this work with what they loaned us, and it won't be necessary to borrow anymore, from anyone, again."

"That's fantastic. Have you been busy since you got the loan?"

"That's an understatement. Yes, I've really been busy. In fact, that's one of the reasons I called you. I could be a whole lot busier. I need you to tell your friends and your clients what I'm doin. Send me all the business you can. The more people see the kind of work and the quality of work we do, the better it's going to be."

"How much work you got lined up? In other words, if they ask me how long it would take before you could start a job for them, what should I tell them?"

"Probably 30 days before we could get started."

"I'll pass the word."

"How's mom? I haven't seen her in a while."

"She's good. I saw her yesterday."

"I'll slip over and see her one of these days. Is your case a tough one?"

"It's turned out to be. It involves a guy by the name of Jack Whitmore. Property division is also one of the issues, and I have no doubt the jerk has hidden money from us. But I've had my hands tied by my client, so there wasn't much I could do to find it. Hope, his wife, is a nice woman. I like her, but she's really getting screwed over by this guy. As you can tell, I'm more than a little frustrated by it all. Unfortunately, that, in a nutshell, is the everyday life of a trial attorney."

"Glad that's your job and not mine. Good luck today. I better go. Send me all the business you can."

"I will. Thanks for calling, Griff. Great talking to you. Glad everything is finally working out."

He had no sooner terminated the call when he saw Hope walking toward him. He motioned for her to follow him into the conference room, which she did.

As she sat down at the conference table, he said, "You all ready for today?"

She reached in her purse and pulled out a tissue as she started to cry. "I don't think I have a choice. I guess I'm as ready as I'll ever be."

"You know, I was thinking about property division. We have nothing to refute anything he says. We have a proposal on the table from them that's never been withdrawn. I think we should take it and resolve that part of the case. While the judge doesn't have to accept it, I think he will if we present it to him, and neither party presents evidence to contradict its terms. That would leave only the issues of custody, support and alimony. Whatta ya think?"

"Well, I think that's probably a logical approach, in light of the fact that I've fucked this thing all up. Sure. Go ahead and tell the other attorney and the judge that's fine. I don't give a damn."

"Okay. Now this morning we're going to hear from three or four people that will testify as to the fact that, based on their involvement with Jack, he appears to be a good father. You need to understand that there's not much I can do about their testimony. I had a chance to check on all of them and they're good people. There's not a bad sole in the bunch. They're here to testify just like our people will be tomorrow—on behalf of their friend. There's really not much I can do to impeach their testimony."

"So, Hope, if I don't spend much time cross-examining them, just know it's because there's next to nothing to cross-examine them about. It will be the same way tomorrow when our people testify and his attorney tries to cross-examine them.”

“I understand.” She continued to dab at her eyes.

David expected she would remain emotional throughout the trial, and anticipated he would just need to deal with it as best he could.

The court attendant knocked on their door a few minutes later. After a short conference in chambers involving the judge and both attorneys, during which the attorneys indicated the only contested issues were custody, child support and alimony, testimony in the case commenced at exactly 9:00 a.m.

All three witnesses testifying for Jack were on and off the stand by ten-thirty. Their testimony was predictable. David had very few questions on cross-examination, which resulted in Jack taking the stand right after a mid-morning break.

His testimony primarily concentrated on custody, and continued until the midday break.

Jack continued testifying until shortly after the mid-afternoon break when David finally got a chance to cross-examine him.

After a number of questions concerning Jack’s life in general, they again reviewed how he would care for the child on a day-to-day basis. The essence of David’s questioning started when he said, “Now Mr. Whitacre, do you actually feel you’re a better parent than Mrs. Whitacre? Is that your assertion?”

“I think I can take care of him on a day-to-day basis certainly as well if not better than she can, yes.”

“Why?”

“Hope is not a strong woman. She’s weak. She doesn’t handle Billy when he’s mad, or upset about things. She doesn't control the situation. She lets him control her. And in my opinion it's only going to get worse as he grows older. Before long, if it continues, by the time he's ten years old, he'll be controlling all aspects of his own life by himself. That won't happen with me."

"Have you ever had an indication she doesn't love Billy or that there is anything in her life of more importance then her son?"

He hesitated, for only a moment before he said, "No, I guess not."

"Would you agree she places him above everything else in her life?"

"I guess so, yes."

"Let's change direction here. I assume during the marriage, she has never had a relationship with another man?"

"No, not that I know of."

"What about you—any other women?"

Jack smiled as he said, "No, of course not."

"It sounds like you have a plan all figured out as concerns the day-to-day care for the child, is that correct?"

"Yes, just as I testified."

"Do you really believe taking the child away from his mother over an extended period of time, and leaving him with a sitter is in the best interest of the child? Do you honestly believe that?"

"Under the scenario I have presented, yes, I do."

"Give me some examples of why she isn't appropriate for full custody?"

"There have been many, many times when I've seen Billy throw a fit and she tries to smooth it over, rather than take control, take charge of the situation. I will not let that happen. I'm not so concerned about him at this age, but as he grows older, if the same thing happens, I can see that as being a recipe for disaster."

"Is there anything else that you can point to that makes you a better parent than her—better for the child in the long run?"

"Not really. That's the major issue, but to me it's a very important issue. Beyond that, I feel I have just as good a plan on a day-to-day basis as she does."

"Nothing further, Judge."

Jack's attorney asked a few questions on redirect, but once they were answered, and neither party had anything further, the judge let him step down.

At that time, Jack rested his case.

Before the introduction of testimony from Hope, the court asked both parties if the child advocate that had been appointed by the judge to do a private investigation concerning the parties, as an independent third party, could introduce her report into evidence without further testimony. Both parties had previously reviewed the report, which indicated either party would be appropriate for custody. Neither party objected and the report was allowed into evidence.

Since it was now approaching four-thirty, the court recessed, indicating they would begin promptly the next morning at 9:00 a.m.

In the conference room, David said, "Why don't you meet me here tomorrow morning about eight and we'll just generally go through your testimony before we start in the morning."

"You know, that bullshit about Billy controlling the situation rather than me was just that—bullshit. That's not the way it is. Sure, I *do* give him a little more leeway than Jack does, but for God's sake he's only four-years-old."

"I know, and the court should know that too. There were no surprises today, and that's a positive. Tomorrow you can take the stand, tell your side, and hopefully that will be the position the judge takes. Nothing happened today that decided the case. Your testimony is extremely important, and we'll just hope it goes as well as it has when we rehearsed it. I'll meet you here tomorrow morning, and we'll give'em all we got in the courtroom. Go home, get a good night's sleep and I'll see you in the morning."

As she left the room, she said, "Oh yeah, I'm sure I'll get a good nights' sleep. Whatever. See you tomorrow."

Chapter 18

David sat quietly while Jack's attorney cross-examined the last of three character witnesses called to testify on behalf of Hope. As he sat, he mentally reviewed Jack's testimony from the previous day. He had made a good witness. He had explained his financial situation in detail, and had presented a believable case for custody. David cross-examined him concerning all matters, but with so little information available about finances, and with Hope's testimony concerning custody much more important than what he might be able to extract from a hostile witness, it took little time to ask the few questions he had.

Jack's position concerning custody, was very basic. His excuse for not spending a great deal of time with Billy, was simply because Hope was always available, and he didn't need to. Now, he opined, if he did become the custodial parent, he was more than willing to expand the time he spent with their child as was necessary. There was really nothing Jack had in his past history that would impact unfavorably on his request for custody, and cross-examination concerning that issue was basically unremarkable.

The three witnesses he had provided which supported his request for custody had testified exactly as expected. They testified Jack was a wonderful father and none of the three could find any reason the court shouldn't consider him for permanent custody.

"Mr. Brenden, are you with us? I just suggested maybe it's time for our noon break. It's a little early but are you okay with that?"

"Sorry, Judge. Yes, certainly that's fine with us."

In silence, both Hope and David walked to the conference room. David indicated he wasn't hungry, and asked her if she wanted him to run and get something for her, to which she answered in the negative. David wanted to use the extra time to review his questions as he continued to prepare for her testimony which would begin right after the break.

Once they both were seated, Hope said, "Well, I thought my three witnesses did quite well, didn't you?"

David said, "Yes." He never looked up, continuing to review his notes, remaining silent.

"Did you see the smirk on that jerk's face?" She leaned forward and stared at David after he provided no response. This time, slightly louder, she said, "Did you see the smirk on that…"

"Yes, yes, Hope, I saw it. Now can you please concentrate on what's important here?" He looked up at her as he said, "Did you listen to them?"

She sat back in her chair, continuing to dab at her eyes.

"Or were you just content to observe the 'smirk' and let what was really relevant go right on by? Did you listen to what they had to say or not?"

She looked away and said, "Yes, yes I heard them. Like I said, I thought they did fine. I'm up next, right?"

"Yes, you are, Hope. Now, listen to me. We have to concentrate on issues that matter here. You can't be off in never, never land, watching his face while you testify. You look at *me*. You think about your responses. You need to do this, and do it right, or your case is history. Don't worry about what he looks like—you look at me and answer the questions like we rehearsed them. *Do you understand?* Your testimony is the essence of this case. This is it—right now, right here. If your testimony goes bad, if you can't concentrate on what you're doing, *we are done*. Do you understand what I'm saying?"

She turned to face him and said softly, "I'll be fine. I'm sorry. I hate him. I absolutely hate him for what he's doing. I'll be fine. I'll get through it. I just needed to vent a little."

David smiled. "You vent well. Just remember why we're here. It has nothing to do with him. It has to do with *you*—with you and your son. This is a chance to tell the court why Billy should be with you all the time, not just part of the time. It's the only chance the judge is going to have to hear the specifics of your request, so don't blow it."

The first portion of the afternoon was spent with Hope testifying as to property matters, at least to the extent of which she was aware, along with other basics concerning herself and the marriage. It was clear to David that Hope had blocked everything out, as he had requested, and was concentrating on her job as defined by him just prior to taking the stand.

By mid-afternoon, testimony concerning most all property and personal questions had been completed. It was now time to discuss custody and all those issues surrounding that particular aspect of the case.

After answering a number of general questions concerning her overall relationship with Billy, David said, "Now, Mrs. Whitmore, let's discuss the custody issue. Are you concerned about Jack's request for full custody?"

"Yes."

"Why?"

"I've always been the primary caretaker. From day one, from the day he was born, it was always me—always me that cared for Billy and took care of his needs. Jack never did any of those things on a day-to-day basis. I don't have a problem with him having visitation, but for him to have full custody, with me only having visitation, is insane. That's just not a viable option, and it certainly isn't in Billy's best interest."

"What was Jack's primary focus while you lived together?"

"Work and making money. That's it. Nothing more, nothing less. He worked all the time. Billy and I were always an afterthought. That's why I was so surprised when he asked for custody."

"What aspect of Jack's day-to-day life concerned you most while you were together?"

"Basically, never seeing him was the biggest issue, but in addition, he was never someone that considered the details involving *anything*. He had a grip on the big picture, but the details escaped him. He never took the time to handle the details. He left that to me. And believe me, raising a child and taking care of him on a day-to-day basis is all about details. That is a problem that would really concern me if he were to get full custody. He might forget to feed him, to take him somewhere, to pick him up from somewhere. He's just incredibly inept when it comes to details. I'm not. That was my role while I was with him, and I handled it well."

"What do you feel would be appropriate as concerns custody?"

"Primary care with me and alternating weekends for him. Maybe Billy could spend a day during the week with him too. The rest of the time he would remain with me. As he gets older, maybe it could be increased if they both wanted that, and regular visitation was working out. But for now, while Billy's so young, no more than that."

"That's all I have, Your Honor."

"Mr. Cruise, you may cross."

Jack's attorney asked a number of basic questions concerning Hope's background, and the property settlement issue already agreed upon. Once finished with that line of questioning, he asked her a few elementary questions concerning Billy, then said, "Was Jack home most every night while you were together?"

"Yes. Whenever he finished what he was doing at the office, he came home. But the office came first. The office always, always came first."

"What about weekends? Was he normally home during the weekends?"

"Yes, unless he had something to do at the office. Then he came home after that was done."

"You were always there, right?"

"Yes."

"So, under those circumstances, he knew he could depend on you being with Billy while he brought home the money, correct?"

She hesitated. "I guess."

"But circumstances have now changed haven't they? And don't you suppose that his approach to work, his approach to Billy, just might also change with it?"

"No, I don't. He's dedicated to his work. Always has been, regardless of the circumstances. In addition, his inability to handle details is and always will be a problem, no matter the family dynamic."

"How do you respond to the child advocate that provided her report to the court and indicated either of you would be appropriate for custody? How do you respond to that?"

She moved forward in her chair. She raised her voice as she said, "You answer a question for me. How many days did she live with Jack? No, I'll answer it for you—*not one*. I've lived with him forever. I know him like I know the back of my hand. She talked to him, what once, maybe twice. I can't object to the conclusion she formed, but I can tell you, and tell this court, that it was wrong. I know him. She doesn't. He can paint a pretty picture in the short run. But in the long run, Billy will suffer if Jack gets full custody, or even if custody is split equally between us. What I'm telling you about him, is the way it is. He is *not* appropriate for anything other than weekend visitation— end of story."

Jack's attorney looked at his notes for a moment, then turned and whispered something to Jack who whispered his response.

"I don't believe we have anything further, Judge."

David asked Hope a few follow-up questions and then rested.

Once he had finished, the judge said, "Folks, I want to review my notes and reread the report made to the court concerning custody. If you'll be back here tomorrow morning, I'm not sure I'll have an answer for everything, but I will have an answer concerning custody. I think that issue needs to be decided as quickly as possible for the sake of the child as much as anything. You be here about nine and I'll tell you what we're gonna do concerning Billy. Court is adjourned for today."

David turned to Hope and whispered, "Do you need to discuss anything further with me or should we just meet in the conference room tomorrow morning about eight forty-five?"

She turned toward him, and said, "I'll see you here tomorrow morning."

Her pain, her disgust were apparent. He didn't try to stop her. She needed time to reflect, to process all that had happened. Perhaps by tomorrow morning, they would be able to reasonably discuss the case, and what would transpire from here on.

Chapter 19

David had discussed the irrelevant until he simply couldn't think of anything relevant *or* irrelevant to say. He figured it was just time to address the elephant in the room and get it over with. When he told Hope what time they should meet in the conference room, he had no idea the judge would be on a conference call for over an hour. If he had known, he would have set the time to meet with her a little later. As it was, it appeared as though the judge would not now open court until near 9:45 a.m.

"So, you ready for this to happen? Are you going to be able to handle the ruling, regardless of what the judge does?"

"I'm more than ready for it to be over. But, as far as handling his ruling, I guess it depends on what the hell he does. I'm anticipating I'll get full custody. If that doesn't happen, you'll have to hold me down, because I'm gonna wanna beat the living shit out of Jack *and* the judge."

David smiled, even though he knew there was most likely more truth in that statement, than fiction.

"You know, if he does get him half the time, it will probably only be a matter of months before he's wanting to make a change. I've seen that happen. The father gets the child for an extended period of time, and soon finds out that wasn't what he wanted at all, but it seemed like that's what he should ask for at the time of trial."

"Yes, and that would be something he would do because he would continue to remain in control from beginning to end—*he* would be the one to initiate the change, and *he* could approve or disapprove whatever the change might be. You're probably right. If he does get Billy more than he should, he'll probably try to negotiate a change in some form or another, as long as, in his own mind, it benefits him and he's in charge."

The knock on the door came at a perfect time, and fortunately, sooner than the court attendant had said it would.

They walked in the courtroom together and took their seats. Jack and his attorney were already there. Neither acknowledged the presence of David nor Hope.

A few moments later, the judge walked through the courtroom door, took his seat behind the bench, and rifled through paperwork as he prepared to make his ruling.

David felt that rush of adrenaline he always felt right before there was a ruling from the bench. He just hoped it turned out favorable, but he was concerned this wasn't going to suit her, no matter how it turned out. Anything less than full custody, with no involvement by Jack in the child's life whatsoever, would most likely be an inappropriate ruling for Hope.

He mentally reviewed the last few months—from the time Hope first threw the paperwork on his desk. The case had not gone well from the beginning, and he had learned long ago if they started bad, they finished bad. He held his breath as the judge began.

"Good morning. Folks, I've had a chance to review the file and review all the testimony along with the report presented by the child advocate. I have come to a conclusion concerning custody, but not as to most of the other matters. I'll file a written ruling in a few days, consisting of my verbal ruling involving custody, but which also embodies all the other elements of the decision, including support, and property."

"First of all, I want to commend both of you for acting like adults during the time prior to this trial. That's the way it's supposed to be, but many times that's not what happens, and the court is drawn into issues involving visitation and other matters concerning the children, prior to the final hearing. That didn't happen here, and you are both to be commended for that."

"Now, first, specifically concerning both parties individually, clearly Mr. Whitmore is appropriate for custody. The record shows he's a hard-working man that loves his son. There is no indication of abuse in any respect, nor was there any testimony other than that he is a good father. There were issues raised concerning his inattention to detail, but I have a feeling that will change, based on his new circumstances."

"He has set up a process for caring for the child while he is working and I can't fault the process he has outlined to the court during the last couple of days. In addition, none of the witnesses presented by either party indicated he is anything but a good father."

"Now, likewise, I believe the respondent, Mrs. Whitmore is an excellent mother. There is nothing in the record that indicates her child isn't the most important element of her life. As concerns the testimony describing her as a mother, not one witness, including Mr. Whitmore, indicated she was anything but the best mother possible, and I concur with what the evidence showed."

"Both of the parents have a good plan for taking care of the child, and Billy is lucky—lucky he has two parents that care for him. I've seen plenty of marriages dissolved where the child or children, came last in discussions concerning dissolving the marriage, not first, as was the case here."

The judge cleared his throat, and David knew he was about to finish off his ruling—his final decision would be the next words out of his mouth.

"As a result of all these factors, I can see no reason not to give both parents equal time with the child—and that will be my ruling. Now, I don't really care how you handle the schedule with each parent. You can do it on a weekly basis, or a biweekly basis, or every other month. I'm going to let the two of you come to an agreement concerning the specifics. Come to a conclusion that works for both of you, let your attorney know, and the attorneys can pass that information on to me."

"However, I want that issue decided right quick. You need to get your heads together yet today, or tomorrow and decide what you want to do. If I haven't heard from one of the attorneys by end of business tomorrow, I'll decide myself. Now, I'd rather the two of you figure this out so it's most convenient for both of you, but if you can't, rest assured I can, and I will. That will be the ruling of the court. We are adjourned. Best of luck to the two of you."

The judge stood and left the courtroom.

No one moved. Finally, David heard Jack ask Hope what she wanted to do. Hope never said a word. She simply stood and walked out of the courtroom.

David turned toward Jack and said, "I'll talk to her. I'll call your attorney later today or tomorrow morning. What are your thoughts? What works best for you?"

"Two consecutive weeks each."

David stood. "I'll contact your attorney tomorrow."

He walked through the front door of his office, and walked past Gail without saying a word. David dropped his files on his desk, and picked up the phone. He called Hope's number, but it went to voice mail. He tried again with the same result. The third time, he left a message telling her to call back as soon as she could.

As he dropped down in his chair, he said, "Damn it."

He looked up to see Gail standing in his doorway.

"I'm thinking that didn't go so well."

"It didn't. The judge split custody between the two of them. She walked out of the courtroom without saying anything and now she won't answer my calls. I need to know how she wants to handle dividing the time between them by tomorrow. You call her every half-hour until she answers."

"Whoa, she really must be unhappy."

He swiveled around to look out his window, as he said, "I think that's putting it mildly. If she wouldn't have been so bullheaded, I might have been able to help her, but she tied my hands all the way through the process. Even in looking for other assets, I might have turned up something about him, personally, that might have helped with the custody issue. Too late now."

"I'll let you know if I reach her."

"Yeah, whatever."

David knew how unhappy she had to be. The custody issue was truly the only issue she was concerned about, and that issue couldn't have turned out much worse. She would calm down. They always did. He would discuss an appeal with her, but he honestly could not recommend she pursue it. The judge's decision was based on firm ground, and he was about as certain as he could be, there wasn't a

snowballs chance in hell the Supreme Court would modify
the ruling Judge Dewitt had just handed down.

Chapter 20

“**J**ack?”

“Yes.”

“Hope.”

She could hear him snicker, as he said, “I know who this is. It hasn't been *that* long. I haven't had a chance to forget you *yet*. It's only been three months. Whatta ya need?”

“Jack, is there some way we could come to some other arrangement? This is killing me. I *know* it's only been three months, but it seems like a lifetime to me.”

“Whatta ya got in mind, Hope?”

“Would you agree just to see him on alternating weekends? I would promise to let you have him if something special came up or…”

“Nope.”

She hesitated. “Is there anything I could do, like maybe give up something I was given in the divorce, to get you to change your mind? I can't handle this arrangement Jack, I really can't.”

“But, I can. I like it this way. Let me think about it. I might like the Lake Tahoe house—I might work something out involving the house—but let's just wait and see. I'll think about it and get back to you. In other words, don't call me, I'll call you.”

“Wait, Jack. How's he doing?”

"He's doing fine. He's always doing fine when you call. Oh, and that's another thing. Quit calling so often. Don't call me, and don't call the babysitter. She's as tired of you calling as I am. I'm going to limit responding to you or taking your calls to only twice a week as of today. Now, you know what—I got one hell of a lot to do here today. I'm still trying to recover financially for all that shit you got in the divorce.   Unfortunately it's gonna take a long, long, time. So excuse me while I recoup. Take care, Hope."

Later that afternoon, she sat at Ann's table, and waited while Ann poured her a cup of coffee.

"You want something in this? Got a great new liqueur that makes coffee just jump out of the cup. Wanna give it a try?"

"No, but thanks."

Hope took a sip, then set the cup down on the table, gripping it with both hands, while she starred into space. After a couple of minutes had passed, Ann said, "You wanna talk today, or is this the day we just stare into space and think? If this is the day for that, I must have missed the memo, because I didn't know a damn thing about it. Now, how does this work? You place your hands…"

Hope looked up, smiled and said, "I'm sorry. I don't know what I was…I'm sorry. How you been?"

"No, Hope, the question isn't how *I've* been, it's how *you've* been?"

"I'm fine. It's been tough. These months since the judge's ruling, have been the most difficult of my life. But, I guess I'm still around."

"Why haven't you been over, or called, or asked me to come visit you? I've seen you once, by chance, at the mall, and you didn't have time for me then, nor have you since then."

"I haven't been able to function since the divorce. Really, today is the first time I've gone anywhere or done anything, other than venture out for necessities, since the trial. I just don't care. Billy was, and is, my life. I just wait for my two weeks to be with him, and nothing else. My life centers around those two weeks."

"You don't look well, Hope. You look thin, you've got circles under your eyes—are you taking care of yourself? You need to do that you know, if for nothing else than for Billy."

"I know, I know, and I *have* recently started doing that. Right after the hearing, I didn't care whether I lived or died. Nothing mattered. I've had to pull myself together and move on, but it's the hardest thing I've ever done. And even now, I live only for those two weeks he's with me."

"You know, you're still a young woman. You have a lot of life left in you. You're a little young to be folding up."

She looked out the window and said, "I called Jack today, before I came over here. I wanted to see if there was something we could agree to, that would leave Billy with me, with him having the right of visitation every other weekend."

"What'd he say?"

"He just laughed at me. He wouldn't even consider it."

"What about David? Is he able to do anything, or is he out of the picture?"

"We discussed appealing the decision, but he said there was a greater chance of failure than success, so we decided not to pursue it any further."

"Were you happy with him, with what he did for you?"

"Yes. What happened, as I told you before, was more my fault than his. He's a good guy, and he did as good a job for me as he could. I would go back to him if I had anything that needed to be done. He's not to blame for any of this. Jack, along with me tying my attorney's hands, are to blame for the mess I'm in now."

"So as concerns the rest of the divorce, where you at?"

"I think everything is finished. I have to clean up a few things, but I think for all intents and purposes, we are done."

"You going to continue to live in the house?"

"Nope—just too big. I'm trying to sell it. I haven't even looked at any other homes yet, because I'm not sure what mine will bring. It's mortgaged, and I need to know how much I'm going to have left before I buy a different one."

"What about the Tahoe home?"

"I'm going to keep it. I'm going to do everything I can to hold onto it. I'll need to live here until Billy gets older, but then I may move out there permanently. I'll probably need to mortgage it to help buy something here if I absolutely have to, but other than that, I'm going to hold onto it for dear life."

Ann leaned back, and said, "Okay, now don't get pissed off when I ask you this. I'm only asking because *I* really need to know what to do. What are your thoughts about other men? I know a lot of men who would love to take you out. How do you feel about…?"

"Stop. Just stop. Thanks for thinking of me, but don't go there. I'm done—at least for now—at least until I can accept this as my new norm. Now, understand, this isn't a suggestion, it's an order. Do *not* set me up, or even consider me as a candidate for dating. When I reach the point where I'm ready to move on, *and I will specifically tell you when I do,* we can then *talk* about dating, but until then I makes me ill to even think about it. Do I make myself clear?"

Ann smiled, and said, "No worries. You just tell me when you're ready."

"Right now, I figure when hell freezes over will be about right."

Later that night, Hope sat in front of a fire she had started in the fireplace right before she poured herself a third glass of wine. She pulled a blanket up over her legs, and while outside, a chilly autumn wind whistled around her home, she again, considered her circumstances.

She could have him murdered—that would teach him.

Hope knew it was time to go to bed. It was late. She was tired. And thoughts of murder were insane. Even in her condition, even though the alcohol had done its duty, she was still able to conclude that murder was not a viable option—a simple murder was too good for him anyway.

She concluded she would bide her time, and just hope that somehow, someway, Jack changed his mind and turned full-time care of Billy over to her. A longshot for sure, but it was the only possibility she could think of that would return her son on a permanent basis.

Hope shoved the blanket off her legs, and started to stand. As she did, she spilled her drink on the floor. She looked down at it, and said, "Fuck. I always did hate these glasses." She threw the glass into the fire, and closed the glass doors in front of the fireplace. She then walked away, figuring the spill would still be there in the morning and she could clean it up then.

As she reached the steps, she reconsidered, concluding the dog could just by god lick it up—what the hell did she care. Hope stopped and grabbed the wall to stabilize herself. As she did, she remembered they didn't have a dog—Jack had run over their dog with his car.

She continued to use the wall to stabilize herself as she concentrated on each step of her slow journey upstairs to the bedroom. Her epiphany they no longer had a dog wasn't going to turn her around and go back to clean up the mess. It would just have to wait until tomorrow, when she *might* then just care enough to clean it up.

Chapter 21

Hope had made a pot of coffee, which she figured would last most of the day, then walked out on her deck. The sun was just starting to top the mountains on the opposite side of the lake.

It was still chilly. She had put on a light jacket to ward off the cool morning air, which was normal for Tahoe this time of year. She sat down and as she did, she thought how enjoyable it was going to be to bring Billy here when he was a little older.

He was now with Jack, which is why she had decided to leave town for a few days. Billy was just too young to appreciate the beauty of the lake, of the basin and all that was Tahoe. She figured maybe in three or four more years, he would appreciate the area, and she would then start bringing him here with her on a regular basis.

"Morning, Hope. How are things today?"

Sam and his wife, Jacki, were neighbors. Both now in their mid-70's, they had been good neighbors for years. She had visited with them when she first arrived a few days ago, telling both about her issues with Jack. Sam admitted he had never been a big fan of her former husband, so he wasn't concerned when she told him Jack wasn't coming back to the cabin.

She smiled. "Good, Sam. I'm good. I'm always good when I'm here. What about you?"

"Just taking my morning walk. As you know, I've walked this same trail almost every morning for the last 30 years, and I'm not about to stop now that I'm 75." He smiled as he said, "Age is only a number. By the way, if you need anything while you're here, whatever it might be in terms of grocery items or anything else, just let Jacki know. She's got every food item that ever existed on the face of this earth—you know, in case we ever get snowed in—again."

"I'll do that. Thanks. Enjoy your walk."

He waived and moved quickly up the trail. It was because of people like him, neighbors all around her, *and the view*, that she would never give up this home. It meant too much to her, and she knew, in time, it would also be an important part of Billy's life.

She looked at her phone to check the time. The differential was two hours, which meant David would indeed be in his office.

Once Gail put her through, she said, "David, how are you?"

"Hope—good to hear from you. Where are you? After you left your message, I tried reaching you, but my messages just went through to voice mail."

"I'm at Tahoe. I was leaving town as I left the message. I was in the air when you tried calling back."

"You still there?"

"Yes. In fact, right now, I'm sitting on the porch with a cup of coffee in front of me. The sun is just rising over the top of the mountains to the east, and the lake is so smooth it looks like a mirror. It's so peaceful, so quiet this morning, that it really makes you wonder if another world outside the basin even exists. The only thing missing is my son."

"Sounds like perfection."

"It is. In the past, I've enjoyed many perfect mornings out here. That's why I've tried so hard, through the transition I'm going through, to keep this place. It helps me maintain my sanity when all else fails."

"Never been there. But it sounds like somewhere I might enjoy."

"It's never too late. It'll all be here waiting for you when you're ready. Now, let's get down to business. Are you aware I bought a new home?"

"Yes. The broker called yesterday. I understand you also sold your present home, is that correct?"

"Yes. However, I'm not going to have enough money from the sale to finance the purchase of my new one. I'll also need to mortgage this one and use the proceeds to help purchase my new one. The mortgage on this house won't amount to much, but it needs to be done. Can you handle all that for me?"

"Yes. When are you coming back?"

"About a week. I'll be there for the closing."

"Not a problem. I should have all the paperwork reviewed by then. I'll make sure the title company is ready for the closings when you arrive. If I have questions I'll just give you a call. So, you don't have Billy with you?"

"No. He's with Jack this week and next."

"How's that all going, Hope? Has he changed his mind concerning some type of compromise involving visitation?"

"No. I haven't spoken with him for months, other than what was absolutely necessary."

"It could be time to discuss all the issues with him again. He may be more than ready to talk."

"I doubt it, but I'll give him a call later this morning to see how Billy's doing, and visit with him about it then."

"Let me know if there's anything I need to do. If I run into any problems with the closings I'll give you a call. By the way, how's the financial situation? I know you weren't happy with the judge's ruling concerning child support or alimony the last time I talked to you. Is that all going to work out for you?"

"No, I wasn't happy, but it's fine. I didn't want to mortgage this home to help purchase the one I'm buying, but it'll all work out. Having two homes to maintain with no other income than I have, will also present a challenge. But if I have to, I'll go back to work. I have a degree in finance, I can surely find work. I'll figure it all out, but I'm going to take my time doing it. Billy is my priority. If he's coming to live with me, I'm not going back to work if I can help it. If it turns out he's not, I'll find a job. Better go. I'll be in touch as soon as I'm back in Nashville."

"Be safe, Hope."

She terminated the call, and tapped Jack's number.

"Morning, Hope. Pretty early in the morning for you isn't it? Aren't you at Tahoe?"

"Yes. How's Billy doing?"

"He's fine. He's got a little cold, but I got that handled. How's the weather out there?"

"Fine. You have a change of heart concerning custody? I'm willing to talk anytime, you know."

"Nope we're fine the way it is. I might discuss some type of change if I were to get the Tahoe house, but it sounds like you're going to have it all tied up with the new purchase you just made."

"How'd you know about that?"

"You know Nashville—big city, small town. News travels pretty fast in the circle I run with. There are few secrets."

She hesitated, trying to figure out a new approach. She quickly concluded there wasn't one. "I'll pick up Billy a week from today. Thanks a lot Jack, you jerk," she said sarcastically, as she terminated the call.

She slammed the phone down on the small table sitting by her chair. He infuriated her every time she talked to him. There was nothing she could do about it—as long as he had Billy half the time they would need to continue to communicate.

Sam was walking near the cabin on his way home as she slammed the phone down.

"Everything okay, Hope?"

"Just got off the phone with Jack. That tell you anything?"

Sam smiled. "Sorry."

"I just wanna smash his face in, the prick."

He stopped, turned to face her, and smiled. "Now you know how I felt every time he showed up here. He's just someone you want to beat the shit out of not long after you meet him. And you don't really even have a specific reason. You just wanna beat the shit out of him for no reason at all. You need to vent for a minute, or cool down alone?"

She thought for a moment, then quickly said, "You wanna cup of coffee?"

Chapter 22

"Have we received the paperwork concerning Hope's house closings?"

"Yes, we have copies of everything. I've got all of it out at my desk. I'm still waiting on a couple of figures from the title company, which they are to send me today or tomorrow, but other than that, we have everything."

The day was almost over. David was just checking on a couple of miscellaneous matters before he left for the night.

Gail said, "Have you talked to her lately? How's she doing?"

"I guess I never told you. She's at Lake Tahoe—at the home she was awarded in the dissolution. She's coming back in a couple of days, and I want to be sure everything's ready for her concerning both closings and the mortgage paperwork on the Tahoe home."

"I think everything's about set. The bank in Reno just needs the amount that's necessary to close here. They'll wire the money when they get the figure. How's she doing?"

David leaned back in his chair and said, "Oh, I think okay. She's still a little discouraged over how it all turned out, but it sounds to me like she's making the adjustments we all need to make when things don't go quite like we expected. She'll be fine, but it's going to take a little time."

"Speaking of adjustments, you all ready for tonight?"

David leaned forward, and said, "Oh, I guess. As I'm sure you recall, after that first time you lined me up, I specifically told you I didn't want fixed up again. Obviously, I should have done the same thing when it came to Henry. I hate to tell a judge to go to hell, even if he is my best friend. He thinks he's doing me a favor and maybe he is, who knows? I'll try this once, and if he sets me up with as big a flake as you did, I'll tell him in no uncertain terms never to do it again."

"By the way, you get a little twinkle in your eyes when you speak of Hope. Something going on there I don't know about?"

David smiled. "Nope. We just went through a lot together. I like her. I didn't when I first met her, but I do now. I really hope everything works out for her in the future. Things haven't worked out very well in the recent past, and she deserves better than that piece of shit she was married to. I just want what's best for her, that's all. I better go. I need to pick up whatshername in about an hour. I'll see you tomorrow morning."

It was early evening, and David had just arrived at the judge's home. Henry had invited him over for a drink. His wife and children had gone to visit her mother—a trip the judge couldn't make because of a trial set to commence the next day.

David walked in the house, and yelled, "Hey, where the hell are you?"

He thought he heard a muffled voice from the rear of the home so he continued to walk on through the house knowing no one, other than Henry, was there. When he reached the pool, Henry was floating near the middle in some type of chair with wooden arms on each side, and a drink in the cup holder of both arms.

"Hey Davy, grab one of those chairs like I have, over there next to the wall. You bring your swimming suit?"

"Got it on under my jeans."

"Take them jeans off, get yourself a drink and grab that chair. This, my friend, is nothin but life at its best."

Once David had discarded his cloths, he fixed himself a drink, and grabbed a chair. He sat down, placed his drink in the cup holder and paddled out to a waiting Henry.

After small talking there way through the first 15 minutes, Henry said, "Well, since you haven't already brought it up, how did last night go? Did she suit you, or were your standards too high for her too?"

"Now Henry, you know my standards aren't *that* high. But in response to your question, she was fine. We got along fine."

"Where'd you go?"

"Oh, I took her to a place on the east side. It's very casual, and we had a good time."

"Going out with her again?"

"Doubt it, but thanks for setting us up."

"Why not? What didn't you like about her?"

David took a drink. "I *did* like her it's just that we don't seem to have much in common. She's not much for the outdoors…I am. I don't like to knit…she does. Even as old as I am, I still may want a child…she's done with children. That's just a few of the areas that we don't see eye to eye on. And they are areas that aren't going to change just because, by chance, we happen to become a couple."

"You know how much money she has? Do you have any idea what she's worth?"

"No not really. I know she's a wealthy woman, but you know me well enough to know that's not much of a factor."

"What the hell *is* a factor for you? I've tried a couple of times to set you up, but you're never satisfied with who I choose."

"Easily solved."

"I know—just quit setting you up. Okay, you got it. That's the last one. You're on your own. I gotta get another drink."

He paddled his way to the apron, and struggled to get out his chair.

"You puttin on weight, Henry? Should you be watching what you …"

"Just shut up, David. I'm fine. I can still beat you at—well, I can beat you at—just shut up. I'm fine."

He slowly walked to the bar, and fixed himself another cocktail. Once settled back in the pool, he said, "Say, how'd that trial go with Judge DeWitt? How'd you get along with him?"

"That's been a while ago. I guess we haven't discussed it have we? Oh, you had him pretty well described. He took the easy way out concerning most issues. He ruled against us on custody, but to be honest, based on the evidence presented, he was probably justified in ruling the way he did."

"You're kidding. Did she lose custody?"

"No. He split the time between both parents, and as I say, based on the testimony introduced, it was probably the right move."

"How'd the rest of the trial go? Did he decide everything the way you thought was appropriate?"

"Pretty much. There weren't many surprises, at least to me."

"Was she upset with the ruling?"

"Hope?"

"Yes."

"Oh, I don't think so much…"

As David was trying to finish the sentence, Henry suddenly got a smile on his face, and said, "Not to interrupt you, but you should know something. This is the second or third time I've talked to you about her. And each time, I've noticed just a hint of a change in your demeanor."

"Now, Davy, you know, that's what we judges are trained to do, at least to some degree anyway—to notice witnesses and how they present their testimony—notice little things about their body language, that might give you an indication of how they are subconsciously feeling about what they are saying. And I'm telling you buddy, I notice a little sparkle in those eyes when you talk about Hope."

David took a drink. "Hmm. I don't know why. We aren't involved in any respect. I still represent her—she's buying a different home here in Nashville, and I'm representing her in the transaction. I have a feeling she's got more issues than I wanna tackle anyway. Sorry, but you're reading me all wrong, buddy. I really hope you're not that far off reading those other witnesses you're talking about. If you are, I don't think I'd wanna be one of them."

David spent the next couple of hours, discussing law, family and politics with his good friend. But on the way home, the one issue that trumped all others, was his friend's observation concerning his relationship with Hope. It was the second time he had heard essentially the same thing in the last couple of days.

David really hadn't subconsciously thought about Hope in that way. He had a job to do when it came to her case, and he did it. But, now, as he considered Henry's observation, he had to admit he was looking forward to seeing her when she returned to Nashville. One thing about it—at least now, with both of their marriages dissolved, their time together would not be spent under quite as much pressure as they had both faced in prior months.

Chapter 23

Griff had left the job before quitting time. The rest of the crew would continue working on the remodeling job, and would work well into the evening. Normally, he would leave when they did. In fact, it was not unusual for work to end for *all* of them, near 9:00 p.m. each and every night.

But Mr. Chase needed to visit, and, after Chase had loaned him money, it had become obvious to Griff all of life must now revolve around him—a fact Chase would quickly confirm if you asked him.

Griff had arrived precisely at the agreed upon time. Now, an hour, and two drinks later, Chase still hadn't arrived. It was always *his* schedule, *his* rules, and *his* terms that dictated relationships, especially if that 'relationship' involved financial issues. But, then again, it was *his* money.

He had just ordered his third drink, when he noticed Chase and the two men that normally followed him around, walk in the front door. Griff motioned so they would notice, and as soon as they saw him, all three began the walk toward his table.

Chase quickly motioned for his boys to take a walk, and he alone sat down, across from Griff.

"Mr. Chase."

"Mr. Brenden."

The waitress started toward their table. Chase shook his head, and motioned for her to turn around and walk away.

"We need to make this brief. I have other people to see, and I'm already running behind this afternoon. How are things?"

Griff took a drink and said, "Good. Things are going good. Why do you ask?"

"When you say 'things are going good,' whatta ya mean? I mean, are you staying sober, staying off all those drugs you was usin, and *that* makes it good, or is your *business* going good? Which is it—or is it both?"

"Well, your money is fully invested, if that clarifies anything. I've spent everything you loaned me, and I could use a little more. I have a number of jobs lined up and plenty of people sending me business—in fact, more than I can really handle."

He leaned back in his chair as he studied Griff. "Well, I understand you been busy, but you see there's a slight contradiction here. You're busy, but you're not keeping up with your payments to me. That really is a serious contradiction, and one that has given me pause, if you know what I mean."

Griff took another drink. "Well, I'm only a couple of payments short and that was because I…"

Chase put up his hand, and stopped Griff in midsentence. "Don't care."

"You don't care about what?"

"Nothin. I don't care about nothin," He leaned forward in his chair, then leaned over the table towards Griff, as he said, "Except getting my money back. When can you make up those two payments you missed?"

"Can I ask you a question? Before I answer, could I ask a question?"

"I don't give a fuck, as long the question you ask is quickly followed by an answer to the question I asked you. Go on."

"Is there any chance of getting just a slight reduction in that interest rate? It seems a little high."

Chase smiled. "Whatta *you* think? The fact of the matter is, now that you've missed two payments, I should raise it. The more risk with the loan, the higher the rate of interest. You know that. And this loan just become a whole lot riskier with you missing them two payments."

Griff thought for a moment then said, "Look, business is really good. I just need a little time to get the cash flow rolling. Could you add the interest I owe on those two payments, to the whole loan and just spread the whole amount over the length of the loan? Could you at least do that for me—just give me a little leeway."

Chase never said a word, as he continued to stare at him. Finally, he said, "Sure, I guess I can do that." He shook his finger at him, as he said, "But I'm telling you not one more missed payment. No more stuff from me either. If you can't repay the loan, you can't buy nothin from me on credit, there's no way."

He hesitated for a moment. "Now, listen to me. I don't want this to happen again. You told me you'd make the payments on time in the amount set out in the note. You haven't done that. I'll spread out the interest over the life of the loan, but don't miss another payment. I'll get the new paperwork ready and have one of my men bring it to you for signature."

Chase stood, leaned over the table, stopping inches from Griff's face. "Don't you let me down here. Be a man of your word and make your payments like you's supposed to. Don't put me in a bad position. That I guarantee, will not turn out well for either of us in the long run."

Griff watched him, along with his two men walk out the front door of the bar.

He had previously decided to visit his mother after he left the bar, since he wasn't far from her home. He still intended on doing that, but he needed another drink and some time to stop shaking before he went anywhere.

"Griff, what the devil are you doing here? Come in. It's been forever. Come in and have a glass of sweet tea, or whatever you want. Come on in the living room."

"Nothing to drink, Mom, I don't have time to do much, but say hi. I had a business meeting in this area and just wanted to stop for a moment and see how you're doing."

"Sit, sit. Griff this is an old classmate, Howard Keating. He stopped in to see how I was and what I've been up to during the last 50 years."

Howard stood, as he shook hands with Griff, and said, "I really need to be going, Betty. I have a few things I need to do yet this afternoon before I go home. I'll give you a call in a few days and see how you are. Griff, nice meeting you."

Howard turned to walk out the door, as Griff said, "Nice meeting you… *Howard*."

As soon as the door had closed, Griff said, "Okay, what's the deal with him? How long has he been coming over? You never mentioned him before. What's his purpose for…"

She smiled and said, "Hold up and listen. It's nothing. His wife died a while back. We were close many years ago. He's stopped by a couple of times just to see how I'm getting along. He knows I have cancer, and he's just concerned. Nothing else, Griff, nothing else. Now tell me what kind of meeting you had."

They talked for about 15 minutes concerning his business and her health. Griff didn't feel comfortable staying any longer with so much yet to finish at the job site.

As he was driving back to work, he called David.

"Hey, Dave, you know anything about a Howard Keating? You ever heard of him?"

"Hmm. I vaguely remember the name, but I'm not sure when or where. Why? What's going on?"

"I just left mom's house and he was there, with her. She seemed a little flustered, and he left as soon as I got there. She said he was an old friend from high school. Did she mention anything to you about seeing some guy?"

"No, she's never said a word. I can't think there's anything going on, not with the condition she's in. I'll mention something to her the next time I see her. How's business going?"

"Good. Oh, and by the way, thanks for those two referrals the other day. We're going to be able to get to them a lot sooner than I thought. I better go. I'll stop in sometime soon, and we'll talk."

As Griff arrived at the worksite, he stopped his vehicle, and sat for a moment as he considered the afternoon's activities.

His mom might just be involved with Howard, or Henry or whatever his name was. He would certainly keep an eye on what was going on. As sick as she was, he didn't want her hurt by some idiot and have *that* issue on her mind, along with all her other problems.

But his real concern was, and would continue to be, Chase. He would need to work harder and finish more jobs to keep up his payments. After today, it was clear he couldn't miss any more of them, or his mother's illness might indeed be the least of his worries.

Chapter 24

David quickly moved from his vehicle to the front door of Worldwide Title Company and darted inside. The heat was intense and easily the hottest day of the summer. It had been hot all week, but today was to the extreme. He couldn't move through the door, into the air-conditioned comfort of the title company's front office, quickly enough.

He was escorted to a conference room where, prior to her appearance, David once again reviewed all the figures and paperwork concerning Hope's transactions.

About 15 minutes after he arrived, Hope walked through the conference room door.

David stood, and said, "Good morning. Hot enough for you?"

She said, "Sit, sit. Yes it is. I'm not used to this. I've only been back from Tahoe a couple of weeks, and this is far from what I enjoyed while I was there. Is everything ready to go?"

As she took a seat next to him, he said, "Yes. I can go through the paperwork with you one more time if you wish, but nothing has changed since we looked everything over at the office."

"No need."

David moved his chair back from the table, angled it toward Hope so he could face her, and said, "So, tell me about Tahoe. We did nothing but talk business the last time

I saw you, and, of course, having all those appointments waiting for me in the reception area didn't help either. What's there that makes you happy? You seem pretty laid back, and, in spite of the results of the dissolution, you seem happy. What's the big deal with Tahoe?"

"I must admit, being there does change my mood. It is so beautiful. The air is crisp, the view is second to none, and while I'm there, I always seem to enjoy the moment, rather than living only for the next day, as I do here."

She smiled as she said, "You really need to try it. You visit once, you'll wish you could stay. It's another world and I love it. That's why I would have never given up our house there—unless it had been as a tradeoff for full custody. But that was the only reason I would have even considered it."

"I need to go there one of these days if I'm ever able to take another vacation. Maybe if you'll rent it out to me, I'll just stay at your place."

"I'll do you one better. As long as I'm not there, you can go for free, anytime you wish. There are just a few personal items I've left there—certainly nothing you haven't seen before. You let me know when you're ready to vacation, and I'll let you know if it's available."

"I'll do that. By the way, how's Billy? How's all that joint custody business going?"

"It's as difficult today, as it was the first day we started it. He's with Jack now. I'm starting to see a little attitude show up in Billy I haven't seen before. Visitation is proceeding as the judge ordered, but I can't accept it any better now than I could the day he ruled. And of course, Jack is just as much an ass now, as he was when we were married. Certainly nothing has changed in that respect. I guess I've gotten used to it. Now, all our schedules have changed to the point it's become a little easier in that respect, but it still isn't right—it just isn't right."

"How's the income situation?"

"Fine. I'll be fine. I need his alimony payments, that's for sure. I've thought about getting a job, but it's tough when I only get Billy two weeks at a time. I want to spend as much time with him as I can. It's tight, but it's working fine. What about you—your divorce finished, and everything cleaned up from it?"

"Finally. Yes, everything is back to a semblance of normalcy I guess, whatever that really means. I haven't seen her in months. I hear about her on occasion, but there's no contact between us whatsoever. I hope she remarries so I can get rid of this alimony obligation."

He hesitated for a moment, smiled and said, "But to be honest, I thank God every day I make one of those alimony payments that it's the only contact I have with her. It's all worth it—making the payment is worth its weight in gold in light of the fact I don't have to deal with her in any other respect."

"You think you'll ever remarry? I know I've asked myself that question many times since we ended our marriage."

"Doubt it." He continued to consider her question, then said, "I shouldn't say that I guess. Sure, if the right person comes along, I'd take a long hard look at it, but she would really need to be the right one. I'll certainly think about that type of commitment in much more detail than I did before I married my ex, but yes, I guess anything is possible. You?"

"Right now, I can't think of anything worse."

David laughed, as he said, "I understand."

The door opened, and for the next hour they reviewed and signed all documents necessary for the purchase of her new home and the sale of her current home.

David arrived at his office early that afternoon, and a few moments later, Gail informed him Griff was waiting to see him. His appointments for the afternoon weren't scheduled to begin until two-thirty, so he told her to send him in.

"Hey Dave, what's going on? I tried to get in to see you this morning, but you were out."

"Yeah, I had a real estate closing outside the office. How's work going?"

As he sat down, Griff said, "It's going good. I've never been busier. But the out-of-pocket expenses I incurred while getting all set up were way more than I expected. That, combined with people taking their time to pay me, keeps me a little short most of the time. I've been too liberal in allowing people to finish paying me for the work I did for them, and it's been a hard lesson for sure."

"Yeah, that's always tough to figure out. It was the same for me when I first started. Knowing when to trust what people tell you they'll do, and when not to, is essential to keeping your business open. Are you still hurting financially?"

"Not too bad, but yes, it's still a problem. That's one of the reasons I'm here. Are you still having financial issues from the divorce? I'm not at the point where a little extra money is an absolute necessity, but I could use a little loan until I get this cash flow figured out."

David leaned back in his chair, considering what he should do. "I'll tell you what. I can loan you a little, maybe a couple of thousand, if that helps."

"Yes, that would definitely help. How soon?"

"Maybe the first of next week."

"That would really help, Dave."

For the next half-hour, they discussed family issues, mostly involving their mother. Griff was definitely concerned about her new friend, and urged David to help him determine if there was anything to worry about.

He left when Gail indicated David's two-thirty had arrived and was waiting to see him. David told him he would have a check for him on Monday and would see him then.

After he left and prior to his appointment, he considered his brother's situation. He actually had more money that he could have loaned him, but he was hoping this would take care of the issue, once and for all.

He would make the promissory note due in 60 days. If it wasn't paid off by then, he would have a good reason not to loan him any more money until the first note was paid. He just wasn't going to put himself in a position to continue to supply him with money for his drugs.

If this was a cash flow problem, he surely could figure it out within the next two months. If he was using the money to purchase drugs, he would be unable to pay the note off, and David would have an excuse for not loaning additional funds.

Hopefully, his brother was being honest with him. If he wasn't, it was only a matter of time before he would, once again, need to find a way to get Griff back in treatment—a responsibility he dreaded almost as much as making each of those monthly alimony payments.

Chapter 25

Martha quickly closed the door behind her, relieved to be inside, away from the stifling heat. It had lasted over a week, and there appeared to be no relief in sight. She was just thankful she didn't need to be working outside, as so many people in Nashville were doing today.

She walked in the living room, and noticed Betty watching the early morning news, with her cup of coffee on the end table near her.

"Good Morning, Ms. Betty. How are you this morning? One hot sucker out there today."

She walked back in the kitchen to start her normal morning duties, and after a few minutes, realized Betty hadn't responded.

She yelled, "Morning, Betty."

Again, no response.

Her heart skipped a beat, as she walked slowly toward the living room. As she approached, she could tell her employer was still sitting upright. As she reached her, it was clear Betty was very much alive and simply ignoring Martha's comments.

Martha put her hands on her hips, and elevated her voice as she said, "Morning, Betty. Is a response to much to ask for when I talk to you? I mean, does it really take that much out of you to say 'good morning'?"

Betty turned her head slightly and said, "Oh, don't get your feathers all ruffled, Martha. Yes, whatever, good morning. Now go on and do your job. I'm busy."

"Not a problem for me, Ms. Betty. Not a problem at all."

Martha walked back into the kitchen and whispered to herself, "That's all you're gitten from me today, that's for sure. You aren't gonna get another chance to bite my head off. Do my thing, and I'm outta here."

Betty continued to watch TV without further comment. Martha continued to do her work-related duties until near 11:00 a.m. Finally, she could stand it no longer.

She walked in the living room, stopping between the TV and Betty. She turned toward her and said, "What the hell's wrong with you this morning? You got a hitch in your gittalong it seems to me. Now, what's the problem? You not feeling good or what?"

"Move."

"Talk."

"Shit. No, I'm fine. Just leave me be. I'm fine."

"No you're not, and I'm not movin tell you tell me what the hell's wrong with you. Did I do something to irritate you? Cause if I did, I don't…"

"No, no just stop. You didn't do anything."

"Out with it then. What's the problem?"

Betty looked away, and when she finally reengaged, she said softly, "I have a date tonight—with Howard. He wants to take me out to eat. I told him I'd go, but now I feel I made a bad decision. I'm just trying to figure out what to do."

Martha smiled, took a deep breath, and said, "Is *that* the problem? You had me worried. I figured something was going on with your health." She sat down near Betty. "Why would you second guess yourself? It sounds like it's only a meal—you're not gonna sleep with him. Why are you torturing yourself about this? Go, have fun, and tell me all about it tomorrow morning."

"I haven't been out on a date since before I was married, and that was a hell of a long time ago. I don't know what to wear…I…"

"Oh, come on now. We'll figure that all out this afternoon. Relax. Quit worrying about it. What the hell do you have to lose?"

Betty turned away, and said nothing, clearly deep in thought.

He picked her up right on time—6:00 p.m.

Martha felt more like her mother than her caretaker, but she knew how worried Betty was. Her curiosity consumed her, and she was more than slightly interested in how she got along. She had decided to stay until Betty arrived home.

Near seven-thirty, the phone rang—it was David. Now, Martha *was* concerned. She had been told not to breathe a word of her date to either of the boys. However, she hadn't anticipated she would need to talk to one of them while Betty was gone.

"Hi, David," she whispered. "How are you?"

He hesitated, then said, "Well, I'm okay, but what are you doing there? You never stay during the evenings. She alright?"

"Well, yes, she's fine, but she had a difficult day. She was really tired most of the day, and she just went to bed. I thought I'd stay with her awhile, and then go home."

"Is this something serious?"

"No, no, nothing serious here, David, nope, nothing at all. I'm just about to leave. She's sleeping now. She over did today. She was helping me around the house, and just overdid. You know how she is.”

David laughed. “I do, I certainly do. Well, leave her a note that I called. I’ll call back in the morning. Thanks for all you do, Martha.”

“No problem.” She quickly terminated the call.

About nine-fifteen, she heard a car door close, and muffled conversation while they both walked toward the house. Martha never said a word, as Betty opened the door, shut it, then turned, leaned back against it, and started to smile.

Martha said, “Apparently, that went very well.”

“It did.”

“Come over here, and sit down. I need to go home, but I wanna hear about it before I leave.”

Betty walked toward the living room, her eyes starting to tear up. But she remained silent as she sat down.

Martha said, “I stayed late because I wanna know what happened. *Now talk.*”

She looked away, as she collected her thoughts. “Yeah, sure. Well, after we had had our salad, and our main course, which was by the way incredible…”

“Don’t want to hear about the damn food, Betty. What happened between the two of you?”

“Well…he told me he still loved me.” Once again, she started to tear up, as she said, “He told me he still loved me—after all these years. He told me he had never stopped loving me, even though he was married to a wonderful woman. I didn’t know what to say.”

“You are kidding me. So what’d you do? How did you respond?”

“I told him to pass the salt.”

Martha laughed, and said, "Okay, so what happened then?"

"It got a little quiet, and then the waitress came and asked us if we were ready for dessert."

"And then?"

"Well, we both ordered…"

"Betty, come on now…"

"Okay, okay, I'm sorry. I said, 'Howard, there's a part of me that has always loved you, too. I never quit wondering about you, where you were, if you were happy, if you had children. I never forgot you, and I never will'."

"And he said? Come on Betty, I don't want to have to keep pulling this out of you. What happened next."

"He said, 'Do you enjoy being with me?' And I said, 'Yes, Howard, I always did, and I still do.' Then he said, 'Maybe we should spend all our time together.' And I said, 'Whatta you mean, Howard?' Then he hesitated for a minute, took a deep breath, and said, 'Let's get married'."

Martha said nothing—nor did Betty.

Finally, Martha said, "Say that again. What'd he say? Did you say 'get married'?"

Betty, her eyes as big as baseballs, said, "That's what he said, Martha. Those were his exact words."

"What'd you say?"

"I told him no. What the hell did you expect me to say. I'm old, I got cancer, I'm dying, I got kids to think about...I got…"

Martha interrupted her, as she said, "Hold on there, Betty. You need to reconsider."

"I do? Why? I'm not getting married. What would people think about me getting remarried at my age, and sick, and…"

"When the hell's what people think ever mattered to you?"

"But the boys, they're not going to…"

"Listen to me. You need to think about what's best for you and what's best for Howard—that's it. Nothing more, nothing less. You know how he feels. He's a smart man. He's thought all this through long before he asked you. It's your turn to think it through and figure out what's best for Betty, no one else. Did you tell him you'd think on it?"

"Well, no, I just told him no. He did, however, tell me to think about it. He said he wasn't taking no for an answer tonight. He was just throwing it out there for me to consider."

"Did you talk about any future plans if it did take place—if you were to marry?"

"Heavens no. I almost threw up when he asked me. I couldn't believe what I was hearing. I was in shock."

"You need to think about this. You two could have such a good time with each other, and hell, you're with each other most of the time now anyway. It really wouldn't mean much of a change."

Martha stood. "Now, I gotta go. You sleep on it. I'll see you tomorrow morning. Oh, by the way, David called."

Betty looked up at her, and said, "Oh my god, you didn't tell him I was out on a…"

Martha smiled, and said, "No, I told him you went to bed early. He accepted that and said he'd call tomorrow. I'll be back in the morning. You sleep on it, and we'll talk then."

Betty looked away, as she said, "Sure, sure we can do that tomorrow morning. I'll be here and we'll just talk about it then."

Martha walked out the front door, making sure it was locked before she walked away. She wanted to make sure the house was shut up tight before she went home. Normally, Betty would handle that after she left. But considering Betty's frame of mind tonight, she just figured she wasn't going to think of anything, but the proposal. She smiled. Martha figured tonight, sleep would most likely not come easy for her good friend and employer.

Chapter 26

Jack Whitmore remained in bed, as he considered all the different issues he needed to resolve during the day. He had been in and out of a restless sleep for over an hour. He knew now, he should have quit thinking about all those problems long ago, jumped out of bed and started resolving them, rather than wasting his time horizontally.

Beth had already started putting herself together to start her day, and was in the bathroom when he walked in to shave and shower.

As he walked out, she said, "You got a lot going on today? What's your schedule look like?"

"Overwhelming." He stopped, turned around and said, "Did you get that child support payment in the mail for me yesterday? It's late after today." He then walked away as he said, "I wish she would just up and die so I could quit making the payments."

"What are you complaining about? It's about half what you should be paying. By the way, it's lying on the table by the door. I forgot to mail it."

"Thanks a lot," he said sarcastically. "I'll take it with me and have Claudia mail it. Oh, and to respond to my complaining issue, I shouldn't have to pay her anything. She gets the kid as much as I do—she should pay for him when I have him, and I should when she has him. It's just not fair the way it is."

"You know you might wanna lower your voice. Billy's still asleep."

"Go get him up and get him ready. I'm leaving early today, and I want him ready to go when I'm ready to go."

Beth finished what she was doing and went in to awaken Billy. She had him ready to go and sitting at the breakfast table 15 minutes later.

As he walked in the kitchen, he said, "You know, it would be a hell of a lot easier if *you* dropped him off today. I got so much to do I can't even think straight."

"I'm not driving near the school." She walked up beside him, and said, softly, "By the way, remember whose child it is. He wasn't ready to get up—I had to wake him up this morning. He'll probably sleep all the way anyway—he's really tired. By the way, if you want beer tonight, you better stop and get it somewhere along the way. We're out."

"Whatever. Just keep adding to the list—as if I don't have enough going on."

Thirty minutes later he strapped Billy into his car seat, and left for the office. The one thing he wanted to make sure and do today was to call his offshore banker. Interest rates were moving. He needed to discuss placement of a large amount of uninvested cash. He knew he would have to fit the call in between appointments, which Claudia had informed him before he left the office on Friday, were booked solid from nine to four.

He pulled into a small mom and pop grocery store/gas station, quickly looked to make sure Billy was sleeping, which he was, and ran inside to buy the beer. The line was long, but they moved quickly, and in just a few minutes, he was back in the car, continuing his rush to the office.

Once he reached the office building, he pulled into the parking garage, and found every parking space on the first floor full. As he drove up the ramp to each level, every floor, much to his dismay, was full. He needed to move along. He didn't need this today.

Finally, as Jack reached the rooftop, he found a spot, and quickly pulled in.

He hurried to his office wondering if this heat wave would ever end—he only had a short walk to the elevator, but he was already sweating through his shirt. Once he reached the office, Jack fixed himself a cup of coffee, and started reviewing files. About 30 minutes after he arrived, he heard Claudia walk in the front door, and start preparing for what would be a very active day.

She walked in his office not long after she arrived, leaned down and kissed him.

"Morning. How was your evening?"

"Fine. Are we all ready for today? You got all the files pulled? I need to talk to my banker too. Don't let me forget to call him. Oh and by the way, I left my child support check on your desk. Mail it for me."

She smiled, as she said, "I will. Everything is all ready to go. I do have a question for you though. Do we get a little time together this week, or are you to busy?"

"No, no, I'll stop at your house maybe Thursday night, after I leave here, and before I go home. Does that work for you?"

"Guess it'll have to, but I would like a little more time than last time. Good gosh you were in and out, in more ways than one, within about 20 minutes."

"Sorry, but for now, that's probably the way it's gotta be every time I'm with you. Oh shit!"

He stood and headed toward the door.

"Where you going?"

"Forgot the Gregson file. It's in my car. Be right back."

He returned with file in hand a few minutes later, and said,

"Will you get the banker on the phone? I wanna talk to him before the rat race all starts today."

The rest of the morning went as scheduled—busy, but all under his control.

With only a few minutes left before noon, and just after the last of the morning appointments had concluded, Claudia walked in his office and said "I just got a strange call from Beth. I told her you were busy, but she said she received a call from school. She said they asked where Billy was and wanted me to ask you if for some reason you kept him at the office today."

"Billy, no I…Oh Jesus, no!"

He jumped up, and ran out the office door. As he approached his car, he noticed two law enforcement vehicles parked behind his vehicle, and an ambulance slowly moving toward the down ramp. He also noticed the driver's window had been broken, and there was glass lying on the ground below the driver's door.

"What's going on? What are you guys doing here? What happened to my car?"

One of them turned toward him and said, "This car belong to you?"

Still out of breath, he said, "Yes, sir. Why?"

"Was that your son in the back seat?"

He had reached the car by now, and looked through the window at the child seat, which was now empty.

"Yes. Where is he? What's going on?"

"Sir, we need to talk. Is your office around here?"

"Yes, but where's my son? What's going on here?"

"Just calm down. We need somewhere to talk—preferably out of the sun."

"Come on. Let's go to my office."

On the way, Jack repeatedly asked about Billy, but neither officer said anything. Once they arrived, one of the officers closed his office door, and said, "Sir, you left your son in the car. He died from the heat. I'm sorry to have to tell you, but your son is dead."

Jack looked out the window, then turned to the officers and said, "Is this a joke? Is this some kind of prank? Because if it is, it really isn't very funny."

"No, Mr. Whitmore it's no joke. You know he was in the vehicle, because you put him there. You know you never dropped him off, nor did you remove him from your vehicle. And you know we would never, ever joke about something this serious. Now tell us about your morning, starting with when you put him in the car."

Jack again turned to look out the window, as he considered his options.

"Am I under arrest?"

"No, not at all. We're just trying to figure out what happened."

"I suppose if I don't answer one of your questions in an appropriate manner, you're going to place me under arrest, is that correct?"

"Well, I suppose so, but neither of us expect that to happen. Now, can you please tell us what happened this morning—how this all came about?"

"You know, I need to think this through—and I probably need to discuss it with an attorney before I say a word. Can we talk later?"

They looked at each other, and finally the officer conducting the investigation said, "You're not charged with anything…yet. I guess so, but no later than this afternoon. We wanna know what happened here, and we're not going to wait until tomorrow."

They both stood. "We'll leave you to do what you need to do, but you need to come to the station no later than three this afternoon so we can figure this out. Don't leave town, Mr. Whitmore."

Jack nodded, and both officers left his office. As soon as they walked out the door, he walked into the reception area, looked at Claudia and said, "Call my attorney. Tell him I need to see him immediately."

Claudia, who was wiping tears from her face, said, "I'm so sorry, Jack. I can't believe this is happening."

"You hear what I said?"

"Yes, yes, I'll contact him right away."

"Have you mailed that child support check yet?"

"No, it's right here."

"Tear it up. She won't be needing it."

Claudia said nothing, as she continued to stare at him.

"Did you hear what I said?"

"Yes, certainly, I'll take care of it."

"Call the service station where I get my car serviced. Tell them I need a window put in my car. See what they recommend. I can bring it in this afternoon, or if they don't handle that type of work, have them recommend someone that does."

"Yes, okay I can do that."

"Now, get Beth on the phone. Make sure whoever answers the phone understands it's an emergency and I need to talk to her right now."

"I'll do that first. I'll let you know when she's on the line."

"Oh, and cancel all my appointments for today and tomorrow. Tell them I've had a death in the family. Reschedule all of them for later in the week.

He walked back in his office and sat down at his desk.

"Beth is on line one."

"Morning."

"Hi, Jack. What's going on? You never call me at work."

"I've got a little problem."

Chapter 27

David had appointments most of the day, but his morning was particularly busy. He was glad to see it come to an end. After a quick lunch at a nearby deli, he was back in his office just before 1:00 p.m.

As he was getting ready for his next appointment, Gail peaked her head around his doorway, and said, "You have a really busy afternoon. I think what you wanted me to do concerning that Davidson trial next week, is all finished. But before you get busy, and I start doing something else, is there anything else for that trial you need me to work on or help you prepare?"

He leaned back, thought for a moment and said, "I don't think so. I think everything's ready to go. Let's wait until Wednesday, and call all the witnesses one more time to remind them, again, of their testimony, and of the time they need to be there. She didn't want me to subpoena them, so I just want to make completely sure they're aware, and nothing has come up that would preclude them from being there."

"I'll do that." She looked down the hallway and said, "I think your next appointment just walked in. How long's he going to take?"

"We should be finished by two. Why don't you go ahead and send him in."

Later that afternoon, he had just finished with his second of five appointments, and had not yet heard the front door open signaling his next one had arrived. As he set aside the file from his prior appointment, Gail walked through his office door. She was obviously upset, and had tissue in hand, as she sat down in front of David's desk.

"Hey, you alright? What's wrong?"

"You're not going to believe this."

David put his pen down, and leaned back in his chair. "What happened?"

"You already know I keep track of what's going on during the day in Nashville. Always have. I wanna know what's going on around the city and especially the traffic situation as we get closer to closing down here for the day."

"Yeah, I know that. You've done that from the first day I hired you. I told you it was fine then and it was…and is now."

She looked away as she dabbed at her eyes.

"It just came over the news that the Whitmore boy, Billy, died this morning."

"What Whitmore boy…who…" He leaned forward, and his voice intensified as he said, "Wait a minute. Not Hope's boy—you're not talking about our Whitmore—not *our* Billy Whitmore?"

She whispered, "Yes."

"Oh my god, no. What happened?"

"It's all pretty sketchy, but I guess Jack had him and he left him in his car. He died from the heat."

"Oh no…no. Are you sure it's our people…our Hope?"

"They just used his name, Jack, and the boy's name, Billy. I can't think there would be another family with the exact same names. I'm sure it's her."

"You say its sketchy, whatta ya mean?"

"They just said it's all under investigation. No charges have been filed and they said it's an 'ongoing investigation.' Those are the words they used."

"This will kill her…I mean literally kill her. I need to go to her."

Gail looked toward the door. "I think I just heard your next appointment come in."

"I'll see him, but call the others and tell them I've had an emergency come up, and reschedule them for some time later in the week."

She stood, and said, "I cannot imagine the pain. I feel so sorry for her, I don't know what to do."

"I'll pass that on to her, but I need to see her and do what I can to help."

"I'll send this guy in and cancel the rest of your appointments."

David drove down her street, watching the house numbers until he spotted the correct one. It was as he imagined it— a small, craftsman style home, but an appropriate size for Hope and her son.

There were a couple of cars in her driveway, and a number of cars parked on the street near the home. David had to drive to the end of the block to find a place to park. He assumed the vehicles belonged to individuals already in her home.

David knocked at the door, but no one answered, He looked inside, and could see a room nearly full of people. He opened the door, and walked in. Hope was seated on the couch with a woman on each side of her. There were other people, standing in small clusters about the room.

With the room already crowded, others that arrived had spilled over into the small dining area.

Hope was seated on the edge of the couch, with a tissue in hand and the box sitting on a coffee table in front of the couch. They had placed a small waste basket on the floor for her convenience, which appeared to be half full of tissues she had already used.

One of the women sitting next to her was holding her hand. As he approached, Hope looked up at him, and her stare told the story. Her eyes were vacant. At first, they showed no sign of recognition whatsoever, but as she continued to look at him, she asked one of the women to move and motioned for David to come forward.

Her face was devoid of any makeup whatsoever. She motioned for him to have a seat beside her. As he reached her side, she extended her hand, and pulled him down beside her.

"Hope, what happened? I can't believe what I'm hearing."

"I don't exactly know."

She pulled her hand away, as she continued to wipe the tears from her cheek. "I only know what the police know and that's apparently not much. They came over to tell me Jack apparently drove to work and forgot to drop Billy off at school. That's all I've been told."

"I am so very sorry, Hope, I just can't tell you how sorry I am."

"I don't know what...I can't think right now." She hesitated and turned away. "You know, I told you how he was with details. He proved me right. Unfortunately, it cost me what I loved more than anything in the world."

"I won't stay long. I just wanted to tell you how sorry I am. I am sick. I am sick about this."

"I don't know all the facts yet, but when I figure it all out, I'll come see you. I don't know whether I'll need you or not, but one way or the other, I'll come to see you—to discuss all this, if that's okay with you."

"Yes, certainly. Just call Gail and I'll tell her to get you in whenever you need to talk. You won't have to wait to see me."

"Thank you."

He squeezed her hand, and said, "I'll see you soon. Hang in there, and call me if you need anything at all."

The next morning, after he had discussed Hope's visit with Gail, he did what he could to concentrate, but it took all the effort he could muster. He was about ready to leave for lunch, having finished his morning appointments, when Gail informed him a detective was waiting to see him concerning the death of Billy Whitmore. He told her to send him in.

An imposing figure, Detective Jim Hoffman was well over six feet tall with a burly build. His handshake was more than adequate, and once introductions were finished, he said, "I need to discuss Jack Whitmore with you."

"From what perspective? I really don't know him personally."

"Did you represent his wife in the dissolution of their marriage?"

"Yes. But again, I can't tell you much about him personally."

"While involved in the case, beyond what the other side was telling you, did you ever get a sense of why he really wanted custody of Billy?"

"Whatta you mean? I don't understand."

"I mean, was it because he really did want custody, or did you ever sense there were other reasons behind his request for custody?"

"Hmm. Let me just say that I personally felt, based on my assessment of the case, he wasn't pursuing custody because of a deep abiding love for the child."

"That's what I'm talking about. Of course, your client, whom I have already talked to, feels the same way. She thinks at was strictly a money issue. It was never discussed between the two of them, but she feels he felt the more time he got with Billy, the less he would pay in child support, and that was the most important factor in his request for custody. You feel the same way?"

"I do. But please understand I have nothing to base it on. I was never told that by him or his attorney. It was a feeling I had all the way through the divorce—that everything revolved around money with him. Nothing was more important than money. Where are you headed with all this? What's going on? Is there more to this than just an accidental death?"

"I'm not at liberty to discuss the case with you. All I can tell you is that I've been asked to investigate the facts. I suppose that, in and of itself, tells you something. But for now, I'm just trying to put the facts together and let the district attorney's office determine where it all goes from here."

Their discussion lasted another five minutes. The detective left his card and told David to contact him if he had anything else to offer.

Long into the night, David continued to consider his appointment with the detective. Obviously, there was more to the child's death than he was willing to discuss. Jack Whitmore certainly wasn't someone he could ever call a friend, but to believe Billy's death was anything other than an accident, seemed to him to be an unreasonable conclusion based on those facts discussed with the detective.

Chapter 28

It had taken David a few days to process and finally accept the passing of young Billy Whitmore. During his lifetime, he never had to handle a death as tragic and as incredibly disheartening as the death of a child so young.

As he sat in his office, not long before Gail would arrive, he continued to wonder why all the questions from law enforcement concerning his death. Since the initial interview, he had heard nothing from anyone concerning repercussions involving the situation.

Gail walked in the front office door at the same time the phone rang. He heard her answer it, then waited for her to peak around his door frame.

"Good Morning. The judge is on line one."

"My judge? Henry?"

"Yes. You wanna visit with him, or return his call later?"

"I'll talk to him."

He picked up, and said, "Good morning, Judge. Still in the swimming pool?"

He laughed as he said, "I wish. I just heard some news you might be interested in."

"I doubt it, but give it your best shot."

"I just heard charges have been filed against Jack Whitmore."

He sat up in his chair. "You're kidding."

"Nope. I heard it through the grapevine. Nothing's out about it yet, but it came from a good source, and I have no doubt it's true."

"What'd they file?"

"Aggravated child abuse."

"Well, if they can establish the facts, that sounds like an appropriate charge. Certainly, no intent to kill, but plenty of neglectful conduct."

"That's what I thought. I figured you'd wanna know. Don't spread it around until he's actually charged."

"No I won't. I'll probably tell Hope. She's not in a good frame of mind right now, and I'd rather she hear it from me, than on the street."

"That the only reason you're telling her?"

"Sure."

"Really?"

"Don't go there, Henry. Thanks for the info."

He called before he drove to her house, so his arrival would be no surprise when he knocked on her door. As fragile as she appeared when he saw her at Billy's funeral, David felt she didn't need another surprise of any kind. She saw him drive up, and was waiting at the door, opening it before he knocked.

"Hi, David. What was so important you needed to see me right away?" She closed the door behind him, as she said, "Come on in. You wanna cup of coffee?"

She looked tired, but other than that, David quickly concluded she was as beautiful without makeup as she was with. She had nothing on but a robe, apparently not having taken the time yet this morning to put on clothes or makeup.

"No. Sorry, but I don't really have time."

"Come, sit down with me." As she sat down on the couch, she said, "Now what is it you need to tell me? Oh, and by the way, thanks for coming to the funeral. I never had an opportunity to thank you for being there."

He sat down near her, and said, "I wouldn't have missed it. Again, I'm so sorry."

She looked away for a moment, then said, "Thank you. I'm just living hour to hour. I really hope I can recover—ever. Overwhelming…it's just…overwhelming, as you can imagine."

"Well, I've got some news for you about the situation I felt you should know. Until it's official though, don't say anything about it to anyone."

"Okay, I won't. What news? Concerning what?"

"I get it from a pretty good source that Jack's going to be charged with a crime—aggravated child abuse."

She never blinked, never reacted in any respect.

"Do you understand what that means?"

"Yes."

"I was concerned they might conclude it was all just a horrible accident, but obviously they have determined it was way more serious than that. Maybe he'll at least have to pay for what happened. Even though the charges are filed, he'll still have to be indicted, but I don't think that will be an issue."

She looked down, and whispered, "Won't bring him back."

He took her hand. "You're right, it won't. But maybe it will at least result in some form of punishment for the man that caused Billy's death."

She continued to sit in silence, until she said, "What happens then—after he's indicted?"

"There'll be a trial, and a jury will need to determine if he's innocent or guilty."

"Will I be allowed to watch?"

"I imagine they'll call you as a witness, but I don't know for sure."

She squeezed his hand. "Will you be able to help me get through this? Can you keep me informed about what's happening, and help me get through this?"

"Certainly. I'll keep you up to date, and walk you through it all. I'll help you with your testimony if you're called to testify."

"What could happen to him—I mean if they find him guilty?"

"He could be sent to prison. In addition, I'm sure this won't help his business."

"Could it affect the alimony payments he's making to me?"

"Yes. If he goes to prison, he'll have nothing from which to pay you."

She nodded, then stood. "I understand. Thank you for all you've done, David. You've been there whenever I've needed you. You're a good friend."

He took that as his signal to leave. He didn't want to leave. He wanted to remain with her, to talk about her future, to talk about issues other than the death of her son. But she was making all the decisions at this point, and it was clear she was ready for him to walk out the door so she could continue to process all the new information she now had.

He stood. "Let me know if you need anything, Hope. You know where I am, even if it's just to have a cup of coffee or a talk in my office. Just let me know."

"I will." She started to walk toward the door.

He said, "I know the way. You don't need to walk with me."

"Thanks." She turned and walked through a doorway into the kitchen, and he let himself out.

"So what's the story with Hope? She getting along or not?"

David had just returned to the office, and was reviewing his messages.

"She'll be fine—I think. She's still trying to accept what happened, but when I have the opportunity, I'm going to tell her that's never going to happen. You never, ever, accept something like that. You just live with it. It's just part of your life, every single day. At least, that's my two cents worth. I'll probably never have an opportunity to tell her that though. We'll never be close enough for me to feel comfortable discussing that issue in depth."

"You'd like to be though, wouldn't you?"

He looked up from his messages and said, "Why do you say that?"

She smiled as she said, "It's pretty clear, David, how you feel about her. Your whole demeanor changes when you talk about her—when you're with her. You have always had a little trouble masking how you feel anyway, and how you really feel about her is no exception."

"You know, I'm not really sure how I feel. I do care for her, but to get back into this relationship business after all I've just been through is not something I want to do, at least not yet."

"You going to help her follow the prosecution of Jack?"

"Sure. She'll have little idea what's going on, and no one to help her understand. That's the least I can do."

"Oh, I imagine if you weren't around, someone would help her. I'm thinking it's really something you're wanting to do, rather than something you feel is an obligation." She smiled. "At least, that's my two cents worth."

He looked up at her and said, "Could we get back to business? We've a lot to go through this morning and you evaluating how I feel about a former client isn't one of them. Now, cut it out and let's discuss the Davidson trial, if that's not too much to ask."

Chapter 29

Griff had been working since shortly after sun-up. His current project involved building a new home. Satisfactory completion would eventually provide a final payment which would greatly assist his cash flow. It was now just a matter of finishing off some of the details, and receiving that payment.

As he prepared to take a short noon break, he noticed a newer model car driving down the lane to the worksite. He watched as it came to a stop, and Chase exited. Today he had none of his men with him, which certainly made Griff breathe a little easier. But a visit from him under any circumstances, was not something to look forward to, especially when he showed up unannounced.

"Mr. Chase, what a surprise. What brings you out here?"

"Oh, I really just wanted to check out your work—to see what my loan helped finance. How are things going for you?"

Griff gestured toward the partially completed home, as he said, "This is my biggest project to date. It's turning out very well. I've got about ten jobs lined up after this one. I think you've received every one of my payments haven't you? I don't think I've missed one."

"No, you've made them all. They are however, always late. And each one seems to be a day or two later than the last. You're up to date, but you might work on getting the damn things to me on time, okay?"

"Sure. Sorry. I don't send them, Kristy, my girlfriend does. I'll tell her to be a little more punctual. Is that the only reason you came to see me—because my payments were a little late?"

"How bout we go sit in the car. To damn hot out here."

Griff wondered if he had a choice—because if he had a choice he wasn't going to sit in his car under any circumstances. He quickly concluded it hadn't been a request. Certainly it had been couched in the form of a request, but he knew better—it was a demand.

"Sure. Let me just tell my men I'll be right back."

As soon as he told his crew to carry on, he walked toward the vehicle, and slid into the back seat—alongside Chase.

"Okay, now Griff here's the deal. I'm in the process of buying a piece of land. I have two or three parcels picked out, but I'm negotiating on each one, so nothing has been finally decided. I wanna build a building on the ultimate site I pick out, and I've selected you as the one to build it."

Griff smiled, as he said, "Great, Mr. Chase. I'd be proud to build it for you."

"As I say I haven't picked the spot yet, and it'll probably be a year or so before I need you to begin. I have a lease on a building which I'm using for another year, but it's downtown, and I want one built beyond the city limits. I'll let you know when I'm ready."

"Great. I'll wait to hear from you, and we'll put it down as a tentative start date for about a year from now."

"It should work out very well for both of us. I get my building and your note balance will drop substantially— maybe even get paid completely off. A win/win situation for both of us."

Griff thought for a moment. "But you're still going to take my regular monthly payments each month, right?"

"Oh no. I'll offset as much of it as I can, based on what I owe you. If I owe you as much as three payments the first month, then I'll offset all three. That's the way it will be done. Should work out well for both of us."

"But if everything you pay me goes toward the note, I'll have no cash flow—I won't be able to pay my men."

Chase stared at Griff, considering his concerns for only a moment.

"Look, you got about a year to figure that all out. How I explained it to you is how we're gonna do it. Figure it all out between now and then. You got time. Save up a little— do what you want, but that's how we're doing this. Now go. I'll let you know when I'm ready for you to begin."

"Oh, and by the way, I expect a low dollar bid on the cost too. I don't want no price that's out of reason. I want it as low as it can be, and don't be trying to screw me on the cost of building it. I got experts to look at such things, and I won't take kindly to you trying to inflate the cost, you understand?"

Griff nodded, opened the car door, and got out. He watched Chase drive away, then slowly walked back to the project.

Later that evening, he sent the crew home. It was eight-thirty before he was able to leave the work site. On the way, he called David and reiterated his conversation with Chase. He asked David if another loan would be available when he started the project for Chase, if he needed it.

Griff figured the first thing David would point out was that he hadn't been paid a penny on the loan he had just made him. As expected, David mentioned that immediately. He went on to say he would see how his finances were at the time Griff needed the funds. He knew that was about the best answer he could expect, based on the fact he hadn't yet paid the old loan off.

Upon arriving home, as he walked through the door, he said, "Hey Kristy, we got any beer…or any booze of any kind?"

She was watching TV when he walked in. She looked up and said, "Hi. Long day?"

"Yup. Booze?"

"I think there's some beer in the fridge. What happened?"

As he walked to the refrigerator, he said, "I had a visitor. Chase came to see me."

Kristy stood, and walked in the kitchen as she said, "What'd he want? We're okay with payments to him aren't we? I mean, I'm sure I've sent him all we owe him."

He opened his beer, and sat down at the table. "Yes, we're up to date, but the bastard wants me to build him a building."

She sat down, across from him, smiled and said, "Great."

He took another drink, but failed to respond.

"That's a good thing, right? More business is good for us, right?"

"He wants to offset our note against what he owes me to build it. That means *all* of it, not just what I might owe him for the month. That means no cash flow for the time I build it. That means there's a chance our employees won't get paid on time."

"Did you explain that to him—that doing it that way could jeopardize our operation? Surely he understood that."

"He told me I had plenty of time to figure that all out, but that was the way he was going to do it. He also made it clear he wanted a break on the price. You know as well as I, what the prick wants, is what he gets. We'll have to figure out something between now and then."

She thought for a moment, and said, "He's right. We'll get it figured out."

"You know, I owe David, I owe your parents, and now this. It just seems like I'm having a hell of time doing anything right. Business is good, but we're not making much progress, financially. Now we have Chase and his building to contend with. It's just a little discouraging."

She stood, and walked around behind him. As she started to rub his shoulders, she said, "Hey, it's going just fine. We got a little time. We'll figure it all out by then."

"I hope so. It just seems like we're always on the edge. Things were looking up until that idiot showed up today."

"Just stay positive. As I look at it, for the first time in a long time, things *are* looking up. We'll just hope it continues, and we have it all figured out by the time you're ready to build his little building for him. It'll all work out, Griff. Just stay positive. It'll all work out just fine."

Chapter 30

She wondered how long this would go on. She couldn't sleep, she couldn't eat, she just plain didn't care—about anything.

Hope sat at her kitchen table as the news on TV rambled on about something that didn't, in any respect, affect her, wondering if she would ever really care about anything or anyone again.

It had been a month. Nothing had changed. Billy was gone, Jack was still around, and she remained unable to move on. She had tried. She had read and watched and listened to everything available concerning how to "move on". Nothing had worked. So here she was. Every morning was the same. No sleep the night before, a couple of pots of coffee during the day, and no relief in sight.

She had now been sitting at her kitchen table since 5:00 a.m. She finally concluded she should do something…anything…to get her mind off Billy. As she mentally sorted through her options, her phone buzzed. The only reason she answered it was because it was from law enforcement.

"Yes."

"Ma'am, this is Detective Hoffman, Nashville police. You got a minute to talk?"

"Several actually. Whatta ya want?"

"Well, you might remember, I called you when Jack was indicted. I just wanted to follow up on that. Right now his trial date is set for early October. I'll keep you updated on that, as to whether the date remains the same or is changed. Of course, you already know I want you to testify. I'll be working with you to set up a time to meet with the assistant district attorney, so he can go through your testimony."

"Can't wait."

He laughed, and said, "No, I'm sure testifying is not high on your list of priorities as it isn't with most people. But the jury needs to hear from you. They need to know how you feel about all this."

"While I don't look forward to that, on the other hand, I'll be a willing witness. I *want* the jury to hear from me, and of course I want him convicted."

"You mentioned that before and so do we, so…"

Just then she heard a knock on the door.

"Someone's at the door. Can you hold a moment?"

"Sure."

She walked to the door, and looked out the window. Ann was standing patiently, with a box of pastries in hand.

Hope opened the door, and said, "Come in. I wasn't expecting you. I'm on the phone."

As she walked away, Ann said, "I figured if I called first, you wouldn't let me stop by, and I wanted to see you."

Hope never turned around. As she walked back to the kitchen with Ann in close attendance, she said, "Mr. Hoffman, I need to go. Stay in touch. Let me know the confirmed date as soon as you know."

"I will, Hope, and thanks."

She terminated the call, and sat down.

"If I'd known you were coming I would have been dressed."

"If you'd known I was coming, you wouldn't have answered the door."

Ann set the box of pastries in the middle of the table, and walked to the cabinet, pulling out a cup. After she had poured herself a cup of coffee and sat down she said, "I figured if I forewarned you, you'd have told me to stay home. I wanted to see you, and I felt the best way to do it was to just drop in. By the way, these donuts are out of sight. Try one."

"Maybe in a bit. I'm not hungry."

"You appear to be having an issue with hunger on a regular basis. You really look thin, Hope. Better eat. Keep your energy up."

"Why?"

"I understand."

"No, you don't. Nobody understands unless they've been through it. Until you've lost a child you'll never understand."

Neither said anything, Ann concentrated on her donut, and Hope starred into space.

Both remained quiet, until Hope said softly, "I'm sorry. I shouldn't have popped off. I'm just lost right now. My life is completely without meaning. I have no past, I have no future. I'm just living from second to second, with no direction of any kind. I don't know what I want, I don't know where to go, and most of all, I don't know how to get some relief from the incredible pain that haunts me every fucking second of every day."

She stood, and walked to the counter, where an open box of tissues had been conveniently placed precisely for the problem she was now experiencing.

As Hope dabbed at the tears, Ann said, "I'm sorry. I can only imagine what you must be going through. I have no idea how I would have handled it. What did the detective want?"

Hope walked back to the table, and sat down, the tears having stopped, at least for the moment.

"He wanted to remind me of Jack's trial. I think as much as anything, although he never said it, he just wanted to make sure I was still on board—that I wasn't getting cold feet and backing out of testifying."

"You haven't, have you? I mean, you still want to tell the jury how you feel, and what you know about Jack don't you?"

She smiled. "I'll do everything I can to convict that fucker. Whatever it takes. If I have to testify for three days, or three weeks, I'll do whatever I can to see him in jail."

"First time I've seen you smile in a month."

"You brought up a topic I can smile about. Nothing else matters to me at the moment—nothing."

"Exactly what is he charged with, do you know?"

"Some kind of child abuse. It's a felony I know that. And I know if he's convicted he'll most likely go to prison. That's just the basics. I really don't know, nor need to know much more than if he's convicted, he'll go to jail."

"Will that affect you? I mean, will you stop getting payments from him if that happens?"

"Sure. I've already taken that into account. I'm going to need to get a job no matter what. I'll just have to work a little harder if I lose the monthly payments from him, but which I'll gladly do with a smile on my face."

"Sounds like you've already thought it all through."

"I guess." She turned away. "Now, if I was just smart enough to figure out how to get my son back that would make it all perfect."

Once again, she started to cry as she said, "You know, I told them about Jack. I told everyone about him—about his inability to handle the details, but no one would listen."

"It just sounded to me like no one thought it was that big an issue at the time."

Hope looked at Ann and said, "I tried to explain time after time. The man would go grill steaks, walk away when they were done, and leave the grill on. He would walk out the front door of our house after Billy and I were already in the car, and leave it wide open. Whenever I was gone for the evening, he would prepare supper for Billy and himself, then leave all the food he got out but didn't use, on the kitchen counter. I would have to throw it all away the next day. He never, ever paid attention to the details that finished up a project—he always left that to me."

"When is his trial?"

"It's scheduled now for fall, October, I think."

"Can I be there with you?"

"I think so, yes. I'll let you know."

"Is David going to help you prepare?"

"I think so. There's so much I don't know yet, but I'm going to figure it all out. *I'll* pay attention to details. Believe me, *I'll* know all about this trial before it ever starts."

Ann thought for a moment then said softly, "Hope, you know, even that trial's not gonna bring him back."

Hope nodded as she said, "I know that. Believe me, I know no matter what I do, nothing will change that, but Jack needs to go to prison for what he did, and I'm going to do everything I can to put him there."

Chapter 31

Ted Carney was an imposing figure of a man. At six foot four, and slightly overweight, he seemed to fill the room, with not only his physical presence, but with his deep voice laced with an unforgettable southern drawl.

"Now, Jack, Whatta ya tellin me, son? Why don't you want yourself a jury? We've been through all this once. I just don't quite understand. Explain your thinkin' to me, if you can."

Jack had done his research. He knew all about Ted Carney long before he retained him for his divorce. Research indicated he didn't take many clients each year, but when he did, they were wealthy, and they didn't lose once he agreed to represent them.

It mattered not what type of case it was—he was equally efficient representing defendants in criminal cases, or in agreeing to represent one party or the other in a civil matter. His success rate was incredible, and Jack would have no one other than Ted Carney in his corner for the criminal proceeding he was about to endure.

"It still just seems to me that I want a judge looking at this and determining whether I am guilty or innocent, rather than 12 idiots who know about as much about the law as my ex did. What am I missing here?"

Ted smiled, looked over the top of his glasses and said, "Let me tell you son, what you're a missin. You have 12 idiots on a jury that have to *agree* you were guilty. That can be damn hard to get done. Otherwise, you got one judge, most of the time—one that's pro law-enforcement—and he's the only one that decides your fate. See what I'm a talkin' 'bout. You got twelve versus one. Get it. Now if I can't convince one of them to find you not guilty, I need to by god shoot myself. And if I can somehow make sure that the one that thinks you're not guilty, also has the ability to convince others, why then, my man, we're home free. Now you understand?"

Jack never responded.

"It's all in selecting the right jurors. I'm a tellin you now, if you *wannna* try this to a judge and not a jury, I'll refund your money and you can move on down the road. Am I making myself clear to ya, boy?"

Jack looked away as he digested all Ted had just said.

"Okay. You know best." He turned toward Ted and said, "Makes sense to me, I guess. Let's just leave things as is, and try it to a full jury. Should we go through what I'm supposed to say one more time? I realize we've been through it five or six times, but would it help if we went through it once more?"

"Who the hell's it gonna help? Not me. It gonna help you? No. Like you say we been through it all 'bout umpteen times. You should have it all memorized by now."

"Okay, I agree. Yes, I think I'm all ready to go. Now, what about that jury list you gave me. I looked it over and made marks beside names of people I know, and that shouldn't be on the jury. There were only about three, maybe four. You gonna make sure they aren't on there because they'll most likely vote against me if they are?"

"Yes, I'll do the best I can to keep them off. You talked to the people that are gonna testify for you? They all ready to go?"

"Yes. They all got their subpoenas and are set to be there on time to testify on my behalf."

"Now, you remember all them rules I talked to you about, don't ya? I mean, there's surely no way you could have forgotten them, but you do remember the basics, don't you? You know, like don't argue with the prosecutor bout anything. Don't answer a question you don't understand. Go ahead and be emotional—something you've never done with me, but if the spirit moves you, go ahead and be emotional—after all you've just lost your son. Don't fidget all around when answering questions—just look right into the eyes of the one askin it, and answer it the best you can. You remember all them things I went through with you, right?"

"Yes. I wrote those all down, and I've gone over them a number of times."

Ted stood. "Well then, I'm a thinkin' we're all set to try the case. Why don't you come in one more time next week, and we'll be ready to go. We'll go through the procedure one more time, and then try the case—let the chips fall where they may."

Jack stood, and extended his hand. "Whatta ya think the odds are?"

Ted shook his hand as he said, "Of gettin you off?"

"Yes."

"I would have never agreed to represent you in the first place if I hadn't intended on getting you off, son. We'll be fine. Just do what I tell ya to do, that's all. Just keep following what I tell ya to do."

As Jack prepared for bed, Beth, mindlessly watching another rerun of House Hunters on TV, said, "I know you don't like to talk much about the trial, but I think I have the right to know a little about what's going on. It starts in a couple of weeks, and you've basically told me nothing. You haven't said a word about your appointment with Ted. So let's talk a bit about it now, okay? Can we visit about this issue for a moment?"

He crawled into bed beside her, and said, "Whatta ya wanna know? There's really not much to tell. Trial starts in a couple of weeks. I'm all ready to go as are all the witnesses. If I'm convicted, I'll go to prison. That's it in a nutshell. Now, what *else* you wanna know?"

"Well, I guess the bottom line is, what does he think our chance of success is? Does he believe we're gonna win?"

"As long as everyone testifies like they're supposed to, yes, he thinks we should win. You all ready to go? You know what you're supposed to say?"

"Yes, I've been through everything multiple times with him, and reviewed it all in my own mind, but I guess I'm still worried."

He turned to face her. "Look, as long as you do as you're told, and testify as he told you to, we should be fine. Just make sure you follow what he told you to do, that's all. Just make sure."

He turned over on his other side, away from her, as he said, "Now turn off that TV and shut the light off. I wanna go to sleep and I don't want that TV blaring while I do."

Claudia walked in his office the next morning, between his second and third appointment.

Jack looked up at her and said, "You ready to testify?

"Well, yes, I think so. I've been through everything with the prosecutor and I've talked to your attorney too. I know what they both want me to say."

"You be sure and remember who you work for. Don't forget who pays your bills."

She smiled. "Is that called tampering with a witness, Mr. Whitmore?"

"Don't think so. It's called 'reminding a witness how their bread gets buttered.' I just don't want you to forget I pay you well. Without me, you got no job."

She leaned down and kissed him. "Nor do I have my lover."

"That's right. You'll lose both. Just do what Ted told you to do and we'll both be fine."

"Oh, I will."

"Hopefully, after the trial, we can get back to normal again. I can start stopping by at least once a week."

"I hope so too. It's been a long dry spell, if you know what I mean."

He smiled. "Just a few more weeks, Claudia. Just hang in there a few more weeks."

Chapter 32

"**B**eth, maybe y'all could go get us some sandwiches at that McDonalds cross the way. Would ya mind?"

"No, I'll be glad to. You guys just want a sandwich each?"

Ted said, "Darlin, I need a bit more than that to keep me rolling. Better get me three if you can carry'em all."

Beth looked stunned, but said, "Okay. Sure. Not a problem. I'll be right back."

Ted looked at Jack, smiled and said, "She clearly doesn't know what it takes to keep a man of my size rollin, does she, Jack? I think I shocked the livin hell out of that girl."

"Can we talk about the case—where we at, how's this all going? What are your thoughts about the jury? It took you long enough to select them. I figured it would take about an hour. You've spent three days pickin them."

"Yeah, but I got the ones on there I wanted. I told you to be patient the moment we started pickin'em. I know you don't understand the whole process, but that's why you done hired me, man. I'll lead you through this thing, but you gotta have faith and listen to what I tell ya. I got on that jury exactly who I want on that jury. Now, you just watched me in action during my opening statement. You *had* to be happy with that. I just laid all that crap out for them in a way a baby coulda understood." He laughed as he said, "I'm a tellin you that's what I did—a baby could have understood what I toldum."

"I would agree with you there. You did a fine job. What about those medical people, and the woman that first found Billy? They didn't really hurt our case did they? I mean, that guy just testified what he died from, which we already knew, and the woman just said she found him. I can't think that hurt us."

"No, they didn't. These guys testifying next could though—one of them—the detective—he could hurt us. That officer that first talked to you won't hurt us because you didn't say nothin to him, but the detective you talked to could. We'll just have to see."

Beth returned shortly thereafter, and they quickly finished their sandwiches. After visiting about the afternoon schedule for a few minutes, they walked back in the courtroom.

Judge Ardmore called the trial to order and testimony continued with the officer that initially interviewed Jack. He simply testified as to his observations upon arriving at the scene. Ted declined to cross-examine him. Jack felt secure in his belief the officer didn't harm his case in any respect. But the next officer concerned him.

Once assistant District Attorney, Randall Flagg, had called the detective to be sworn, and all the foundational information had been entered into the record, he said, "When did you first meet with the defendant, Detective Hoffman?"

"The day after the incident."

"Did you talk to him at all the day it happened?"

"No. He wanted to see his attorney before he talked to anyone."

"When you talked to him, what did you notice, if anything, about his physical and mental demeanor?"

"Lack of any emotion."

"What did you observe in that respect?"

"He just was very businesslike about it. He showed no emotion of any kind. That surprised me."

"What did he say happened?"

"He said he left the house with the baby sleeping in the back of the car. He got out to purchase some items at the grocery store, and noticed Billy was still sleeping. He got back in the car and drove to work. He just forgot the child was there. He said he had a million things on his mind. He said it took forever to find a place to park, and he never thought a thing about Billy until his wife called and asked him why the child wasn't at school."

"So, he said it was all just an accident, but one in which this boy died, is that it?"

"Yes."

"Did he ever deny the fact that he just forgot the child? Were there ever any other excuses given for the boy's death?"

"None."

"And as I understood the situation, he didn't forget he had the boy *once*. He had an opportunity to take care of him a number of times during that time sequence, and just failed to do so at any point in time, is that correct?"

"Yes, that's correct."

"Your Honor, that's all I have."

"Cross examine, Mr. Carnie?"

Ted stood, as he said, "Thank ya, Your Honor. Now Mr. Hoffman, let's make sure of one thing before we go any further. This was just a horrible accident, correct? I mean there's no facts anywhere out there that indicate this was intentional, isn't that right?"

"There is nothing to indicate he did this intentionally. But he *neglected* him on numerous occasions and that caused his death."

Ted sat down, as he said, "So you're saying it wasn't an accident."

"I'm saying it was gross negligence to leave that child in the car that day. In addition, he never ever acted like it *meant* anything to him. No emotion at any point in time. He acted like it was just another day at the office."

"Well now, we all have our own way of showing our emotions do we not, Detective Hoffman? I mean, you express them one way, I express mine another, is that a fair statement?"

"Certainly."

"Did you know this man before the incident?"

"No."

"So, you can't compare his 'before' demeanor, to his demeanor after he lost his child, can you? I mean, you can say he was emotionless, and that it shocked you, but maybe this is the way this man processes everything, correct?"

"I guess. It just wasn't what I would have…"

"Now hold on there officer. You don't need to supplement your response. Your response was 'I guess,' is that correct?"

"Yes, that's my response."

"Does this same situation happen a lot around the city? I mean is this the first time you've investigated this type of case in Nashville?"

"No."

"Fact is, officer, we all live our lives anymore at an insane pace, don't we? I mean is it fair to say that this type of case has exploded on the scene in just the past couple of years—people forgetting their children because they have so much on their minds?"

Detective Hoffman looked away for a moment before reengaging in his verbal examination. "It doesn't happen often, but yes, it is more frequent now than it used to be. Any more, people are very busy living life. But that doesn't mean they should be excused for starting the process that killed their child, accident or not. And each case has to be reviewed on its own merits. This one was different."

"Is there any doubt in your mind the defendant was remorseful for what happened?"

"No, not really. I was at the funeral. I watched him then, and for a while after. He was definitely upset, just not in the way I expected."

"He lost his child—his only child didn't he?"

"Yes."

"You really think after all he's been through, he needs to be punished again? I mean really…is this all…"

"Objection, Your Honor. That issue belongs to the jury and only to the jury, not to this detective."

"Sustained. Move on, Mr. Carnie."

"Nothing further."

"Anything further, Mr. Flagg?"

"No, Your Honor."

"You may step down detective. Folks, we've done enough for the day. I'm going to terminate the proceedings, and we'll reconvene tomorrow morning at nine. Remember the admonition I gave you concerning having no discussions about this case with anyone. Court is adjourned for the day."

Back in the conference room, Jack said, "Well, what about today? What are your conclusions?"

"We did fine. He said just what I expected him to say. There were no surprises. But tomorrow, ya know Hope is scheduled to testify. That will be tough for her to do. I'll have to handle her carefully, so don't jump up and down when I let a lot of what she has to say, go unchallenged. We'll clean it all up in the closing statement."

"That 'emotion' issue gonna hurt us? I don't show much emotion in any aspect of my life. I wasn't raised that way, and I'm afraid that's just who I am."

"We'll handle that when you testify. I got that part all figured out."

Beth said, "So what about tomorrow? Is Hope the only witness?"

"No. Claudia is also to testify, along with a couple of other officers that were in the interview room with Detective Hoffman. I'm not concerned about them. We got in the testimony we needed to through Detective Hoffman. The two key witnesses tomorrow will be Hope and Claudia. Claudia mention anything about her testimony to you?"

"No. She just said that she was going to testify for the state. I asked her about it a couple of times, but she said she was told to discuss nothing with me, and that's what she needed to do. I'm not worried about her. She needs the job and I pay her more than she most likely could get anywhere else."

Ted smiled as he said, "You see them old ladies on the jury wipen their eyes during Hoffman's testimony about you losing your child? That's *exactly* the reaction we needed. That's why jury selection is so important. That's why you can't rush it."

"So, you're thinking everything is going okay?"

"I do, Jack. Yes sir, I certainly do. Your testimony will save your own life. Just wait and see, my friend, just wait and see."

Chapter 33

Together, they sat through the prior day's testimony. As Hope would question some procedural issue, she would whisper her concern or ask a question. David would simply listen or provide an answer.

They agreed to meet at a small coffee shop the next morning before walking to the courthouse together and listening to the testimony of witnesses on the stand prior to her testimony.

Now, as they sat quietly, she could hardly hold her coffee cup steady enough to keep the coffee in the cup. They discussed how, at this moment, her nervous appearance was clearly obvious, but later this morning, she would need to remain completely under control. David did all he could to try to help her remain focused upon exactly what her role would be today, while also trying to keep the conversation somewhat light.

She, however, was *completely* focused on the business at hand—the business of convicting her ex- husband, and she made it quite clear that was exactly where her focus would remain until the job was finished, regardless of her physical appearance.

She wasn't certain why they needed her testimony. David told her the prosecutor wanted the jury to hear from the mother of the child. He felt it might help the jury understand exactly how devastating Billy's death was to those around him. He told her the prosecutor wanted the jury to hear specifically how she felt—how upset she was at Jack, and that the situation went way beyond simply a horrible mistake.

They arrived at the courthouse twenty minutes before proceedings were to commence. The jurors were all present, but no one was yet seated.

Once court convened, they listened to a couple of witnesses testify they had seen Jack exit his vehicle that day, but noticed nothing unusual about his demeanor. He didn't appear to be in a hurry, or overly stressed in any respect. Of course, they didn't see the child he left in the back seat as Jack walked away.

They took a fifteen minute break near 10:00 a.m. After the break, the assistant district attorney called out the name of Hope Whitmore. She grabbed David's leg and squeezed. He turned to her and nodded. She let go of his leg, rose slowly, then walked forward to be sworn in and take the stand.

After foundational questions had been asked and answered, attorney Flagg asked, "Can you describe the relationship between your former husband and Billy?"

"There wasn't much of one. Jack was always too busy for Billy."

"Busy with what?"

"I could say work I guess, but it never mattered much what it was—*everything* always came before Billy."

Hope had anticipated the questions would take their toll on her before she concluded her testimony, so she carried a small handkerchief in her purse. Initially it was not needed, but now she used it frequently to dab away the tears.

"How much time did the defendant spend with him?"

"As little as possible."

"Did the situation which gave rise to Billy's death surprise you?"

"The situation giving rise to Billy's death didn't—his death..." She paused, dabbed at the tears, took a deep breath, and said, "His death...yes, his death obviously surprised me. I told everyone that would listen when we were going through our divorce, that Jack was the world's worst when it came to details. No one other than my attorney would listen. And that's what killed Billy—Jack's lack of attention to details. The only difference between the day we were married and the day Billy died, was that while we were married, I learned I always needed to be there to clean up after Jack—to clean up the details. The one time I wasn't there, cost me...my son."

"Would you like a moment to..."

"No, no, I wanna get this over with."

"Were you surprised when he asked for full custody?"

"Yes. He never, ever had much to do with Billy. I had no doubt his demand for custody had much more to do with reducing his child support payments then it did spending time with our son. His request for custody was certainly not consistent with the amount of time he spent with him while we were married. He was never with him."

"In summary, you seem to be saying he had no interest in the child other than how Billy could in some manner save Jack money. Is that an accurate statement?"

"The only language Jack knows is the language of money. Nothing else has ever mattered to him. There is no doubt in my mind the only thing Jack was thinking of when he walked away from that car, was how much money he could make during the rest of the day. And that—that mindset—cost me, cost us our son."

"Nothing further, Your Honor."

"Cross?"

Ted stood. "Well now, ma'am you're not here a tellin this jury the defendant didn't love his child are ya? Whatta you basing that on? He tell you that?"

Hope moved forward in her chair. "Not in so many words, sir, but I lived with him a long time—actually too long. And it was crystal clear his God was money, and he, sir, worshiped it every day of the year, morning, noon and night. He didn't give a shit about Billy. I lived with him. I knew, *know* Jack like the back of my hand. Nothing ever mattered then, nothing matters now, but the almighty dollar, and you can by god take that to the bank…sir."

The judge leaned over, and softly said, "Ma'am you need to watch the language. Just tone it down a notch please."

She listened quietly, and as soon as he finished, she turned and said, "Judge. That man murdered my son. Makes no difference whether he shot him with a gun or left him in the car. He murdered him. Now, I'm sorry if my language is a little salty, but I want everyone to understand exactly how I feel. Let me make this real simple. Because of that man over there, because of his actions and his actions alone, my son is gone forever."

The Judge leaned back, and said, "Now, ma'am, let *me* be '*real simple.*' I understand how you feel. But you need to answer only the questions you're asked and nothing more. In addition, your language needs to be toned down in this courtroom. Another outburst like that, I'll find you in contempt and have you removed, you understand?"

"What the hell do I care whether I'm *removed* or not. You, and everyone else in the *system,* just don't seem to get it. First, out of spite, he gets Billy for half the time, and then because he didn't give a shit about him anyway, he kills him. *This is all insane.* He should be in prison! Instead he's out spending his money, enjoying life and my son is dead. I'll never see him again because that bastard killed him. You incompetent idiot, do you understand what..."

"Officer come up here. Ma'am you're out of control. You're also in contempt. Officer, remove her from the courtroom. Mrs. Whitmore don't come back in here for any reason until this trial ends or I'll have you incarcerated. Now get her out of here."

David watched as they removed Hope, and then walked out the back door of the courtroom to find her. She was leaning against the wall of the hallway, handkerchief in hand, sobbing uncontrollably.

David walked up behind her, and put his arm around her back, as he said, "I'm so sorry, Hope. Do you want me to take you home?"

She turned toward him, her mascara running down her face, eyes red from crying and said, "Hell no. I'll wait for you out here. Go back in there and listen to the next witness. I need to know what she has to say."

"Okay. I'll be out as soon as they adjourn for lunch. There's a bench right outside the courthouse. I'll meet you there near noon."

David walked back in the courtroom just as Claudia was sitting down in the witness chair. He listened as the assistant district attorney walked her through the obligatory foundational issues, and then continued with direct examination as specifically concerned the facts.

"Were you in the office the day Billy died?"

"Yes."

"What did you observe about the defendant's demeanor when he was told his child was dead?"

"Nothing."

"Did he show any emotion of any kind?"

"No."

"What did he say to you?"

"He asked me if I had mailed his child support payment."

"What was your response?"

"I told him I hadn't."

"And his response?"

"He just told me to tear it up—she wouldn't be needing it now."

"At that time did he appear upset or emotional?"

"No."

"Did he ever show any sign of emotion?"

"No."

"Did you have any discussion with him after he told you to tear up the check?"

"He told me to reschedule all his appointments, and to get his attorney on the phone. He said to tell him he needed to see him immediately."

"Prior to Billy's death, did he ever visit with you about his son? Did he ever tell you what his son was doing, or what he did with him during the weeks Billy was with him?"

"No."

"I have nothing further, Judge."

"Cross?"

Ted stood and said, "You never had any doubt, but what this was just a tragic accident did you? I mean, you never felt he left him in the car intentionally did you?"

"I wouldn't know."

Ted looked down at Jack, then at the witness.

"We all process a situation in our own way now don't we? You talk about him being so unemotional, but in fact, ma'am, we just all process everything a little differently don't we?"

"I guess."

Ted was quiet for a moment, before he smiled at the witness and said, "Nothing further, Judge."

David watched as Jack's attorney took his seat, then leaned over to whisper in Jack's ear. Obviously, Jack's secretary had not testified as expected.

The judge recessed for the day, having other matters to take up outside the courtroom involving a different case. Court would reconvene tomorrow morning, when Ted indicated the defendant would testify.

David found Hope where he expected her to be, and walked her to her car. She was now well under control.

"David, are you coming tomorrow morning?"

"No, I can't be here. I guess based on what the judge said, it probably would not be a good idea for you to be in the courtroom either, unless you wanna spend a night or two in jail."

"I realize after today, it's not good for me to be there anyway. I'll stay away and just hope the jury does the right thing. I'll tell you one thing. They better find him guilty. The evidence is pretty clear-cut. I'm not sure what I'll do if they don't find him guilty. He needs to pay for what he's done, David, he needs to pay, one way or the other."

Chapter 34

Jack had been at the office since 5:00 a.m. There was no way he would finish all that needed to be done before he left for the courthouse.

It was hard to believe, but his business had actually increased since he had been criminally charged with the death of Billy. However, because of frequent meetings with his attorney, and now the trial, some of his new *and* old clients were starting to complain. Most of them needed a babysitter as concerned their finances. In fact, many times that role was more important to the customer than whether they actually made money. But, right now, with all his legal issues, it was a role he was finding very hard to fulfill.

He heard the outer door open, and Claudia start to prepare her work space for the day's activities. He had been waiting for her to arrive. Jack had a few issues they needed to discuss after her testimony yesterday.

He never asked her to come in his office. He just waited for her to walk in on her own.

"Morning. You all ready to go? What's supposed to happen in the courtroom today?"

"It's my understanding it's now our turn to present evidence, so first off will be me, then Beth. Have a chair."

As she sat down, he said, "Your testimony was interesting yesterday."

"Really? How so?"

"I wonder if you could have described me in any darker terms than you did."

"Sorry." She hesitated. "Now hold on—what are you talking about? I just told the truth. What I told them is what you said, and what I told them about your physical appearance through it all, was the truth."

"Did you have to paint me as being so cold? Did you really need to go as far as you did, and paint me so unemotional—so uncaring?"

"No, I didn't need to, but that was how you appeared to me. What was I supposed to do, lie?"

"Wouldn't have hurt anything. You made me appear as an uncaring, fucking monster, Claudia." He leaned back in his chair and said, "I'm thinking it's time you look for another job, and I mean right now."

"What the hell are you talking about? Why should I?"

"Because it's time for you to go. You need to start looking and right quick."

"You firing me? Are you firing me because of yesterday?"

"You got it. I'll give you a few days to find something else, but then I want you out of here."

She looked away, then slowly stood, and walked to the door. She turned around as she reached the doorway, smiled and said, "Beth know about us?"

He stared at her, but said nothing.

"Because if she doesn't she's in for a big surprise if I leave here under these circumstances."

"Get out. We'll discuss this once the trial is over."

"Do I still need to look for a job today?"

He hesitated, before he said, "No, not today. Now get your ass out of here."

There wasn't a sound from the jurors or the spectators as Ted had Jack testify as to his background, and other matters necessary to establish a foundational basis for his testimony, before he jumped into the facts concerning his son's death.

Once that procedural requirement was satisfied, he said, "Now, in your own words, tell us what happened the day Billy died, from the time you left the house, until you found out he was dead."

"Well, I strapped him in, and drove to a small grocery store. I needed a few items from the store. As I got out of the car, I looked at him. He was sleeping. After buying what I needed, I got back in the car, drove to work, and when I got there, all the parking spaces were full. I was really stressed because I knew I had so many projects I needed to finish before the day was over. When I finally found a place to park, I quickly jumped out, and ran in to the office." He looked down and said softly, "I left him in the car."

"What was your relationship with your son?"

Jack started to cry. "I loved him with all my heart."

"Your former spouse says you didn't give a hoot about him. Is that the truth?"

"Absolutely not. I loved him as much as any dad loves his child. I wanted full custody of him in the divorce, but she wouldn't let me have him. We had a very contentious divorce, as I'm sure you could tell from prior testimony. But there's nothing on this earth I loved more than my son. I miss him every day."

"Had you taken him to school before? Was this part of your normal morning procedure?"

"No. Normally, Beth took him. But she was driving a different direction that day. It was to be a shorter trip for me, and I told her I'd take him. It wasn't a responsibility I normally handled, and that was another reason I forgot him." Again he began to cry. "I just didn't normally take him—she did. And if she had, I'm sure none of this would have happened. So many things could have changed what happened. I still can't believe I forgot him. I just can't accept..."

Jack put his hands over his face as he sobbed.

The judge said, "Mr. Whitmore you wanna take a break here?" He shoved a box of tissues at the witness.

Jack took one, wiped away the tears, took a couple of deep breaths, and said, "No, Your Honor I wanna go on, but thank you."

"Now Jack, this was your first and only child correct?"

"Yes."

"So you haven't ever been down this path before— having to take kids to daycare, to school, or nothin like that right?"

"No. In fact, as I said, this was the very first time I had taken him. Beth always did it before."

"So the process was all relatively new for you?"

"Yes. Not that that is an excuse for what I did, but it was the first time.

"Is there anything else you want to explain to the jury, bout what happened here, Mr. Whitmore?"

He looked at the jury, once again started to cry, and said, "I'm sorry. I'm so sorry. I would give anything to be able to go back to that day, and do it all over again. If you feel I'm guilty, certainly do your duty. But I can tell you, for me, it really doesn't matter what you do. I'll never forgive myself for what I did, for the rest of my life. No matter what you do, guilty, not guilty, whatever, I will never, ever get over what I did."

Jack watched as three of the jurors, all women, started to remove tissues from their purses. Just the desired effect they wanted.

Cross-examination took most of the morning session. Attorney Flagg basically just went through testimony already entered into the record on direct-examination. The facts were relatively simple, and there were very few elements of it left to discuss that hadn't already been discussed.

With about an hour left in the morning session, and after Jack had stepped down, Ted called Beth Whitmore to the stand. After dispensing with foundational issues, he said, "Tell us about Jack's relationship with his son, Mrs. Whitmore."

"He had a great relationship with him. He spent as much time as he could with him, and actually tried for full custody when they were divorced. He took him to the park, he took him to feed the ducks, and he spent time with him every night after he came home from work. They had a great relationship. I did too. I loved Billy. I'll miss him as much as Jack will."

"Jack really hadn't been divorced all that long when this happened had he?"

"No, and that was part of the problem. We were both just still getting used to a complete change in lifestyle when this happened. We were just getting into a routine that worked for all three of us when Billy died. In fact, this was the very first time Jack needed to take him to school. I always took him. It was on my way to work, so I just dropped him off."

She hesitated, took a deep breath, and continued. "But that day, I had to pick up some files from another office building, and it was the opposite direction of the school.

So I asked Jack to take him rather than me." She started to cry. Again, the judge pushed the tissue box toward the witness stand. "If I had taken him as I always had, this would never have happened."

"Any doubt this was nothin but a horrible accident?"

"No, of course not. The sad part of it is, neither of us will *ever* get over it. The jury can do as they wish. To be honest, I don't think Jack really cares. This will literally haunt him for as long as he lives. They could never sentence him to anything worse than his own self-imposed sentence he'll live with the rest of his life."

Ted ended her direct testimony shortly thereafter, and cross-examination by the assistant district attorney was unremarkable . The facts, as Beth knew them, were brief, and it was obvious any additional testimony from her would only benefit the defendant.

The defense called only a few more witnesses to testify as to their observations concerning the relationship between Jack and the child, then rested. The state had no rebuttal, and presentation of evidence was then closed. The judge would submit the case to the jury tomorrow morning after closing arguments by both sides.

As Jack walked in the door, later that evening, Beth met him with a glass of wine, and a kiss.

Jack smiled and said, "You did a good job up there today. I was proud of you."

She walked toward the kitchen and said, "I just told the truth. Can't much go wrong when you do that."

"Whatta ya think? Am I gonna walk or are they going to send me to prison?"

She started putting plates on the table for supper, as she said, "I know there are a couple of women on the jury that are really emotionally disturbed by the testimony, but beyond that I can't read them. Hopefully they'll come to a conclusion quickly. I can't stand much more of this."

He grabbed her as she walked by, and pulled her close. "I just want you to know how much I appreciate what you did."

She kissed him and pulled away. "Hopefully, it'll keep you out of prison. I sure as hell wouldn't wish that on anyone, Jack, not even you."

Chapter 35

David Brenden felt conflicted. As he reviewed file after file, he felt he should be in court, following up on the Whitmore trial, either with Hope, if she dared set foot in the courtroom, or without her. After his discussion with her last night, he had come to the conclusion it was probably best for her not to venture back into the courtroom. Even though she would have no direct contact with the judge, she was afraid, as was David, she simply couldn't control her own emotions if something did happen during the proceedings which she felt was unfair, inappropriate or untruthful.

He heard Gail walk in the office door, and it wasn't but a few moments later she walked in his office and took a chair.

"So, you heading back to the courthouse? What's on the agenda with the trial today, do you know?"

David looked up from his file, and said, "Good morning. I only know what the clerk's office told me on the phone before I left here last night. They thought closing statements would be this morning and the case would be submitted to the jury after the judge read them the instructions, most likely near noon."

"You got a lotta people coming in today. I know you didn't tell me to move their appointments, so I assume you're not going to go today?"

"No. I've got too much to do. I talked to Hope, and I don't think she's going either. It's just too tough on her, and it's hard for her to remain under control. I could somewhat help keep her in check, but once she gets upset, especially about this case, she's pretty much uncontrollable. I'll try to keep her updated. I know she's been in touch with the clerk's office. They'll also help keep her updated as the trial progresses."

"Whatta you think they'll do?"

"No idea. You know, Ted is a hell of a defense attorney. He knows how to pick a jury and he knows how to play one. He's as good as it gets in Nashville when it comes to juries. But the state's obviously got a strong case, so we'll just have to wait and see."

"I assume Hope will call today. You want me to put her through if she does?"

"Find out what she wants, and if it's serious, or she seems out of control emotionally, put her through, and I'll do what I can. Otherwise, if it's neither of those two, I'll just call her back."

David had finished up with his last appointment of the morning, when Gail informed him Hope was on line one. She said Hope wasn't out of control, but just wanted to visit for a moment.

David told Gail he would take her call, since he had finished his morning appointments and now had time to talk.

As soon as he picked up, she said, "Morning. You heard anything yet?"

"No. I was hoping you had. It was my understanding they would submit the case to the jury after the noon hour, but that can all change in the blink of an eye in the courtroom. I haven't called the clerk's office yet this morning. I've just been too busy."

"Any idea how long they'll take to decide after it's given to the jury?"

"Not a clue. They could take an hour, or they could take a week."

"Okay. Sorry to bother. I'll touch base with you later today if that's okay."

David paused for a moment. "Tell you what. *If* the jury deliberates into the evening trying to come to a conclusion, why don't we just meet somewhere for supper? We're both waiting for a verdict anyway, might as well wait together."

She hesitated.

"Look, all we're doing is waiting for a verdict. Don't consider this a date. I know you don't wanna get involved again, this soon, with anyone, and to be honest, neither do I. But, at the moment, we're both interested in this verdict, both waiting to hear from the jury. We might as well wait together, at least for supper. I'll buy. Whatta ya say? If they reach a verdict before supper, we'll just cancel."

Again, she hesitated. But finally she said, "Alright. That sounds fine. You want me to meet you somewhere?"

"Why don't I just pick you up? No need for us both to drive. I'll just pick you up about six-thirty."

He could hear her take a deep breath. "Okay, see you then. Let me know if you hear anything before then."

He laughed. "Why, so you can call off our meeting for supper?"

"No, no, not really. On second thought, it would probably just be a good idea to meet for supper no matter what. We can celebrate if they convict the bastard, and if they find him not guilty, someone's going to need to drive me home after I down a full bottle of whiskey—might as well be you. Just keep me up to date."

David had only just returned from an abbreviated lunch and sat down, grabbing the file for his next appointment, when Gail said, "Your mom's on line one. You wanna take it or not?"

"Does it sound important?"

"I really can't tell. I don't know her that well. Whatta you wanna do?"

"I'll take it."

He picked up, and said, "Hi, Mom, what's going on?"

"Hi, David. Can you come over?"

"Sure. What time? I got a dinner date, well, kind of a date, at six-thirty. I could come over before that, or after we're done. I don't have much doubt dinner won't last long."

"No, I mean now."

David could tell there was something a little strange about her voice—there was a breathiness, an upbeat tone he hadn't noticed in a long time.

"Mom, no, I have appointments all afternoon. Can't this wait."

"No."

"Is it an emergency?"

"No."

"Right now?"

"Yes."

He hesitated. Gail would have to move the next three appointments and…"See you in a few minutes."

He never even knocked. David's thoughts were on all the appointments Gail had needed to change, and, in addition, he was having a difficult time trying to determine what in the world was so important.

He walked in the front door, and stopped dead in his tracks as he reached the archway between the kitchen and the living room. His mother was watching TV on the couch, and holding hands with a man he had never met. He folded his arms, and said, "Excuse me, what's going on here? Who's the man, Mom?"

It was obvious Betty hadn't heard him come in. Startled, she pulled her hand away, and both of them stood.

"Oh, hi, honey. Come on in. I want you to meet someone."

As he walked around the end of the couch, she said, "David, meet Howard Keating, an old friend of mine."

Howard extended his hand, as David said, "So you're Howard. Mom has told me a little about you."

David shook his hand, as Betty said, "Sit down, David. We've something to tell you. We wanted you to be the first to know."

David sat, as he said, "Okay what's going on. This is a first. You've never ever called at work during the day, and had me come over. What's going on?"

She looked at Howard, he smiled, and as she turned toward David, she said, "We're getting married."

David looked at both of them in disbelief. "I'm sorry, you're what? I misunderstood. Where are you going?"

Betty laughed. "We're going nowhere, David, we're getting married."

David sat back, and said, "Now wait a minute. Why? Do you have to? What are you doing, Mom—do you even know? Howard, is it? It's Howard right? Who are you? I don't know a thing about you."

Betty said, "You don't need to, David. I'm the one marrying him, not you. I've known him all my life. Now, just relax. We're both terribly excited. We wanted you to be the first to know. We aren't going to wait long before we do this—probably a month or so. Just long enough to set everything up. It's going to be before a magistrate, and not a church wedding so there won't be many there, which is what we want."

"But, Mom, you're not well. Does he know that?"

"You know, David, I've never felt better in my life. Yes, yes, he knows all about the cancer. Doesn't matter to him. But, in terms of how I feel, I haven't felt better in a long time. We've been all through this many times, and we've come to the conclusion we want to live out our lives together no matter how long either of us have. We don't want your approval. The decision's already been made. We want you to be as happy as we are."

They both were smiling, as they continued to hold each other's hand. Clearly the decision had been made. She was as happy as he had seen her in a long time. He wasn't going to be the one to burst their bubble. They were old enough to decide, and they had obviously done just that.

He looked at her, then at him. Finally he said, "Okay. Okay. Obviously there's nothing I can say that's going to change either of your minds at this point in time. You got the coffee going? Before I head back to work, I think I wanna know a lot more about you, Howard. Before you marry my mother, I feel I really need to vet you. I need to know a little more about where you been, what you've been up to, and why you two decided to take this step. I been cross-examining people a long time. Get ready to go, cause I got a whole lot a questions."

He watched as his mother's prospective husband shifted in his chair, and said slowly, "Well, okay. I'll answer the best I can, I guess."

David stood, turned toward the kitchen, smiled and said, "Now, don't you move, Howard. Let me get a cup of coffee and we'll begin."

Chapter 36

David's interrogation lasted only a few minutes. He would have stretched it out, and continued to question Howard if he felt it necessary, but it was clear his mother already knew all she needed to know.

He was still concerned about this "marriage" business, but at this point in her life, he had ultimately decided he would just do all he could to support his mother whatever direction she traveled. If Howard could provide her with days of happiness, along with a glimmer of hope while fighting the disease, so be it. As soon as he reached the office, he called Griff.

"Hey, Griff, I just got back from a visit with mom. Did you know she was seeing this guy, Howard?"

"I think I told you that already, David. Yes, I knew. I've met him. Seems like a nice guy."

"Well, I hope so, because they're getting married."

Griff remained silent.

"David said, "You still there?"

"Oh, I wasn't sure you were still on. I think we had a glitch in the line. I'm just sure I didn't hear what I thought I heard. Now, what were you saying?"

"They're getting married."

Again, Griff remained quiet. Finally he said, "Did you say 'they're getting married'? *Is that what you said?*"

"Yes. I was just over there. That's what they told me."

"Holy shit, you have to be kidding me. Do I need to go talk to her? Would that help? She can't get married. She's not well. She can't…"

"Hold on, Griff. I went through all that with her. I've not seen her this happy in a long time. I've heard it can be therapeutic if people that are sick, experience a substantial change in the direction of their life, or a change in attitude for some reason. She's obviously in love with the guy, and she's got some of that spark back she used to have. Let's let them run with this for a while and see what happens. We can both keep tabs on her. Be excited about it when she tells you. Let's just follow along for a while."

"Okay, if you think that's what's best."

"Better go. I gotta meet a client for supper in a bit. Talk to you soon."

"Is it a *woman* client? You got a date?"

"Yes, it's a woman, but *no* it's not a date. I'm just babysitting with her while we wait for a verdict in her husband's trial. She's the former wife of Jack Whitmore. I think I told you about him leaving their child in the car and the charges against him. Just another negative event in the pathetic life of that bastard. He's a real peace of work."

"I remember you talking about him. I gotta go. Thanks for the info bout mom."

David terminated the call, then quickly punched in the number of the clerk of court. He wanted updated information concerning the trial before he left the office to pick up Hope.

David watched her walk to his car a few minutes later. They drove to a small restaurant on Westend Avenue where he had eaten many times. It wasn't fancy, it wasn't flashy, but it was always quiet, the dining area dignified, and the food memorable.

After ordering drinks, Hope said, "So what specifically did they tell you when you called the courthouse? What's going on?"

"The last time I talked to them was right before I picked you up. They were still deliberating. The judge said he was going to let them continue until about eight, and if they hadn't come to a verdict by then, he would send them home for the night."

"Can this go on forever? How long will he let them deliberate?"

"Up to him. But, no, it will eventually come to an end one way or the other. It won't go on forever. If they don't convict and they don't acquit, then they'll have a hung jury and end it."

"I don't understand. What's a hung jury? What if it *is* a hung jury? What happens then?"

"It happens when the jury can't come to a unanimous decision—when they can't all decide whether he's guilty *or* innocent. If that happens, the prosecutor's office will need to decide if they wanna retry him."

"In that event, they don't *have* to retry him?"

"No. If for some reason or other, they don't feel they can get a conviction, they'll let it go. But hopefully they'll convict him, and we won't have to worry about such things."

The waiter brought their wine, and they each ordered supper. As they ordered, Hope looked at the waiter and said, "Now, I want you to split these checks. I'll pay for mine, he can pay for his."

"Hold on, Hope. I asked you here tonight. This is on me." He looked up at the waiter, and said, "Just bring us one check."

"But, David…"

"You've paid me enough to represent you. You've also got some money issues. Just let me do this. If we eat together again, you can pay, if that will make you feel better, okay?"

She remained silent, as she took her first sip of wine.

"Let's talk about something positive. Tell me, again, about life in Tahoe. Is it as wonderful as you say it is?"

She started to smile, as she said, "You cannot believe how beautiful it is there. It's beyond words. The scenery, the people, the weather, even in winter when it can be pretty rough—it's just beautiful. My home isn't very big, but it's big enough for one—or two if need be."

"What are your thoughts concerning a permanent home? You staying here, going there, or doing both?"

"Probably both for now. If Billy had died before I bought the home I just purchased here, I probably would have moved, but for now, I'll use both—unless something happens to change my mind."

The waiter brought salads, and as both began to eat, he said, "What about marrying again? Is that a possibility for you or are you done?"

She was about to take a bite, when he asked the question. She stopped, with fork in midair, and said, "Probably done. Why do you ask?"

"No reason. I didn't mean to put you on the spot—just making small talk, that's all, just a little small talk."

She hesitated, smiled and said, "Okay, sorry. I might have taken that wrong. At this time, that is truly the furthest thing from my mind. No, marriage is definitely not in the cards for me. And if I did for some reason reconsider, I would sure as hell research the man better than I did Jack. He swept me off my feet. I did nothing to determine what kind of man he really was before we married. That won't happen again, I can guarantee you that."

David reconsidered his next question, which was going to involve having children. He figured all of her personal issues involving life after Billy were simply too sensitive to delve into that subject at this point in time.

"What about your money concerns? I know right after the divorce that was a problem. Is it working out alright for you?"

"Yes, I'm fine. I don't have a lot of leeway with spending, but I'll be fine."

The waiter brought their main course, and as he sat the plates down, she smiled and said, "What about you? You staying here the rest of your life, or you going to venture out?"

"I'll probably just hang around here. I have a great practice, and of course my family, what's left of it anyway, is all here. They need me. My brother has a few drug issues—my mother has cancer. I wouldn't feel comfortable leaving either of them. Of course, I also have alimony to pay, which is consuming a large amount of each month's income."

As she sliced off her first cut of beef, she said, "So where would you go if you did decide to leave here?"

He smiled. "You know, you make Tahoe sound nice. Might have to look there before I looked anywhere else."

"It's best for me, but I'm not sure how you would feel about it. Could you practice in California? Could you get your license there?"

"I have no idea what their requirements are. Knowing California, they would most likely be different from any other state. I'm not even sure I would continue to practice law. One thing about getting a law degree—there are lots of available jobs in the business world that you're qualified to do. You don't have to practice law just because you have a degree. I don't know what I'd do, but since I'm pretty well locked in here, at least for the foreseeable future, guess it doesn't much matter."

Later that night he drove her home. He started to get out of the car to walk her to her door, when she put her hand on his arm, and said, "I'm fine. You don't need to walk me to the house. Just keep me updated tomorrow concerning the jury, will you?"

He drove home thinking about the evening. He needed to forget about her, and just move on, but it was becoming difficult. There was something about her that, at least to him, was special. But, in spite of those feelings, he simply didn't want to become involved again. Not now. Not yet.

In addition to all his own issues, certainly she had made it clear, at least for now, she was not interested in a relationship with anyone either. He had no doubt that "*anyone*" included him.

Chapter 37

Griff needed to make a run for supplies. On the way, he thought about David and his dinner date last night. Of course, according to David it wasn't a "date" but Griff had little doubt there was more to the evening than David wished to discuss.

"Morning. How's your day starting out?"

David said, "Good. Where are you? You workin today?"

"Absolutely, but I needed to make a run to pick up a few supplies so we can finish this job up yet this week, and I thought I'd use the drive time to call you."

"How's it going—I mean, not only that job, but your business?"

"Fine. What about last night? That's why I called. Who did you say you were with?"

"Oh, just a client. A client and I went out for supper. Just a client."

"You told me who it was, but I really didn't know the name. Who was it, David? Who was the client."

"It was Hope Whitmore…is… who it was. Why?"

"You seeing her now? You know, as I recall this isn't the first time you've mentioned her name."

"No, I'm not seeing her. Absolutely not. A while back, I told you about her husband's trial. The case has now been submitted to the jury, and we're waiting to see what they do."

"So, how'd it go?"

"We're not sure. As I told you, we're still waiting to see what they do. They didn't come in last night, and I doubt they've reconvened yet this morning. They'll probably start deliberating about nine this morning."

"You know what I mean. How'd the *date* go?"

"Wasn't a date, Griff. But as concerns Hope, I do like her. She's a good woman that's been through a lot. Yesterday, we were both waiting for the jury to come in, and we decided, since we were both anxiously awaiting the verdict, to wait through dinner together. That's it, no more, no less."

"Let me ask you one question—did you sleep alone?"

"Sure did. Let's move on. How's business? You got plenty to do?"

"Just hold on a sec. While we're on the subject of the Whitmore family, is this Jack Whitmore as bad as you make him out to be, or is your assessment of him based somewhat upon the fact that you're more than a little involved with his former wife?"

"I am *not* involved with his former wife, Griff. But as concerns the issue of Jack Whitmore, he is, in my opinion, as worthless as a human being can be. He hid money from his wife when we were trying the divorce, I have no doubt he was seeing another woman while he was married to Hope, and he was stupid enough to leave his child in the backseat of his car, killing him. He's a real piece of work, Griff, a real piece of work."

"Good thing she's rid of him."

"She's really struggling right now. I guess I'm doing what I can to help get her through it, although I'm afraid I've done about all I can do. Of course, this criminal case has not helped in putting all the issues behind her. I'll be glad for her when the trial concludes and she can finally move on."

"You think the jury will finish up today?"

"I do. I think there'll either be a verdict today, or the judge will declare a mistrial, one way or the other. Now, let's move along. How's business?"

"Oh, it's fine. I'm doing…okay, I guess."

"Do you have a lot of jobs lined up?"

"I do. It's just tight right now. I'm still learning quite a bit about the other side of this business that I never was involved in before—the boss part. As you can imagine, it's a far cry from just showing up at work as an employee and doing your job. The key to it all for me now, is making sure the bid is correct—making sure I don't overestimate or underestimate the job I'm doing. Unfortunately, so far, I've underestimated a lot of them, but I'm working on it. It's gotten better. I'm still hopeful it'll all work out."

"I need to go. I got someone waiting for me, and appointments lined up every half hour until noon. Good hearing from you. Keep me updated on the business."

Griff finally walked through their apartment door at eight-thirty. Kristy was watching TV in the living room, as he walked in.

"Getting home a little late aren't you?"

"Long day."

He walked in the kitchen, and pulled a beer out of the refrigerator, then sat down at the kitchen table as he took his shoes off.

Kristy walked in the kitchen, sat down next to him, and said, "How'd it go today? Making any progress on the house?"

"Yeah, we got along good. We should have it all finished up in about a week. I haven't heard from Chase, but I'm thinking he's probably about ready for me to start his building. I've got five estimates to get out tonight, but not knowing when he's going to want me to start on *his* fucking project makes it difficult to know when to tell these other people that might accept our bid, when I can start for them."

"Can you contact Chase and explain the problem? Would he understand?"

"Hell no. As long as I owe him, it's his rules…period."

Griff downed his beer, and walked to the refrigerator to pull out another. As he sat down, she said, "So how does the overall picture look? Are we making any money? Is this all going to work out the way we hoped it would?"

"I'm really not sure. I just don't know. Right now, I feel a little like we're robbing Peter to pay Paul. I'm pulling funds from one job to apply to another. It's just tough, Kristy. I underestimated a couple of jobs and they're killing us." He ran his fingers through his hair. "I really don't know if this is going to work out."

"Well, I don't want to add to our troubles, but mom called today. You know we promised we'd pay them back before now. They aren't rich. She hinted around about when we might be able to pay them. They need the money. What should I tell her?"

Griff stood as he said, "Goddammit, Kristy, I don't know. I'm working as hard as I can. I can't commit any more hours to the job than what I'm doing now. I don't have any idea what to tell her. I know one thing though— we can't pay them now. I just don't have it."

"Well, you know, I can't bring in any more than I'm making either. I'm working all the hours they'll give me. There's nothing else I can do to help us."

"I know that."

"Do you think it would be better if you quit doing this, and went to work for a contractor as an employee? Would that help us?"

"You know I've already tried that. The problem with that at this stage of the game, is that it would probably help us on a day-to-day basis with our own expenses, but I still need to pay off Chase. Where would that money come from? I can't borrow from a bank and pay him off because I have no collateral to put up for a loan."

He looked away as he said, "I don't know what to do anymore. I'm not going back to David or mom either. I'm no longer a fucking child. I should be able to make it without my families help."

"Should we just leave town—move away and start over?"

"I've thought about that, but I'm afraid with all the contacts Chase has, he'd find us. I don't think either of us wanna travel that road. It's probably better to stay here and just work through it."

"So we just keep doing what we're doing and hope it turns out? That never works does it? Isn't there something we can change in the way you're doing business to make this work? I mean, there are contractors all over Nashville getting rich." She stood, put her arms around him, then smiled as she said, "We need to be one of them."

"I'll see what I can do. I'll start bumping up my estimates a little and see if that helps."

She gave him a hug, turned and walked away as she said, "Hope so. I don't think we have a lot of options left."

Later that night as Kristy lie sleeping near him, and after Griff had tried to fall asleep for a couple of hours, he considered her comment concerning their remaining options, which were, indeed, becoming somewhat limited.

Maybe he would try adjusting his bids one more time. But if that didn't work, he had no idea what he was going to do.

Of course, in addition to all his other problems , Chase and his new building waited in the wings. Even if he found a current solution to their financial problems, he was afraid constructing Chase's building using the method of financing Chase had suggested, would most likely ruin them, no matter what plan he came up with in the near term.

Chapter 38

"**S**o what takes priority today, your appointments or the verdict?"

"The verdict. I really thought the judge would terminate their deliberations yesterday. He surprised me by letting them carry it over until today. Of course, that's not the first time that's happened. Judges confuse me all the time, as you, of all people, should know."

Gail and David sat quietly, just prior to 8:00 a.m., waiting for his first appointment to walk in the front door.

"How's Hope doing?"

"I haven't seen her in a day or two, but I've talked to her a few times, and she's fine. She's anxious, as everyone associated with the trial is, but she's fine. I feel maybe she's a little stronger now, than she has been. I think she's finally accepted the fact the pain is never, ever going away, but now understands she still has to go on, to put one foot in front of the other and live her life. Of course, that's not easily understood and even more difficult to accept, but she's doing better."

The office phone rang. Gail picked it up, mumbled a couple of words and hung up.

"Apparently the judge had the jury come in early. That was the clerk's office. She says they've concluded their deliberations."

David took a deep breath. "Did she say what they did?"

"No. She said the judge had a couple of matters to take care of first, but he would have them brought in the courtroom within the next half hour. She wanted me to let you know. She knew you wanted kept up to date."

David stood. "Call Hope. Tell her what's going on. I'll pick her up in 15 minutes. Tell her to be ready and waiting outside her door."

"I'll move your early appointments to this afternoon."

He yelled, "Thanks." as he walked out the front door of his office.

Thirty minutes later they were seated in the courtroom. It was virtually empty. David and Hope sat down on one of the bench seats next to the back wall. He hoped the judge didn't happen to see them. David remembered his stern admonishment to Hope when he kicked her out of the courtroom. But he figured the judge would have enough to do without looking toward the back of the room, evaluating who was and wasn't there.

The jury was just being seated. Once they were in the seat each had occupied during the course of the trial, and the parties were seated at their respective council tables, the court attendant walked through the chamber door, followed by the judge.

Everyone rose, and he opened court. He looked at the jury, and said, "Mr. Foreman, it's my understanding you have completed your deliberations, is that correct."

One of the gentlemen seated at the end of one of two rows of jurors in the jury box, stood and said, "We have, Your Honor."

"It's my understanding you have been unable to reach a verdict in this matter."

David could feel Hope tense up. She reached over and gripped his leg.

"That's correct, Your Honor. I sent you a prior message stating that we were deadlocked, and you told us to continue to deliberate, but we just aren't going to be able to come to a unanimous conclusion, Judge. There's just no way."

"Alright then. If that's it, that's it. The jury is dismissed. Check with the clerk's office before you leave the building."

The judge turned toward the parties and said, "Gentlemen, you heard what I heard. I guess it will be up to the district attorney's office as concerns further proceedings. Court concerning this matter is concluded. The bond concerning the defendant will remain as is, pending further proceedings in this matter. Anything further, Mr. District Attorney?"

"No, Your Honor."

"What about the defense? Anything further?"

"No, Your Honor. Nothin from us."

"Then we are adjourned."

David watched while Jack and his attorney quickly exited the courtroom. Assistant District Attorney Flagg remained motionless, head down, obviously distraught and apparently assessing his options.

Hope turned to David, and said, "Okay what the hell does this all mean?"

"It means that for now, the proceedings are over. The question is what happens from here on."

"How are we gonna know?"

"I'm going to go ask Flagg right now. If you'll let go of my leg, I'll go do that."

She looked down, and said, "Sorry. Didn't realize I was still clamped on."

She removed her hand. David stood and walked to the front of the courtroom.

As he approached from behind, he placed his hand on Flagg's shoulder and said, "Sorry, Randy. Lots of work for nothing. Did you know the jury was deadlocked?"

He looked up at David, and said, "I knew yesterday there were some problems. There were two or three older women that just could not find him guilty. They had mentioned he had suffered enough, and God would punish him if he were of such a mind. But I really thought the remaining jurors could convince them to change their vote. Guess they couldn't."

"You gonna retry him?"

"I suppose we will. I'll have to talk to the boss and see what he wants to do, but my intention now is to retry him. We'll talk to a couple of the jurors and see what they thought, but yes, for now, I definitely intend to retry him."

"Keep me informed, will you?" He extended his hand, which an obviously discouraged Randall Flagg then shook.

"I will. Tell Hope I'm so sorry it all turned out this way."

"I will."

As soon as David reached Hope, the questions began.

As they stood to walk out of the courtroom, she said, "What'd he say?"

"He tells me there were two or three ladies on the jury that just could not find him guilty. They held out until the end. He told me to tell you he was sorry."

"So, what now?"

As they walked down the steps and out of the courthouse, he said, "Randy said it's his intention to retry the case. He's not obligated to do that. He'll need to discuss it with his boss, and he's the one that will make the final decision. He told me he'd let us know when he knew."

After considering his response and as she slid in the passenger seat of his car, she said, "Why *wouldn't* they retry him?"

"Hope, you have no idea how busy that office is. They're all overworked and underpaid. They all have multiple trials they are preparing for every day, and this case, since it's not a murder, or a rape, or a high-profile case of some type, just might not carry with it the high priority some other cases might. It's up to his boss."

"They *have* to retry it. There has to be some justice here David, for me, for Billy."

"I agree. I understand. But it's all up to them now."

"Is there anything I can do to pressure them into retrying it?"

"No. It's an inner-office decision. They'll make it based on conversations with some of the jurors from this trial, and an evaluation of whether they believe they can be successful the second time around."

They drove in silence the rest of the way. As he came to a stop in her driveway, she said, "You wanna come in for a cup of coffee—or something stronger if you follow my lead?"

He smiled. "Can't today. I had appointments scheduled for all morning and I'm sure by now, Gail is ready to pull her hair out. Another time?"

"Certainly. Sure. That's fine. Let me know what you hear. Thanks for providing transportation and clarifying what went on today."

He nodded. She got out, closed the door behind her, and he watched her as she reached the door of her home.

As he backed out of her driveway, he had to admit he was as surprised as she was. Certainly, he was disappointed with the result. But where the case might proceed from here was anyone's guess.

The district attorney's office was overworked, and he knew it wouldn't take much for them to decline to retry the case. He would need to be there to comfort her if that happened. One issue was a certainty—Hope would, without doubt, have a very difficult time accepting the conclusion that office would not retry Jack for Billy's death.

Chapter 39

Hope seldom ventured out of her home. From the moment she learned Billy had died, it had become her sanctuary. She felt uncomfortable around people. She had no desire to discuss his death or to have people she had known for a long period of time, continue to ask how she was getting along. She had discussed it with others long enough—it was just much easier staying home, and suffering in silence.

However, Ann had called and wanted to meet downtown. Her proposal was that they would do a little shopping, drink a little coffee, and just in general, have a girl's day out.

Hope rejected the whole idea repeatedly, until she told Ann if she didn't quit pushing the plan, she would hang up. She knew what Ann was trying to do. She appreciated her efforts, but Hope just wasn't ready. She finally made that very clear to her while using language she would have preferred her son not hear, if he were still living and in the room.

Ann finally gave up, and instead, suggested she drive to Hope's home. They could talk in the quiet surroundings of her kitchen, and not have to worry about contact from other people. That idea was agreeable with Hope, and she had just sat down, when Ann, as she set a cup of coffee in front of her, said, "So give me the details concerning the jury verdict. That's one of the reasons I wanted to talk—your sketchy, abbreviated explanation of what happened was unclear. What happened?"

"They just couldn't come to a conclusion. It's called a hung jury. All twelve of them just couldn't come to an agreeable verdict. I guess it happens, but I had never heard of it before."

"So now, it's a matter of whether they want to retry him, is that what I understood you to say?"

"Yes. That's it in a nutshell. David has no idea what they'll do."

Ann was quiet. She took a deep breath, and said, "How's everything working out with David? He still representing you, or…or what exactly is your relationship with him?"

Hope smiled. "Always lay it on the line don't you. We're fine. Yes, he's still representing me. And he's still only my attorney, if that's what you're asking."

"Nothing has developed beyond that?"

"Absolutely not." She paused, looked away, and said, "You know, another time, different circumstances, a different situation, he and I…" she turned toward Ann, who clearly was hanging on each and every word. "He and I might have become an item. But the way things are now, I…"

"Hope, you two seem close. You talk about him a lot. You get that look in your eyes I've seen before—that look I saw when you first met Jack. It may not be the perfect time for this to happen, but if I were you, I wouldn't push him away. Has he suggested how he feels about you? Has that ever come up?"

After she had considered the question for a moment, she said, "No. There's been a time or two when he's grabbed my hand, or once or twice I grabbed his leg when something strange happened in court, but other than that, no, there's never been anything discussed concerning the two of us."

"At some point, you know, this whole legal battle is going to be over. When that happens, you're going to have to decide whether you really want to spend more time with him or let him go, you know that don't you."

"Well, that's kind of interesting too. He told me this morning when I talked to him…"

"Do you talk to him every day?"

"Yes—most of the time it's more than once. We have become close, there's no doubt about that. I would miss him if we were no longer with each other or talked each day. But it's not good timing. I'm just not ready yet, I'm really not."

"I interrupted you. What were you telling me he told you this morning?"

"Oh…yes, he said this morning we may not be done with Jack even if the state doesn't retry him. He said we could sue him. He said I could file some kind of case for wrongful death against him—sue him for damages for the loss of Billy. I don't know much about it yet, and he said there's no need to discuss it unless they decide not to retry him. But he said we might be able to hurt Jack where it would hurt him the most—in his bank account. We just have to wait and see what the state does first."

"When do you think you'll know?"

"David said we can't push them. They promised to let him know as soon as they make an inner-office decision. I'm hoping it's soon. This is all about to drive me nuts."

"You planning on staying around until they decide? Don't you normally go to Tahoe sometime during the summer or fall?"

"Yes, I always have. I'm planning on going near the end of the month, but I'm going nowhere, nor even *planning* a trip anywhere until I know what the district attorney is going to do."

"Let me know as soon as you know."

"I will."

Later that evening as she was getting ready for bed, she reconsidered her discussion with Ann concerning David. She had not focused her thoughts on him, as a man, since the first time they met. Her thoughts of him had been, and continued to remain, focused upon his legal representation of her. He was her attorney, and she was the client he was obligated to protect.

But the conversation with Ann today had somewhat changed that. Maybe she needed to focus a little more upon him as a man, and not just her attorney. That would be so very easy for her to do, but until today, she hadn't dropped her guard. She had not allowed herself to think of him in that way.

As she lie in bed, mindlessly watching some science fiction movie on TV, she thought perhaps it was time that changed. Maybe it was time she thought of him as that good looking, kind, considerate…

Her phone rang. She looked at caller ID. Speak of the devil…She smiled. "Calling pretty late aren't you, Mr. attorney?"

"I'm sorry. Did I wake you?"

"No, no. I had plenty of coffee today. Unfortunately that normally leads to late-night, nonsensical movies, which is exactly where it led me tonight. Are you still at work?"

"No, no, I've been on and off the phone most of the night, either with clients or trying to get to the bottom of a little problem we might have."

She sat up. "A little problem *we* might have?" Her heart skipped a beat. "You mean literally you and I?"

"No, no not us. The state's case against Jack."

"Why what happened?"

"When I caught the news at six, I heard them say one of the detectives from the Nashville police force had been involved in a car accident. I didn't think much about it right away, but then during one of those little breaks at the top of the hour, you know, the ones where they give you a quick look at the upcoming news at ten, they mentioned his name was Detective Hoffman."

"Oh no, not our Detective Hoffman? Was it our detective?"

"I wasn't sure, but I assumed there was only one Hoffman on the force. I waited until ten for the rest of the story, and I just heard it a few minutes ago. It *was* our detective and…and he died from his injuries, Hope."

"Oh my god—his family. How sad for his family. What about our case? Will it have an impact on our case?"

"I wasn't sure. Right after I heard the story, I called Flagg. He told me he had little doubt that the case against Jack would be dismissed. He said retrying it was a little shaky anyway, and now with the lead detective dead, he was almost certain they would dismiss it. He's to let me know in the morning, but it appears to me it's over."

Hope started to cry.

"Now wait, Hope, I know you're upset, but let's don't rush to any conclusions. Let's see for certain what happens tomorrow. In the meantime, I'll continue to do a little research concerning the civil action we could file against him. Don't give up yet."

"Okay, David, I won't. It's just that…"

"Hang in with me, Hope. Let's just wait a day or two before we come to any conclusions."

"Okay. Thanks for calling."

She terminated the call, looked up at the soundless movie, and used the remote to turn it off.

Hope got out of bed, and walked downstairs to the kitchen. She poured herself a half glass of bourbon, and walked into the darkened living room, sitting down on the couch. As she sat there she thought of all the times Jack had gotten away with it—with something. He was always very creative at finding a method of slithering out of a problem, or an issue of some type.

But that wasn't going to happen—not this time. He might get out of those criminal charges, but she decided even if he did, this wasn't over by any means. David figured he had a way, a possible alternative, to go after Jack. If it held any promise whatsoever, she would push it, along with every other option she had available, until one of them gave up. But *this* time, for the *first* time, it by god wasn't going to be her.

Chapter 40

Jack had enough work lying on his desk to keep him busy day and night for a year. He didn't even know which file to start with—they were all important and they all needed his immediate attention.

He had been reducing the pile of files since 6:00 a.m. but had hardly made a dent. He had just finished making a second pot of coffee, when he heard Claudia walk in the front office door.

She leaned around his office door frame and said, "Hi. How was your night?"

Jack looked up and said, "Unfortunately, it was without you."

She smiled as she said, "Well, you know I'm available. You just have to pull the trigger, cowboy."

He smiled, and said, "I'm waiting to hear from Ted today—Ted Carnie. Be sure and put him through if he calls."

She walked in his office, and leaned down, kissing him before she took a seat in front of his desk.

"Do you know what's going on with the trial? Is it over?"

"I'm not sure. He was to call today. As early as he gets to work, I'm surprised he hasn't called me by now. He was going to discuss a few issues with the district attorney's office, and then give me a call. I'm hoping they're dismissing it, but I'm not sure yet. They may not even give us an answer today—they may just let it hang there for

239

who knows how long, before they decide what to do. To be honest, I was so damn glad the jury didn't convict me, the fact they are even considering dismissing the whole thing, is just frosting on the cake."

She stood. "I better get ready for the day. You going to stop by after work?"

"Absolutely. I should be there a little after five. I feel like a party, so be ready to rock and roll."

As she walked away, she said, "Always am."

The call he was waiting for finally came about ten-thirty.

"Morning, Ted. I've been waiting for you to call. What've you found out?"

"Well, I don't know if you've heard the latest or not. Did you know our detective, Detective Hoffman, was involved in a car accident?"

Jack leaned back in his chair. "How bad was it?"

"Bad enough to kill'em."

Jack smiled as he leaned back in his chair. "You have got to be kidding. When did that happen?"

"Last night. That's what's taken me so long to call you. I couldn't get in touch with Flagg until just a few minutes ago. They're tryin to figure out what they're gonna do with all his cases."

"Did he know what they're gonna do with mine?"

"They're gonna toss it, Jack. It's all over. They weren't sure what they were gonna do anyway, but now with the detective's death, they're just gonna dismiss."

"Thank God. Then it's all over?"

"Congratulations, Jack. Yes, it's over."

They discussed a few other business matters which Ted was handling for him, and once he terminated the call, he yelled, "Hey Claudia, come in a minute."

She quickly walked through the door. "What's wrong? What's going on?"

He stood, walked around his desk, took her in his arms and kissed her. "They're dismissing the case. It's over."

A few hours later, Jack swung his bare legs over the edge of Claudia's bed, then, as he sat there, turned, looked down at her, and said, "Let no one ever say you didn't know how to screw a guy. You're the best, baby, absolutely the best."

She kicked off the sheet, held out her arms, and said, "Wanna go again? I'm ready if you are."

"No I can't. I need to go home."

She ran her fingers down his back, and said, "You have to be *so* happy that trial and everything associated with it, is finally at an end. I've seen a big change in you today. You're back to who you were before this all happened."

"This has been one of the worst situations I've ever lived through. First, Billy dies, which was bad enough. Then they turn a bad situation into an absolute nightmare by charging me with his death. It's like jumping from the frying pan into the fire."

"You know, that's kind of strange you would put it that way. Most people would have considered the worst of the two incidents as the death of the boy, *not* being prosecuted for it."

"Maybe I got that backwards. Anyway, it was the worst period of my life, I know that."

"Well, your business never suffered. We're as busy as ever."

"That's at least partially because of you. You did a fantastic job of holding things together for me."

"If that's the case, maybe I deserve a raise."

He smiled. "You got that from me about twenty minutes ago."

"You know what I mean."

"We'll talk about that tomorrow at the ..."

His phone rang, and caller ID indicated it was Ted Carney.

"Hmm, wonder what Ted wants?"

"Hi. What's going on?"

"Well I've got some interestin news I felt you should know."

"Okay. Is it about the criminal case?"

"No, that's over. That's a done deal."

"So what's the '*new*' news you got for me?"

"I had a long conversation with Hope's attorney. He called to let me know the criminal case was over, which I already knew, but while talkin' to him, he informed me he was most likely gonna sue you on behalf of Hope for the wrongful death of Billy."

Jack stood, cleared his throat and said, "I guess I don't understand. I thought this was it. Once the criminal proceedings were over, I thought everything was at an end."

"It is as far as criminal court is concerned. But he could sue you in civil court for damages—for causing the death of Billy. It can be done, and he's tellin me that's what Hope wants to do, at least at this point in time. We'll let it set for a while. Maybe she'll change her mind."

"So, how much could they sue me for?"

"How much they could sue you for and how much they actually got, could be a long ways apart, *if* they got anything. I'm pretty good at defending those types of cases, depending, of course, on the facts. But they could sue you for millions. Now, as I say…"

"Wait a minute. Did you say millions?"

"Sure. They can sue you for as much as they want, but that don't mean they'll get it."

Jack started to pace back and forth across the room. "So should I call her and warn her not to do this? Should I go see her? What should I do?"

"Don't contact her. Let's just wait and see what happens. The relationship between the two of you being as it is, she could be just sittin on the fence as to what to do, and your conversation with her could spur her on. Do *not* communicate with her at all. Let's just see what they decide to do. You contacting her could actually irritate her into filing. I'll let you know what they're doin when I know."

"Thanks for calling."

Jack terminated the call not knowing whether Ted might have had more he wanted to say. Didn't matter—he had heard all he wanted to hear.

He looked down at Claudia, as he pulled his pants on, and said, "That insane former wife of mine may be suing me—*for my money*. I can't believe this. I fucking can't believe this."

"Can she do that?"

As he pulled on his shirt, he said, "Apparently so. At least according to Ted she can."

"What for? What can she sue you for?"

"I guess damages for the loss of Billy. I gotta go. I gotta research what she can and can't do. I can't believe she's doing this. I'll see you tomorrow."

Chapter 41

Hope had questioned David about the possibility of filing a civil suit against Jack on more than one occasion. In fact, she had called him three times during the last couple of days. But he had continued to defer discussing the specifics with her, believing it necessary to do just a little more research before he discussed filing in detail.

When she called a fourth time, he suggested, as he had while they were both awaiting the jury verdict, that they meet, and discuss the potential civil action over supper. She had initially rejected that proposal while awaiting the verdict, but this time she offered no resistance whatsoever.

They had just finished eating, and were having an after dinner drink—one for the road. They had yet to discuss the details concerning possible litigation, choosing to discuss their families or other issues, both, at least for now, avoiding the elephant in the room.

Finally, he said, "Okay, let's get down to business. We might as well talk about the civil action against Jack and get it over with. First of all, you should know that this will be a fairly long process, but…"

"Hold on. We need to discuss one specific aspect of it first, before we get into the legal issues. I don't have the money to do this. I'm fine, as concerns my personal finances, but it's still a little tight, and I just plain don't have any extra to pay you. So if it's an expensive proposition, there's no need in discussing any further, because I just plain can't afford it. Maybe later, but not now. That's one of the reasons I've been somewhat hesitant to discuss it tonight."

He smiled. "I assumed you had avoided the subject for a reason. You called three or four times to discuss it, and then tonight you avoided the subject like the plague. I understand your concerns, but you needn't worry about that. I'll take the case on what's called a contingency. I'll collect if you collect. You win, I win. My fee will be 30% of whatever you are awarded by the jury. You won't have any cost, other than some out-of-pocket expenses to pay for. I can't legally advance those, so that'll be up to you to pay."

"You're kidding. You'll take the case that way? I mean without me paying you?"

"Without you paying me, *unless* we win. Then my share comes out of your share. Now, don't get me wrong. There'll be some of those expenses, as we prepare for trial, that won't be cheap, but I honestly believe they'll be small enough that you can weather the storm. I'll keep you informed when they're coming up, so you can budget accordingly."

"Well, that certainly eases my concern. Shall we have one more drink before we go?"

"Sure." He motioned for the waiter to bring one more for each of them.

"Okay, so what is the process once we're ready to begin?"

"This is called a civil case versus the previous proceeding against him which was a criminal case. In the criminal case, the burden of proof was beyond a reasonable doubt, but here the burden of proof is just by a preponderance of evidence, a majority of the evidence, so it's a completely different standard. In that respect, it's easier to win a civil case."

"What needs to be proven with this kind of case?"

"This is an action for wrongful death, so obviously the first thing we need to prove is that Jack wrongfully caused Billy's death. That won't be hard to do. But the second major issue is that we have to prove how much you were damaged. Now, in Tennessee you can recover damages in a wrongful death action, for loss of love, society and affection of a child. Those are the elements you need to show to establish damages. The actual amount we ask for will be determined by an expert who we will use to quantify the damages."

"That sounds hard to do—to put a value on those types of losses."

"It is. That's why we need an expert—someone who specializes in this field and has done this before, in other cases, for other people. I'll handle that. I'll find the right one and make sure he knows what he's doing—that he's been successful before."

"How long will this take—I mean from beginning to end?"

"Well, this is January, so I would hope it might be over by the middle of the year. It's really hard to tell. But, you know Ted. I'm assuming that's who will represent Jack. He's a good one for padding the bill, and I'm sure he'll work the case for all its worth. Realistically, it could take until the end of the year. We're not going to hurry it. We'll take our time and do it right."

"Will I have to testify?"

"Yes. You'll have to tell the jury how much you miss your son, and why you feel Jack should pay for your loss."

"That won't be hard to do." She turned away and said nothing. David could tell she was weighing the pain of going through the process one more time, versus the joy of punishing Jack for what he had done.

She turned toward David, and said, "Let's do it. Let's get it filed and see what happens." She smiled. "I would love to be there when he's served with the papers. I shouldn't say that I guess, but that would warm my heart."

"He's definitely not going to like it. Anything that might affect his status, his money, is going to hurt him. I'll start working on the paperwork tomorrow, and let you know when it's ready to sign. Now, let's change the subject—enough business for one night. Do you have anything enjoyable planned during the next few weeks? What are your plans?"

"I really think toward the end of the month, I'll fly to Tahoe. It's time for me to get back out there. I miss it."

"How long will you stay?"

"Probably a couple of weeks. I'll need to check the cabin and make sure everything is in working order, and I'll probably just stay a couple of weeks. I'd like to get this lawsuit filed before I leave."

"I can handle that. We'll get it on file before the end of the month." He smiled, as he said, "You know, I haven't been away for a while, and, as I've mentioned, I've never been to Tahoe. Maybe I'll just meet you out there. You can show me around."

She studied him as she considered his idea. Finally she said, "Yes, that would be nice. We'll just have to see how all that works out."

A few minutes later, both finished their after-dinner drink, and he drove her home. Once they arrived, he got out of the car, as she did, and started to walk her to the door.

As they walked, she said, "David, you needn't walk with me. I know the way just fine."

"I know I don't, but I want to. I really don't want to get back in the car and drive home. I really… don't want to leave your side."

Both remained quiet as they reached her door. He put his arms around her. She didn't resist. He pulled her near, and kissed her.

As he started to back away, she put her arms around him, and kissed him again. This time it was more than a good night kiss, and David for the first time, had some idea how she really felt.

"Can I come in?"

She backed up, and remained silent for only a few seconds, before she said, "Don't misunderstand. I care for you. But I'm not ready for all this, I'm just not. I love being with you, I love what just happened, but for now, can we just leave it at that? Give me a little time, David. Is that okay with you? Are you upset with me? I really am sorry, but…"

He gently placed a finger over her lips, as he whispered, "You need go no further. I understand. I wouldn't even consider pushing you into something you're not ready for. I too, love being with you, but if you're not ready for this, I'll be glad to wait until you are. I better go. I'll talk to you tomorrow morning."

He leaned forward, kissed her, then walked down the sidewalk and got in his vehicle. As he drove away, he looked back. Hope was still standing there, watching, as he drove away.

Chapter 42

"Get me the Jackson file, " Jack yelled. A few moments later, she walked through his door, and he said, "Are they coming in today? I thought I saw a note that said they would be in today."

As she laid the file down on his desk, Claudia said, "You did, they are. I think they're on the schedule to come in at two."

As she walked back to her office she stopped, turned around, and said, "Oh, by the way, I haven't had an opportunity to thank you properly for the raise. I'm available tonight, if you wanna stop by."

He continued to try to locate a telephone note on his desk, under piles of files. He never looked up as he said, "May do that. I just…might…do…" He looked up at her and said, "Where the hell did you put that Jackson file?"

She walked back to his desk, picked up the Jackson file, and held it out to him.

"Oh, thanks."

"You gonna stop by tonight?"

"Might, yes I might…"

"Your wife have any idea we're an item? Does she have a clue?"

"Nope, nope, she sure doesn't. I need to go through a few things before my first client gets here. Let's talk about that other thing later today."

Claudia thought for a moment, then said, "Other thing…that other thing…okay, sure, whatever."

Jack had appointment after appointment, until noon. He had just sat down with two of his best clients. It would be the last of his appointments during the morning. As he was listening to them outline their investment needs, there was a knock on his door. It opened slightly, and Claudia stuck her head through, just far enough to say, "Jack, I think you need to come out for a moment."

He leaned forward in his chair, looked at her in pure disgust and said, "Claudia, I'm a little tied up right now. I'll be out when I'm through here."

"No, Jack, better come out now." She disappeared, then quietly shut the door.

He knew she was fully aware of the rules of the office. He was never, ever to be interrupted while with clients unless…unless it was really important. He stood and said, "Folks, hold on just a moment. I better find out what's so important. Be right back."

Jack walked out into the reception area, and saw a man standing patiently in front of Claudia's desk. He stared at him, then at Claudia, as he said, "What's so damn important?"

As he finished his sentence, the man walked up to him, handed him some papers, and said, "This, my friend. This is what's so damn important. You've been served."

As the process server walked out the office door, Jack started to review the paperwork. As he read through the document, he looked up at Claudia, and said, "She sued me. I can't believe this. She sued me. I'm gonna kill her."

Claudia stood, and reached over the reception desk, grabbing the paperwork from his hands. He looked at her and said, "What the hell are you doing? Give those to me."

She whispered, "Finish up your appointment. Take care of those clients, Jack. They've been with you forever. Do your job. I'll review these, and we'll talk about them when you're done with your clients."

"Don't you dare…" He looked away, as he tried to evaluate all that was going on. When he reengaged in conversation, he took a deep breath, and said, "You're right. I'll finish up first, and we'll go from there. Call Ted. Tell him not to leave for lunch until I have a chance to discuss this with him."

His appointment lasted through the noon hour, and Claudia hadn't waited to leave for lunch. He sat alone, in his office, reviewing the paperwork Hope had served on him. As he read them, line by line, he became more incensed with each word. Finally, he picked up the phone, and touched Hope's number.

As he heard her say, "Hello," he said, "Hope, I just got served with papers. Are you serious? Are you really suing me? What's going on?"

"Yes I am, Jack."

"What the hell are you doing that for? Why would you do this to me? You know I lost as much as you did with his death. Why would you continue to carry this on? I was basically found not guilty by that jury and had to endure all that shit, and now this. Come on Hope, let's just move on."

"That's what I'm doing—moving on."

"You're going to go through with this? This isn't going to turn out any better than the criminal case did. You're not going to win this. Would you please just dismiss it, and let each of us go our own way?"

"Let me make this simple Jack—you know—so you *get* it. I'll carry on like this until you pay for what you did. You killed someone. No one gets away with something like that. I'll take the case as far as I can, and if this doesn't work, I'll find a way that does, until you pay for what you did to our son."

He smiled. "I'll see you in hell before you get a penny from me."

"Got a pretty good idea I'll probably see you there no matter what happens with this lawsuit, Jack."

He terminated the call, and quickly punched in Ted's private number.

"Hi, Ted. I just got served. She's suing me just like you thought she might. I have the papers right here. I can fax them to you. I just talked to her. She's insane. I always knew she was. From the first time I…"

"Hold it, Jack. Good god man, y'all sound like a fricken machinegun. Fax me the paperwork, and I'll call you back. By the way, do *not* call her again. Now do you understand me—do not call *or* talk to her again for any reason."

The rest of the afternoon crept by, until around 3:00 p.m., when Ted finally called back. Jack stepped out of the room, and away from his clients, to discuss the case on his phone while standing in the reception room, near Claudia's desk.

"Whatta you think, Ted?"

"Well, Jack, she's sued ya, that's for sure. She's asked for an unspecified amount of money as a result of the wrongful death of her son."

"Can she do that? I mean, I thought I was off the hook when that criminal jury wouldn't convict me."

"She has a right to do what she did. Now, we better get together and discuss this, because she could definitely prevail in this case. We gotta do what we can to prepare and prepare well, or you could be in danger of a losin all the assets you've put together over the years. Better come in tomorrow morning if possible."

Jack set up a time to meet with Ted, and then asked Claudia to get Beth on the phone.

Claudia walked in his office and said, "She's on line one. Before you pick up, are you planning on stoppin by after work?"

"Yes. Yes I am."

As Jack picked up the phone, Claudia smiled, and walked out of his office.

"Beth, first of all I'll be a little late tonight. Second of all, you're not gonna believe what my ex has done now."

Chapter 43

It had been a couple of weeks since David filed the paperwork and started legal action against Jack Whitmore. He called Hope to tell her the lawsuit had been initiated, but had to leave a message—she wasn't home. She never called back. He hoped that kiss hadn't adversely affected their relationship, legally or romantically. David had thought of her every day since, but he was concerned how the change in their relationship might have affected her. Absolutely no feedback worried him.

He had just written down the data necessary to start another dissolution of marriage, his fourth this week, when Gail informed him Hope was in the reception area and wondered if he had time to see her for a moment.

His heart skipped a beat, as he told Gail to send her in. He stood before she walked in the door.

She closed the door behind her, smiled and said, "Hi."

He walked out from behind his desk, and as he reached her, he put his arms around her and kissed her. She never resisted. In fact, he felt her arms close around him, as she pulled him close during the kiss.

David leaned back, smiled and said, "Better now."

She smiled. "Can we talk a minute? I'm sorry I just walked in without making an appointment, but I've been somewhat busy, and I was driving by, so I thought I would surprise you and walk in."

"Best thing that's happened all day." He backed away, and walked around the end of his desk, as he said, "Have a seat."

As she sat, she said, "How's everything coming along? I know he got served."

"How do you know that?"

"He called me. He wasn't happy. I wasn't very nice. It wasn't a friendly conversation."

"Yes, he was served. I've had a chance to discuss the case with his attorney. Since we all know most of the facts and the witnesses involved, other than the expert we hire, there won't be much discovery—depositions and things of that nature. That will help shorten the time before trial."

"Good. You still think it'll be done by Christmas?"

"Hard to say. I've been wrong many times concerning the time this type of litigation takes. It's just going to have to take as long as it takes. That's really hard to predict."

"What's our chance of success in your opinion?"

"Good."

"Is that it? Just good?"

He smiled. "You'll find I'm normally pretty conservative about my assessment of a case until it's over. However, once it's concluded, I'm really an expert at how it all turned out."

She laughed. "Is there anything I need to do?"

"No. I'll take it from here. I've talked to a couple of experts about the case, and one in particular, interests me. I'm to visit with him again next week. We'll determine what we want to do with him then. I visited with him briefly before I even talked to you about filing. He's extremely competent and has been very successful in cases of this nature in the past, so we'll just try to tie down a few details and go from there."

"Okay, I guess that's all I needed to know."

"No problem."

Neither said a word, until she said, "Oh, just one more thing. I was…thinking… about going to Tahoe in a couple of weeks—just getting out of here for a few days. Maybe for a long weekend like Wednesday through Sunday."

David noticed she appeared somewhat nervous as she explained. "I remember you mentioned that the last time we were together."

"That was when you said you had never been in that vicinity before. You …wanna come along?"

He smiled as he sat forward in his chair, and said, "Well, I don't know. Let me check my schedule." He never took her eyes off her. "You know, I think I can make it. Let me work out a few issues just to make sure I'm good to go. I'll call you later today to iron out the details."

She stood. "Certainly. Just give me call when you know for sure."

He stood and walked around the end of desk, took her in his arms and kissed her.

"You know, I could get in a little trouble doing this. I'm not supposed to be romantically involved with my clients."

She smiled. "I've got a feeling I'm no longer *just* a client, Mr. Williams."

The plans had changed. Hope had flown out on Tuesday, but he hadn't been able to free himself from a hearing scheduled on Wednesday morning, so they had not been able to travel together.

David landed in Reno, rented a car, and had just driven over the rim of the Tahoe basin. For the first time, he had an opportunity to observe what Hope had discussed in such glowing terms so many times in the past—he had just seen Lake Tahoe.

He continued to drive around the south end of the lake, following the GPS in his vehicle, which he anticipated would take him straight to Hope.

It was nearly dark when he pulled up in front of her cabin. He grabbed a small bag containing a few clothes along with his personal items, and walked up the steps to the front door of a beautiful log cabin.

He knocked, and she smiled as she opened the door. "Come in, come in. How was the trip?"

He set his bag down on a chair next to the door, took her in his arms and kissed her.

"It was long. I was anxious to get here. Seemed like it took forever."

"I'm glad you're here. I've been waiting all day."

He said, "Where should I put my bag? You want me to put it…"

"In the bedroom. Let me show you around first."

She then escorted him through the few rooms the cabin had, which included two bedrooms, living room, and a small kitchen.

"This looks pretty cozy. Nice cabin. I can see why you love to come here."

"You hungry? You wanna go get something to eat. There's a small restaurant down by the lake that…"

He took her in his arms, and said, "No, I'm not hungry. Food isn't on my mind at all. You are. And you've been on my mind for a long, long time."

She said nothing. She seemed hesitant as she looked away.

After a few seconds of an uncomfortable silence, David said, "Let's sit for a minute, Hope We need to talk." He led the way, and they both sat down on the couch. He continued to hold her hand.

"Look. We've both been involved with difficult relationships. Mine was almost as bad as yours. We've both been trying to move on—put aside the pain, and move on. But it's hard to do—it's not an easy task. I see it all the time in my line of work. Everyone, and I mean everyone, has a problem with putting a bad relationship behind them, and then moving on."

She said nothing.

"But you know, it's time we *both* move on. I've known for a long time I was in love with you. I just didn't want to admit it. But this is *our moment*, and it just seems to me it's time we accept it."

"But I find myself wondering how this is going to end. I'm afraid. Are we going to end up the same way as…?"

"Wait. Just wait. We can't possibly anticipate how this is going to end, one way or the other. No one can figure out, in advance, how *any* relationship will end, and I'm certainly not smart enough to do that either. We need to take it a step at a time. Small steps, one at a time. I know I couldn't wait to see you. I know I'm in love with you. I know *nothing* was going to come between me being with you, in this cabin, for the next few days. That's what I know."

David hesitated for a moment. She remained silent, as he continued. "Where we go from here, what happens from here on out, neither of us can predict. But I also know this. I wouldn't want to be anywhere in the world right now other than here—with you. Who knows where this relationship goes tomorrow, or next week, or next year? The only thing we're absolutely certain of, is today, right now. And to be honest, for the first time in a long time, that's all that's important to me."

Once again, she looked away.

He began to wonder if he had made a serious mistake meeting her here. He continued to assess his situation, until she turned toward him, smiled, then kissed him.

She stood, and pulled him up with her. "You know, you couldn't have said that any better. I've known I've been in love with you for a long time, but just plain didn't want to admit it. Time to accept it and go with it, wherever it may lead."

She took his hand, and led him through the bedroom door.

Later, he lie with his head propped up by a pillow, while Hope rested her head on his chest, both facing the small fireplace in the room. The only light came from the fire Hope had started prior to David's arrival.

Both remained quiet, until David said, "You know, I really never thought we were ever going to reach this moment. I knew how I felt about you, there was never much question about that, but there were so many issues and problems that kept coming between us. I just didn't think we'd ever make it to this moment."

"I feel like I have been living a nightmare for a long time. First with the marriage, then the divorce, then Billy. Just one thing after another."

"You definitely needed an attorney. I'm just glad you came to see me and not someone else."

"I could feel myself wanting to become involved with you, but each time I started to let myself go, something else came up. And each time that happened, I would try to put you, as a person, out of my mind, and continue my involvement with you only as my lawyer."

"I understand. And with as much as you were going through, I wasn't going to be the first to change the type of relationship we had—until I finally just said the hell with it and kissed you that first time. I just felt it was time to find out how you felt, and either make a move, or let you go. I'm glad I made the move."

"So am I. I really never wanted this to happen. I really didn't. With so much going on I just didn't feel I could commit myself to anyone. Not now. Maybe later, but definitely not now."

"And yet, here we are."

"Yes, here we are."

"You know, my grandmother was a wise woman. My grandparents didn't have much. They farmed outside Nashville, and never really had much of anything except kids. But my grandmother was full of wisdom, and I remember one thing she told me about love a long time ago."

"What was that?"

"Oh, I'd come home from college and she'd be there. And she'd ask me about my love life. I'd tell her I really cared for so and so, but I just didn't want to become involved right now—you know, because of school or for some other reason. Kind of like you not wanting to become involved with me while all this was going on."

"I can certainly identify with that."

"One time she was listening to me tell her about some girl I really, really liked, but was just hesitant to become involved with. I told her I would have something going on, and then suddenly, out of the blue, I would be thinking of her. She said, 'You know, I've found out through the years, a heart that's committed is hard to control.' Since then, I've found those words to ring true more than once."

Hope remained silent, until she finally said, "You know, I think that describes both of our situations perfectly."

A few minutes later, David felt her relax as she fell asleep. With the faint glow from the fireplace filling the room, and the woman he loved close by, for the first time in a very long time, he wanted a moment in his life to last forever.

Chapter 44

David loosened his tie, and took another long drink of bourbon and water. He had poured his first one right after Gail had shut out the lights and left the office. Now, an hour and a half later, he was on his fourth. His friend Judge Armstrong, had now joined him, although he had only been there long enough to be on his second drink.

"So, this party of two is being held why? I mean, is it because you *are* or *aren't* happy about your mom getting married. Maybe it's the booze doing the talkin, but I'm sorry, I just don't quite understand."

"No, no I'm glad she's getting married—aren't I? I mean, *shouldn't* we be? I mean why *shouldn't* she enjoy this...this..."

Henry smiled. "Forget where you were going did ya?"

"Absolutely...could have...I guess." He took another drink.

"You know, you've probably had enough. You still have to find your way home. How you gonna do that? Did you think about that while you were pouring your third or fourth one?"

"Yup, sure did. Uber. Uber will getcha where ya need to be and on time too."

"You bet. So, David, on the eve of the event, how do you really feel about your mom getting married?"

He took a sip, looked at Henry and said, "I couldn't be any perkier."

Henry smiled and said, "You mean happier? Is that what ya mean, counselor?"

"Don't you put words in my mouth, Judge. You know that's not allowed in this courtroom."

"Sorry bout that. Are you aware enough of your surroundings that you can tell me what time you want me there tomorrow?"

"I am. I certainly am." He concentrated. "The wedding is at, let's see, it's at four, so I need to be there about three, and that means you need to be there…" He smiled. "About three."

"Hmm. Wonder if I should accept that as gospel."

"Sure you would...should. Wedding's at four. You and me need to be there bout three. You can take that to the bank, Mr. Judge. Now drink up. I still got a little some of this bourbon left, and we're not gonna waste it."

"David, are you back there? I saw your light on and you're not answering your cell. Can I come on back?"

Hope had just walked through the unlocked front door.

"Sure, come on in, Hope."

David heard her steps down the hallway, and as she walked into his office she said, "Why don't you answer your…oh, I didn't know someone was with you."

David smiled. "Hope, Judge whatshisname, whatshisname, Hope."

The judge stood, smiled and held out his hand. "As you can see, Hope, our friend has a little issue this evening. It's nice to finally meet you. I've heard a lot about you."

"As I have about you. I was just checking on the status of my case with …"

Henry said, "Have a seat, Hope. By the way you can quit the charade. I knew all about you and David long before the two of you even became involved. Ever since the first day he met you, he's had a hard time talking about much else, other than you. He still hasn't filled me in completely, but I assumed the two of you were involved when he wouldn't tell me why or where he was going when he left town a few weeks ago. I had my suspicions you were together."

"Great guy."

"He is. Drunk or not, you're right, he is."

She smiled, as David poured just a little more bourbon in his glass. She nodded toward him, looked at Henry and said, "Whatta we gonna do with him?"

"He said he was taking an Uber home. Does the episode we're going through right now…this event…have to do *only* with his mother getting married?"

David said, "You two know I'm right here, don't you? I mean I hear what you're trying to say. You get that don't the two of you?"

Hope looked at Henry and said, "Yes. He's concerned. After what he's told me, he shouldn't be, but he is. I'll just take him home." She turned toward David and said, "Is your car in the parking garage? Can you leave it there all night?"

David leaned forward in his chair and said, "Do you want that spot? I own it, but maybe I could transfer it to you. You want it?"

Henry smiled, stood and said, "He told me to be there about three. You think that's close to accurate?"

"Yes. He did tell you it's a church now, and not before a magistrate, didn't he? They changed their minds. I have to be there early too, and he told me when he was sober, that was the time…about three.”

“Yes, I did know the location had been changed.”

She stood and smiled. “Thanks for babysitting.”

“No problem. I’ll see you tomorrow.”

David and his mother sat quietly bside each other, in a small meeting room, down the hall from the sanctuary of the church where Betty was about to be married.

David leaned forward in his chair, taking his mother’s hand.

“Now look, Mom, you still have time to pull out of this. Nothing is final until you say those words, those two words, ‘I do’.”

“But why would I pull out, when I want to go through with it? That doesn’t make much sense to me.”

“Mom, are you sure this is what you want?”

She squeezed his hand, before she pulled it away.

“Never been so sure of anything in my life. I was rotting away in that house before Howard. All I was doing was waiting to die.” She looked away. “He changed all that. He’s givin me at least a breath of hope…hope that maybe, somehow, my change in attitude, my positive approach concerning life, will put this disease I have on hold—give us a few good years of life.”

“I was lost, David I really was. Howard found me, gave me a life, and I am forever grateful to him.” She turned toward him and said, “I don’t know now what I would do without him, or to be frank, what I ever *did* without him.”

David sat back in his chair and smiled. “Well, I imagine Henry and Griff have about got everyone seated.”

He stood, and faced her. He then reached out, took her hand, and pulled Betty up out of her chair. As he hugged her he said, "Let's go get this party started, Mom."

It had been five days since the ceremony. Now, between appointments, David leaned back in his chair, and thought about the wedding. He smiled, as he remembered walking her down the aisle—she looked like a kid in a pet shop.

Gail interrupted his walk down the aisle, as she informed him Hope was on line one.

"Hey. What's going on?"

"Miss you."

"It's been awhile."

"Whatta you hear from your mom? How are they doing?"

"They're still in the Smokies. I talked to her last night. They were coming home today, but have now extended a few more days. Let me put it this way, so you have something to compare it with—they are having almost as much fun together as you and I do."

She laughed. "Thanks. That's certainly couched in terms I understand. Now, what about the trial—how are we doing?"

"Good. However, I'm really thinking we might not finish it all up as early as I originally thought. It could be right after the first of the year when we try it. Everything's going well, it's just taking a little longer than I expected. I've told you about Ted—whatever he can do to pad his bill he does."

"Certainly, no surprise. Okay, I won't bother you."

"What bothers me is when I *don't* hear from you, not when I do."

She laughed. "Sleepover tonight?"

"Your place or mine?"
"Yours."
"Supper first?"
"Sure. Your place or out?"
"Out. Pick you up about six?"
"See you then."

Chapter 45

A cold late October wind seemed to push Chase as he approached Griff at an ever-increasing speed. Griff waited for him inside the framework of a large structure located just outside the city limits of Nashville. He needed to continue to remember to keep his emotions in check. He was on edge. But he needed to remain calm, business like, sure of himself, even though he was concerned everything in his world of business was about to come crashing down around him.

"Morning, Mr. Chase."

"Griff, how we coming?"

"Fine. We have it pretty well framed in. The rest of the framing should be done by the end of next week."

"Let's walk."

As they started walking, they discussed construction of the inner portions of the structure.

Once they reached the far end of the building, they sat down on a pile of lumber.

"What's your projected completion date?"

"I'm really not sure right now. I'm hoping in a couple of months."

Chase looked down for a moment, then said, "You know, I'd really like to have it done in about thirty days. Does that fit your schedule?"

"Not very well. I'm hurrying as fast as I can. I want it done right, and I really don't think hurrying will help. I'm thinking I need at least two months to finish up."

Chase looked around the structure for a moment, before he said, "Tell you what. Let's compromise. I don't do that very often, as you know, but in your case, I will. I'll give you six more weeks to finish up. I really need the space. I don't wanna wait two more months. I'd like to use it right now, but I'll give you six more weeks." He smiled. "Is that going to work for you?"

"Guess it'll have to."

"Now you get the idea." He stood. "Let's walk back. It's too cold to sit here very long."

As they walked, Griff said, "Can we visit about the payment plan you're using?"

"What's there to visit about? It's working fine. You've about got half that note paid off. It's working the way it's supposed to."

"Well, maybe for you, but it's not working so well for me. I'm having trouble paying the men. In fact, I'm behind in payroll as we speak. Is there any way we can just apply what you owe me to each month's monthly payment only, so I could use the rest to catch up on my employee's pay?'

"Oh, I don't think so, Griff. It doesn't make sense to pay you, when you already owe me. Let's just keep doing what we're doing."

Griff stopped walking. "This really isn't working, Mr. Chase. I'm short every week. I'm really concerned these guys are gonna walk out on me if I can't start paying them soon."

Chase turned to face him as he said, "Now look, Griff. You knew how this was going to go down. This is no fucking surprise to you. I told you in advance how this would all work. You've had plenty of opportunity to figure it all out. Don't come crying to me now when you knew from the beginning how this was going to work. Come on, let's walk. I wanna get back in the car and warm up."

As they continued toward his vehicle, Griff said, "I need to make a buy. I need just enough for me this time. You okay if I buy a little on credit?"

Chase turned to look at Griff for a moment, frowned at him and said, "Oh, I suppose. Go talk to John. He'll get you squared away. I'll add it on to what you owe me."

He never arrived home until after 8:00 p.m. Kristy was watching TV when he walked in.

He looked at her and said, "Hi. I need to shower. Anything to eat?"

"Leftovers in the fridge. Tough day? You look beat."

"My conversation with Chase made it a long day. I'll tell you about it when I shower and eat something. Maybe my attitude will improve once I smell better and have something in my stomach."

He showered, ate some left-over, warmed-up pizza, and drank a beer. As he walked in the living room and sat down, Kristy said, "What'd Chase have to say? You going to be able to change the way you're paying him?"

"I don't think so. He's insisting I do it his way."

"Well, did you insist back?"

"You know, I've told you a thousand fucking times Kristy, he controls everything he touches. You don't tell him what to do. You do what he tells *you* to do. I still owe him, and until I'm paid up, it's gonna be his way, *period*."

"So whatta ya gonna do, Griff? How long are your men going to stick around if you're not paying them?"

"Good question. I have no idea. I hope until this job is over, and I can get them paid out of the next job we do, which of course, will then, again, leave *us* a little short. I don't know. I'm handing this day-to-day. That's all I can do."

"Can you borrow more money from David?"

"I can try I guess. What about you? You got any other source of funds we could fall back on?"

"No."

He leaned back in his chair, and thought for a moment. Finally he rubbed his eyes, as he said, "You know, I'm not sure this is going to work. I thought we had the perfect plan, until Chase got in the way. But any more, it seems like there's always some fucking fly in the ointment. There's always something that I hadn't figured out in advance or that just comes up out of the blue."

"You know, Griff, I'm getting a little tired of it all too. I didn't sign on with you to live a life where every day is a drama. I sit here and wait for you to come home every night, hopefully with good news, and every fucking day it's the same—we got some mountain to climb—there's another problem we need to solve—you need to figure something out real quick or 'somethin bad is gonna happen.' I'm getting tired of living this way."

"Well, isn't that a surprise. How do you think I feel? It affects me the same way it affects you. We're both in the *same boat here, Kristy.* I'm as tired of it as you are."

"Heres the deal." She stood. "It's really getting old sitting in that *damn boat* with you. We better get this figured out right quick, because I'm not gonna sink to the bottom of the river with you, Griff, I'm just not."

She walked in the bedroom and slammed the door.

He yelled, "I guess that means I'm sleeping out here again, right?"

He didn't have to ask. He already knew. Griff stood, and walked across the room to the jacket he had left on the chair. He pulled out his purchase from Chase. He looked at it a long time, before he whispered, "What the hell. How could this *possibly* make things any worse?"

The next morning, he woke up on the couch when a slender ray of sunshine struck him in the eyes . He got up and walked into their bedroom. Kristy had already left for work. He checked to make sure her clothes were still in the closet, which they were—at least for now. After last night, however, he had no idea how long they might remain there.

Chapter 46

Last night, before he left the office, David had reviewed the list of appointments he had for today. He noticed Griff was on the list. That concerned him. Griff never made an appointment. He never felt he needed to. David was his brother, and, as a result, Griff felt he had the right, the privilege, to walk in his office door any time he wanted.

Setting up an appointment seemed a little unusual, but no more unusual than the phone calls between the two of them during the last few weeks. They were all brief, to the point, and covered only the essentials—they never talked about anything that didn't need to be discussed. Griff made sure that happened. He discussed nothing, other than what he felt was absolutely necessary. David hoped that changed today. He loved the *old* Griff—the fun-loving, over-the-top comic—a joy to be around. David hadn't seen that side of him in a long time.

His appointment at 10:00 a.m. came and went, with Griff failing to appear, nor contacting him by phone. Finally, almost an hour late, he walked down the hallway to David's office, leaving behind him, in the reception area, a couple that had made an appointment for 11:00 a.m., but would now need to wait beyond their scheduled time, because Griff was an hour late.

As he walked through the door, David said, "Hey, how are you? Everything okay? You don't normally make appointments to see me—you normally just walk right in."

As Griff sat down, he said, "I know, but this time I wanted to make sure you were here, and available. How you been?"

"Oh, fine. Same old issues I guess. Still fighting that idiot Jack Whitmore, but that's quickly becoming a life-long chore I'm afraid."

"You're kidding. You were fighting him the last time I talked to you—and the time before that. How long is this situation with him going to go on? What are you doing that's taking so long to finish?"

David smiled. "Well, actually it's more than one thing. There was that criminal charge filed against him for causing the death of his child, but now, I've sued him for Hope, and we have this civil case going against him."

"You never told me about that."

"It really isn't something I enjoy discussing. I don't like the guy, never have. But, because of Hope, I just keep butting heads with him."

"You and Hope involved?"

David smiled and said, "We are. Have been for a while now."

"You never told me. Isn't that something worthy of discussion? I can't believe you haven't told me."

"You know, to be honest, it's not something I'm discussing with *anyone*. I'm having a relationship with a client. That's not supposed to happen. She's actually the only one that could raise the issue if, for some reason, the two of us were at odds, but still, it's not supposed to happen. So, we've tried to be as discrete as we could be."

"You love her?"

He looked away for a moment before turning toward Griff and saying, "I do. I'm not real sure where it's all going, and won't be until we get this idiot former husband of hers out of our lives, but yes, I love her."

"How long's this litigation supposed to take?"

"It's already taken longer than I thought it would. I figured it might be done by Christmas, but here we are in February. It's set for trial the beginning of next month, so hopefully there'll be no more continuances and we'll get it out of the way."

"You two discussing marriage?"

"It's been discussed, but both our lives are just on hold while we go through this with Jack. The case will be over before long, but, for now anyway, all of her attention, along with most of mine, is concentrated upon getting the trial started and finished."

"You can take a lesson from mom on how to marry well. They seem to be enjoying life to the max. I'm really happy for both of them."

David smiled. "I have never seen her this happy. She knew what the hell she was doing, that's for sure. What's your situation right now? How are things in your life?"

Griff smiled. "You don't wanna know. Really, you don't wanna know."

"That good, huh?"

"Yup, just fucking unbelievable."

"Well, give me a few details. What's so good, what's not so good? I just discussed everything going on in my life, now tell me what's going on in yours. How's Kristy doing?"

Griff hesitated for a moment before he responded. "To be honest, I'm not really sure."

"Whatta ya mean?"

"She moved out a couple of weeks ago, and I haven't seen her since. I've tried to contact her, but she won't answer my calls. I have a feeling she may have gone to her parent's home in Michigan, but they won't answer my calls either. I've given up trying to contact her."

David figured he knew the answer to this question before he ever asked. "What happened, Griff?"

"I know what you're thinking, but it wasn't drugs—not this time. It was money. Things aren't going all that well, and she just buckled under the pressure. I don't blame her. I thought I had this all figured out, but it's really not working out according to plan—which is, by the way, consistent with the rest of my life."

David cleared his throat before he asked his next question. "Do you need some money? I can loan you a little if you do."

"No, not this time. It's time I figure this out on my own, without help from family, friends or anyone else. Thanks, but I need to figure out how to make this work on my own."

"What's causing the problem? Out of all the issues you have, what's causing the biggest problem?"

"I owe this guy some money. I'm building a building for him, and he's putting the squeeze on me to offset what he owes me against what I owe him. It's really running me short when it comes to paying the rest of my bills. Instead of just taking monthly payments, whatever he owes me at the end of each month goes against what I owe him. It runs me short in payroll every month. I just had a couple of men quit last week because I couldn't pay them. I'm down to a skeleton crew now, and will be until I finish the job."

"Why don't you just let me help you get through this time period? I can help you without squeezing my finances, and then you can repay me once the guy has been paid in full."

"You know, I'm not gonna do that this time. I need to figure these kinds of problems out myself, without my mother or my older brother helping me out. I'm a big boy now, David. It's just time I figured it all out."

David leaned forward in his chair and said, "I hate to ask this again, but are drugs an issue? What are they costing you each month?"

"No, they're not an issue at all. The financial problems I'm going through now have nothing to do with drugs. It all centers around the man I'm working for. If I can just get through this project, I'll be fine. Don't worry about me. I'll be fine."

"You able to pay your rent, put food on the table, things like that?"

"Oh sure. Well, I'm behind in rent, but I've talked to the landlord and he's giving me a little leeway. It will all work out fine. I didn't come here to talk about *me*, I came here to get an update on *you*"

"I just feel bad about what you're going through. Let me help you. Even if it's only to pay your rent for a few months."

Griff stood, and smiled. "Nope. I'm doing this myself this time. Don't worry 'bout me. Let's get together and have supper with mom and Howard before long. I think they would enjoy that and so would I. Bring Hope. She already knows both mom and Howard from the wedding. We'll have a good time."

David stood, hands on hips, and said, "Please let me help a little financially."

"I'll handle it. Stay in touch. Let me know when you want to get together with mom."

David nodded, and watched Griff walk out his office door. As he sat down, he concluded Griff was a man near the end of his rope. He would make it a point to remain in touch with him at least every other day from now on. Even with that smile, David could clearly see he was not in a good place right now. Hopefully, everything would turn around for him. Because if it didn't, with Griff not accepting any help, he was really concerned his life might be moving in an extremely dangerous direction.

Chapter 47

He hurriedly jotted down a few notes which would remind him of questions he needed to ask Hope to help her prepare to testifiy. As he leaned back in his chair, and took a drink of his lukewarm coffee, he glanced at his desk clock. She would be here any minute. David hadn't seen her in three days—since last weekend—and it seemed like an eternity. He was more than anxious to spend time with her, even if it did only involve preparation for trial.

He heard the outer office door open, and then heard her voice as she discussed clothes with Gail. She now frequented the office on a regular basis, and as a result, had become good friends with Gail. There had even been a couple of times within the last month when they had gone shopping together.

It was but a few minutes later she walked into his office. He stood, walked around his desk, and into her arms. He kissed her, then leaned back and looked at her. Again, he kissed her, but this time he didn't back away, until she did, as she said, "Hold on. We need to stop. We have work to do."

He smiled, "Okay, up to you. I could stand here doing just this until it's time to go home for the day, but if we must go to work, we must, I guess."

She took a chair, as he walked around the end of this desk, sat down, and started shuffling his paperwork, looking for the sheet upon which he had outlined her direct examination.

She said, "Okay, where do we begin?"

"Even though you and I have been through many of these particular elements of the trial before, let's start at the beginning, and I mean the *very* beginning. Now, do you recall picking the jury in the criminal case?"

"Yes."

"That's the first thing we're gonna do tomorrow morning."

"How many are selected? Is it the same as in the criminal case?"

"Yes. In Tennessee, twelve jurors decide a civil case. They are selected in a manner similar to the procedure we followed in the criminal case. We'll be involved with that for at least the first day."

"So, does it just take a majority of them to determine who wins?"

"No. It takes all twelve to determine which side wins— they have to be unanimous."

"What exactly do they decide? How does that work?"

"First of all, they decide whether the plaintiff—you, or the defendant—him, wins the case. Then, if they decide he wins, it's over, but if they decide you win, they then figure out how much you're entitled to. That's what their job consists of."

"Okay, so when do I testify?"

"You'll be the first witness, followed by other witnesses that will testify he left the child in the car. That will be the easiest portion of the case to prove. He's admitted it. The portion of the trial that establishes he was responsible for Billy's death will not be a difficult issue to establish."

"You keep saying '*that portion*' will not be difficult. Obviously, you believe there's a portion of it that *will* be difficult to establish. What part of it is going to be difficult to prove?"

"The damages—the sum to which you're entitled."

"Okay explain why that's so difficult."

"Because a loss like you have suffered is tough to quantify. It's not as if someone stole your car, destroyed it, and you want paid for it. It's not easy putting a dollar figure on the loss of life."

"And that's why we have an expert—to do that very thing, right?"

"Yes, but they have one too. They'll be experts everywhere, but the jury still has to accept our version of damages for them to rule appropriately for us. It won't be hard to establish you're entitled to something, but for them to determine you're entitled to the amount we're asking for, will be considerably more difficult. It's not enough that they determine he was responsible. That's just the first part of the equation. The jury then has to establish damages that are appropriate, and not let his sob story control their conclusion. If it does, we may end up with a few bucks, but not enough to make it worth our time."

"What's the jury going to think of me suing him in the first place? I mean, are they going to think I'm some money grabbing ex-spouse that's just in it for a buck?"

"Might. We'll try to offset that by establishing that you're doing what's legal, what's correct, and what you're entitled to do under the law. No one will be able to get the criminal verdict into evidence, so testimony concerning that trial and the way it ended, won't be something for them to consider. But through you, we'll establish you have the right to do this, and that you have the legal right to be compensated for what he did to you."

She considered his remarks for a second, then looked away and said, "I can't believe this is happening. It's like a bad dream. At least I've reached the point where, when we're together, when were alone, I forget, or at least I gloss over all this. But his death, going through one trial, now *another* trial—it's a non-ending nightmare."

"One way or the other it's almost over. Now, let's just quickly go through the different items we've discussed before, concerning your demeanor on the witness stand."

"You mean like don't ever answer a question you don't understand?"

"Exactly. If you don't understand it, ask the one that asked the question to rephrase it until you understand it. Stay calm. Put your hands in your lap—don't be waiving them all over the place. Speak loudly enough so everyone can hear you, including every member of the jury."

"If I have a question for you concerning what's going on—a question that I want to ask you at that moment—can we break while I ask you?"

"No. It will need to wait."

"What about the judge? Do I know him? It's not Henry is it?"

"No. It's Judge Ardmore. He's a good judge, and he'll be fair to both sides. He won't be an issue for either party. Now do you want to go through the questions I'm going to ask you one more time, or do you think you're ready?"

"I think I'm ready. I have the printout of your questions and probable questions from Ted that you gave me. I've gone through both lists a number of times. I think I'm ready to go."

Later that night, he tossed and turned trying to find a position which was comfortable. He did as he always did the night before a trial—he worried about everything it involved, until he was fortunate enough to drop off for a few hours. Tonight, however, there was one significant difference—he was in love with the client he represented. That created a whole new set of factors to worry about, and he had been through each one multiple times while trying to fall asleep.

David opened his eyes, and grabbed the remote. He would try falling asleep with the TV on. Maybe that would do the job.

He waited anxiously for Hope to arrive. All the preliminaries had been dispensed with during the first two days of trial. The jury had been selected. Opening statements had been made, and all procedural matters had been handled. It was time for Hope to testify. She was late. He looked at his watch. She was at least six minutes late—now seven. As he continued to stare at his watch, there was a knock on the conference room door. He opened it, and said, "You're late. I was concerned about you."

She frowned at him as she walked in. *"I'm here now. Let's go through everything one more time before I need to get up in that damn chair and testify."*

Chapter 48

David called out her name. Only the actual participants heard him. No one else was in the courtroom. All witnesses were sequestered—they could listen to none of the testimony prior to testifying. In addition, absolutely no one was present as a spectator.

Hope walked to the front of the courtroom and was sworn in. Once all foundational requirements concerning her testimony were satisfied, and preliminary testimony of a general nature was concluded, David's questions began to focus on her son, Billy.

"Describe Billy for us, Mrs. Whitmore."

She smiled. "He was an adorable little boy. We've already introduced his picture into the record, so anyone could see how cute he was. He was so much fun to be around. Full of life, curious, full of wonder, just a good kid, a fun child to raise and to be around."

"Who raised him?"

"I did. And really I don't say that in a disparaging way. It's what I wanted to do. I didn't care if Jack worked all the time. I didn't care whether he paid any attention to Billy, which most of the time he didn't. It just didn't matter. I loved him. I loved being with him every day of the week."

She looked down, and whispered, "We were very close—in fact, beyond close." She looked David and said, "We were virtually inseparable. I didn't even like to take him to the babysitter when there was something I needed to do without him—that's how close we were."

"And now?"

"And now? Well, hasn't that all changed." She thought for a moment, then said softly, "I still have many of his toys. I kept many of his clothing items, just because I don't want to forget. It's just hard to let him go."

"You've lost his love, his association, your relationship with him forever."

"Obviously. I also lost a good part of myself when he died. These past months since his death, have changed me. I no longer wanna go anywhere. I don't want to hear friends of ours tell me again and again, 'I'm so sorry.' I don't have people over to my home. I seldom visit with anyone on the phone. Life changed radically when he died. I'll never be the same. I lost a huge part of myself when he died in that car."

"Have you considered having other children, or adopting in the future?"

"No."

"Why not?"

"I'm afraid. Afraid someday I might have to go through this pain again. I'd rather have no more children and live my life alone, than go through this again."

"Okay, Mrs. Whitmore, tell us why you're here today."

"We're here to determine whether Jack is financially responsible for his actions."

"Is money something that you think will help you accept the loss of your son?"

"No, it has nothing to do with helping me get over it. I'll never get over his death. But the law is pretty clear. Someone responsible for another's death, can be held financially accountable for what they did, and I feel he should be held accountable. It's not me that made up this law. People a lot smarter than I, decided this remedy should be available, and I'm just following what the law says you can do, nothing more nothing less."

"You haven't asked for a specific amount?"

"No. I left it open for the jury to come to a conclusion they believe best fits this case. Of course, the expert that will testify has his own ideas as to an amount, but he can testify to that at the appropriate time."

"I have nothing more, Your Honor."

"Cross examine, Mr. Carnie?"

"Your Honor, I would like to meet with my client for a few moments prior to cross. I realize it's a little early for a noon break, but would that be in order anyway?"

The judge looked at his watch and said, "Certainly. Let's break a little early, and then return a little early. Jury members remember the admonition I gave you at the beginning of the trial, and I'll see you back here at one. Court is in recess."

Hope walked through the conference room door, with David close behind. He shut the door, then turned around, put his arms around her and kissed her.

"I assume that means I did a good job."

David smiled, and said, "You did." As he motioned for her to sit, he sat down, and said, "But this afternoon isn't going to be as easy. Just remember what I told you. Stay cool, remain calm, and answer from the heart. Don't lose your temper when he starts discussing Jack, which he probably will. You'll be fine, you'll do just fine, no problem, but remember…"

"Hold on, David. You're the one that needs to take a deep breath. I'll remember what you said, and I'll be fine. Now lean back, and relax."

He smiled, and said, "I am a little nervous I guess. I don't know why though. You're getting pretty good at this—at testifying."

"I'm not sure how good I'm getting, but I'll tell you one thing. I'll be glad never to have to look at him at that table again. Hopefully this will be the last time I ever have to look at Jack for *any* reason. He does upset me. I'll give him credit for that, he really does upset me."

Once the noon break ended, Hope returned to the stand, ready for cross-examination. Ted took over two hours just questioning her about her background and relationship with both Billy and Jack.

Then he became more specific. "Let me ask you, Mrs. Whitmore, why are you suing Jack?"

"*Why* am I suing him?"

"Yes, I mean, I guess I really don't understand your reasoning."

"It's really quite simple. Because he killed our son."

"But what do you figure to gain by suing him? It's never gonna bring your son back."

"I know. But, sir you know, we all gotta pay for our sins. Some way or the other, we all gotta pay. And hopefully, this is how Jack is going to pay for what he did to another human being. Happens all the time. You know that. People get sued over car accidents and over the loss of someone's life all the time, because the law says that's what they should do and can do. This case is no different. He killed our son. He's responsible for ending a life. He cost me my relationship with my child. The expert is able to turn that loss into a monetary figure and that's why we're here— time for him to pay up."

"Is that going to scratch your itch is it, Mrs. Whitmore— making him pay?"

She teared up, as she said, "No amount of money is going to replace Billy. But on the other hand, your client killed somebody. He should pay for that."

"Don't you think he already has? He lost a son too."

"You know, I lived with him for a lot a year's, sir, and the only thing he ever knew was money. I honestly don't think he gave a damn about either Billy or me. That's why he left Billy in the car. Getting to his office that morning and making money was way more important than the welfare of his son."

Ted shuffled papers around for a moment before he said, "Were you satisfied with what you received in your divorce?"

"Objection. Relevance."

"Judge, I'll connect it all up. There's a reason for asking that question, I can assure you."

"Please proceed, Mr. Carnie. If it reaches the point I can't figure out how it's relevant I'll stop you and ask the jury to disregard that line of questioning."

"Fair enough, Judge. Now ma'am, were you satisfied with how your property division ended up in your marriage?"

"To be honest, no, I wasn't. I knew Jack was hiding money, and that we had way more than he said we did."

"Well, now, was that ever proven?"

"No."

"But you thought he was concealing assets didn't you?"

"Yes."

He hesitated for a moment, then said, "So, is this a way to backdoor him—to get a little more money and offset what you thought you lost in the dissolution of marriage?"

She smiled. "Absolutely not. This case has nothing to do with that one."

"Really?"

"*Really*, Mr. Carnie."

"Do you think Mr. Whitmore has suffered just as you have over the loss of Billy?"

"I have no idea."

"Whatta ya *think*? I mean, Billy was his son too."

She leaned forward in his chair, and said, "You want the truth?"

"Well, certainly we want the truth."

"I don't believe, knowing him as I do, he lost one minute of sleep over Billy's death. That's what I think and what I believe to be the truth. He didn't give a shit one way or the other."

Ted stood and said, "And you're here to punish him for that, aren't you, Mrs. Whitmore? You want money from him you never got in your dissolution of marriage. You feel he really never did care whether your son died, and it's for those reasons you're in court here today aren't you—has virtually nothing to do with the loss of Billy. His death is just a convenient method for y'all to get what you really want isn't it?"

"Objection, Your Honor. That's ridicules. That's improper…"

"It is, Mr. Brenden, it is. Those last few questions are for the jury to decide and for you to argue in your closing, Mr. Carnie. Objection is sustained. Anything further?"

As Ted sat down, he said, "Nothing further."

David asked a few follow-up questions to clean up some of the issues that were not properly addressed during cross-examination.

Later that night, as he sat at his desk reviewing his notes and getting ready for witnesses that would testify tomorrow morning, he knew Ted had made his point—in fact, he made numerous points. It was going to be a dogfight all the way to the end. There remained no debatable issue concerning liability, but a determination as to the amount of damages, was, and would continue to remain completely unpredictable until the final verdict.

Chapter 49

Hope arrived only a few minutes after he did. They both sat, each deep in thought, at a table within one of the conference rooms, waiting to walk in the courtroom and continue another day of trial.

David smiled, and said, "Had enough haven't you."

Hope, now staring out one of the windows, turned to David and said quietly, "More than that—I've had about all I can handle."

"Sorry we filed?"

"No, not really. It needed to be done. I needed to know I had done all I could do to make him pay for what he did. If you hadn't told me this procedure was available, and I would have found out from someone else, I would have definitely been upset. No, I'm glad we filed, but mentally I'm a mess. We just need to get it over with, and move on one way or the other."

"Well, we're close, we're really close to a conclusion. All the other witnesses have testified, and we have only Jack left to take the stand. It's been a long week and a half, but we're almost done."

"You haven't said much about the outcome. Any thoughts? Any idea what they'll do?"

David smiled. "Not really. As I told you, I have a perfect record in assessing what juries do because I never give a prediction until *after* we have a verdict. Seriously, I know we won't have a problem with the jury determining he's responsible. But unfortunately, that's only half the battle.

What they come back with as concerns damages is the other issue, and as concerns *that* issue, I don't have any idea. Ted's good at what he does, but so am I. Jack's testimony will be important. How he comes across will affect the jurors one way or the other, I know that. We'll just see what he has to say."

"The jerk will lie all the way through. Or he'll be overly emotional like he was during the criminal trial."

"Hopefully, the jury will see through all his emotional antics and do what's right."

Hope once again turned to stare out one of the windows, while remaining quiet.

David reached out and took her hand. "What's on your mind? You're definitely much more quiet today than you normally are."

She looked down as she said, "I'm just so sick of all this. Sometimes I think it's time to leave Nashville and just get away from all these memories that remind me of a horrible marriage, and the loss of Billy." She looked at him and said, "But I know I can't afford that, and besides, now there's you. I don't want to leave you—leave what's developed between us."

He squeezed her hand. "Let's get through this. Maybe once this is over, you'll feel differently about everything."

The knock on the door indicated Judge Ardmore was ready to proceed.

She smiled. "Maybe. Maybe you're right. Hope so."

Jack's testimony had gone basically as anticipated. He had played the emotion card all the way through his testimony. Direct examination was over and David was re-examining a few of the issues Ted had already covered.

"Mr. Whitmore, there's no doubt, but what your actions caused the death of this child, correct?"

"No, I guess not." Jack wiped his eyes, as he began to cry while answering the question.

"And there's really no doubt under the law, that your ex-wife is entitled to recover monetarily for what you did, correct?"

"I guess. I assume that's why we're here."

"Now, there seems to be an issue concerning what she received in the dissolution of your marriage—that maybe this is really all about getting back at you for that. Your attorney raised that issue, didn't he?"

"Yes."

"You know and understand she had the right to appeal that decision, but that she never exercised that right, did she?"

"No."

"So, wouldn't that draw you to the conclusion she was happy or satisfied with the way it turned out? Wouldn't that make your argument about her getting back at you as a result of the dissolution a little weak, Mr. Whitmore?"

He looked away as he said, "I guess."

"What was Billy's life worth to you in monetary terms?"

"Billy's life?"

"Yes."

"No value. There's not a value you can put on his life."

"Try. Put a figure on it."

"I can't. I'm sorry I can't."

"Was it worth more than five hundred dollars?"

He looked at his attorney, then at David. "I cannot put a figure on it. I don't know." He looked at the jurors for a moment then at David. "You know, everyone seems to forget here—I lost a son too." Again he started to cry.

"Because of me, I lost my son. She isn't the only one that lost someone in all this." He whispered, "I did too."

The judge looked down at the witness and said, "You wanna take a short break, Mr. Whitmore?"

"No, no let's move on."

"How much time would you say your former wife spent with Billy?"

He wiped away another tear with his sleeve as he replied, "You mean as a percentage?"

"Yes."

"I don't know, maybe fifty percent."

David leaned back in his chair and smiled. "Who you kidding, Mr. Whitmore? More like ninety percent wasn't it?"

"I don't know. What's the difference?"

"Well, the difference is you not only took her son away, you took away a constant companion, didn't you?"

"They were with each other out of necessity. I was working."

David increased his level of intensity when he said, "He *was* her constant companion, wasn't he?"

"Yes, yes I guess he was. But why can't you understand this was just all an unfortunate mistake, an accident, I didn't do anything intentional."

"I do understand and so does everyone else, Mr. Whitmore. But we all have to pay for our mistakes, in some form or another, and it's time you paid for yours— it's time you paid for yours, Mr. Whitmore. That's all I have, Judge."

"Mr. Carnie, any redirect?"

"No, Your Honor, and the defense rests."

"Mr. Brenden are you going to present any rebuttal evidence?"

"No, Your Honor. The facts have all been submitted. There's no additional evidence to submit on behalf of the plaintiff."

"Alright then, all evidence on behalf of the parties has now been submitted. Tomorrow morning we'll hear closing statements, I'll go through the instructions of the court to the jury, and we'll submit this case to them for a verdict. We are recessed for today."

In the conference room, once they had discussed the day's testimony, Hope said, "So tomorrow it's all submitted to the jury?"

"Yes."

"How long until we have a verdict—any idea?"

"No. The facts aren't that complicated, but the issue of the amount they may award you could take a while. That expert of ours did an incredible job of testifying. I would only hope the jury listened, and that they follow his final conclusion."

"You're right, he did do a wonderful job." She stood to leave. "Should we just meet here tomorrow morning?"

"Yes, that's fine with me, unless you don't want to be alone tonight. I can stop by after I finish up at the office, and we can come here, together, tomorrow morning."

She smiled, as she said, "You know, I think I need to be alone. I have a lot of things to catch up on. I've just really got quite a bit on my mind right now."

He stood as he said, "Yes, that's pretty obvious. Okay. Why don't you go home and relax. I'll check with you later tonight, and then we'll meet here tomorrow morning about eight-thirty and wrap this all up."

She kissed him, and said, "You were wonderful in the courtroom, David. I couldn't have asked for better representation."

"Cross-examination of Jack was difficult for me. In a case like this, you need to just make your points and quit. I feel like I continued to hammer the same points, just to emphasize them to the jury, but his answers never changed. He was tough to cross-examine. But, thank you. I guess the jury will decide how good I was."

"Not really. The facts are the facts. You can't change those. We are fighting the king of all liars. He's always been good at that and at being an incredible actor. Jack always performs well when under pressure and he did again today. I only hope the jury sees through it all, and makes him pay dearly for what he did to Billy."

"So do I, Hope, so do I."

Chapter 50

"Well, David. Good Lord, how long's it been?"

"Ya know, Mom, it's not *my* fault you're gone all the time. I've tried to reach you a number of times. My calls all go to voicemail, and you never seem to have time to return them—any of them. Since you answered this one, maybe I'll start calling you early in the mornings. Does that work better for you?"

"Sure sweetheart, that works fine for me. However, you should know I don't most often answer when we're gone, and lately we been gone quite a bit."

"What have you been doing? Are you *always* busy? Obviously, you're never home."

"Oh, I don't know—I guess we've been a little bit of everywhere. We went up to Kentucky to see some of Howard's relatives, and…oh, we went back to Gatlinburg for a few days. What have you been up to? How's Hope? I just love that girl."

David laughed. "That's not hard to do, Mom. Actually I've been with her a lot lately. I told you about filing suit against that idiot former husband of hers. We're waiting for a verdict. The jury started their deliberations yesterday and I'm waiting on a call from the clerk telling us they've reached a verdict. I have no appointments because I don't know when I'll have to go to the courthouse."

"Is Hope with you?"

"No. She's home. I told her I'd call her, and take her to the courthouse when the jury came to a conclusion. I'm thinking it will be sometime today,"

"So when are the two of you going to stop over?"

"You know, every time I call, it's to make sure you're going to be home so I can stop by, but you're never there. Sounds like you're having a good time. I'm really happy for you and Howard. I hope…"

"Well, for gracious sakes, David you won't believe this, but Griff is at the door. I'll call you back, honey."

She opened the door and said, "Hi, Griff. What a surprise. How long's it been?"

He walked in and embraced her. "Been a while, Mom. I've driven by a couple of times, but it was pretty obvious no one was home."

She motioned toward the table, and said, "Sit, sit. Let me get you a cup of coffee. Howard, Griff is here. Come on in and sit with us."

Both men sat, while Betty poured three cups of coffee. As she sat the pastry's down on the table, she said, "How's everything going, Griff? How's that construction business coming along?"

"Not bad. But, way more important than that, what have you two been doing? I know you're darn hard to run down."

Howard smiled and said, "Your mom and I have been all over. We spent some time in Kentucky, we've been in the Smokies, near Gatlinburg, and we've been all over Nashville. We've had one hell of a good time since we got married, I can tell ya that."

"Mom, how you been feeling?"

She hesitated for a moment, before she said, "Good, good, I'm feeling good."

Griff caught her hesitation and moved forward in his chair. "Have you, Mom? You wouldn't tell me that just so I wouldn't worry, right? Are you feeling okay?"

"Oh, I get a little tired is all. Sometimes we have to slow down because I get a little tired. I'm sure it's nothing, but I do get somewhat weary. When that happens, we just stop what we're a doin, and I sit for a while before we move on. Certainly nothing to worry about. We're having the time of our lives. We head to Charleston next. I've never been there. We're only going for a few days. Just long enough to eat some of that good Charleston food, and see the sights. Then it's back home. Got a party to go to a few days after we get back."

Howard said, "Griff, how's Kristy doing? She getting along okay?"

Griff looked away and said, "Actually, we're no longer together, Howard." He hesitated for a moment. "I'd rather not talk about her, if that's okay."

Howard looked at Betty, then turned toward Griff and said, "Sure, that's fine. I understand."

Betty watched Griff for a moment. He never moved. He said nothing.

She turned toward Howard and said, "Howard, I think that show of yours you like to watch is on TV. Can you give Griff and I a moment?"

"Oh, sure. Certainly. I'll just be in the other room watching…that…show."

Once Howard had left the room, Betty said, "Okay Griff, what the hell's going on?"

"Not worth talking about. It's much more fun listening to both of you talk about what's going on in your lives. I'm so happy for the two…"

"Stop it, Griff. Just stop. What's the story on Kristy?"

He looked away for a moment before he turned toward her, and said, "It just didn't work out. Too much pressure. She couldn't take it. I don't blame her. It's been pretty rough lately. Business isn't going very well, and she had had enough."

"How long has she been gone?"

"Long enough to be certain she's not coming back."

"You still talking to her? Would it help if I called her?"

Griff laughed. "Still trying to fix my messes huh, Mom? No that wouldn't help. She wasn't taking any of my calls, and now, she's apparently changed phones. I get nothing when I try to call. I've called her folks, but they won't pick up. No, our relationship is over. I do hate it, because I still love her. But the 'love' business has gotta be a two-way street and right now, unfortunately it's only running one-way. I don't expect to ever see her again."

She reached out and took his hand. "I'm so sorry, Griff."

"It's fine, Mom. I'll move on."

"What about the business? How's it going?"

"Not well. I got crossways with a guy I'm doing work for. I owed him a little money, and he wanted a building built. To make a long story short, I've had to terminate the crew, and shut down construction. He's not happy. I'll get him handled some way, but it's gonna take a little time. I just have to figure out what I'm going to do and act on it."

"So are you working at all?"

"Not right now, but it's fine. I have a couple of job prospects I need to look into this week. It'll all work out, but I'm just in between everything right now."

"Can we help you? I've got some…"

"No, absolutely not. You've helped in the past. Those days are over. I'll figure this out without family help this time. Don't worry about me. You take care of yourself—make sure you're doing okay. I'll be fine."

He stayed but a few more minutes, and as he walked out the back door, Howard walked in the kitchen.

He watched Griff walk out, and shut the door behind him, at which time he looked at Betty and said, "Is he all right? It sounds like his life is a mess. Is his business okay?"

"He's got some real problems right now, Howard. I tried to help him, but he doesn't want any help. Kristy left him and his business is failing. I don't think he has any idea what his future holds. But, even beyond that, I'm not real sure he cares. He's a damn mess, Howard. I am really…I am really concerned about him."

Chapter 51

"**S**hould we go a little faster?"

"No, we're fine. They won't start without both parties sitting at the council tables. Besides that, I told the clerk I was going to get you, and we would be there as soon as traffic allowed."

The distance from Hope's home to the courthouse wasn't all that far, but as horrendous as the traffic situation in Nashville had become, he had no idea how long it would take for them to travel the relatively short distance.

Hope fumbled through her purse looking for something. Finally she just said, "Screw it. Do you have any kind of breath mint with you? I just finished a drink, and I don't want the smell on my breath."

He smiled, glanced at her and said, "No, sorry, I don't. But just to reassure you, your breath smells fine." He hesitated before he said, "You okay? I mean I can tell you're really nervous. You going to be able to handle this?"

She continued to look straight ahead, as she said, "David, I just want this to end. Hopefully, it will end the way we want it to, but more importantly, I just want this all over with."

They drove in silence the rest of the way. Upon reaching the courthouse, he let her out. He told her he would be in as soon as he parked and to go ahead and take a chair at the council table.

As soon as he sat down, the court attendant notified the judge and shortly thereafter, they ushered the jury into the courtroom.

Once the judge took his place, he said, "Ladies and gentlemen of the jury, it's my understanding you've come to a conclusion, is that correct?"

A younger woman, seated at the end of one of two rows of jurors, said, "We have, Your Honor."

"Please provide it to the court attendant."

The court attendant took the verdict and handed it to the judge. He read it over, then said, "As concerns the issue of liability, the jurors have found in favor of the plaintiff."

David turned to look at Hope and winked.

"As concerns the amount of damages, the jury has awarded the sum of one hundred thousand dollars." The judge turned to look at the foreperson, and said, "Is this the verdict of all of you?"

"It is, Your Honor."

David heard some movement at the other council table, and then heard Jack whisper loud enough for the whole courtroom to hear. "What the hell have they done? I'm not paying her one red cent. Are they crazy?"

The judge heard his remarks, looked at Ted and said, "Get your client under control Mr. Carnie or I'll find him in contempt. He can pay the amount from a jail cell."

David heard whispering between both individuals at the other table, but there were no more comments loud enough to be heard, from either of them.

The judge looked at the jurors, and said, "Ladies and gentlemen thank you for your help concerning the case. You are free to go, but please stop by the clerk's office on your way out. Folks, this case is now concluded. We are adjourned."

Hope looked at David as the jurors left the courtroom, and whispered, "Is that it? We end up with a hundred grand for a murder? What the fuck, David, I don't get it. How could that happen?"

"I don't know. Meet me in that conference room, where we've met each day. I'll be along shortly."

She walked out the back door of the courtroom, and David noticed as Jack watched every move she made.

He stood, walked over to their table, and said, "Does your client want to just write the check today or does he need some time."

Jack looked up, smiled and said, "This case will never end. My attorney told me I could appeal, and that's just what I'm going to do. I'll appeal the verdict if I have to spend every last red cent I have. She's getting nothing from me."

David looked at Ted, and said, "Is that what you're going to do—appeal?"

"That's what we've discussed, yes. I'm not real sure there's much in the way of grounds for an appeal, but if that's what he's inclined to do, I'll probably do it."

"I'm not paying her one penny, and you can tell…"

David placed both hands on the table and leaned toward Jack. He said, "You know Jack, you couldn't have come out of all this any better. You got away with murdering a human being, you've put your wife through a living hell, and now this. You keep your fucking mouth shut or I'll shut it for you, and if you don't think I can, you try me."

Jack started to respond, but thought better of it, and just turned the other way.

David looked at Ted, and said, "Let me know what you wanna do. I'll discuss all of the remaining issues with Hope, and maybe we can somehow conclude this. I must admit, this is the first time in a long time I've been involved in a case where nobody won, and everyone was unhappy. Stay in touch, Ted."

David opened the door to the conference room, finding Hope looking out one of the windows. He said, "Let's sit down and discuss where we're going from here."

He sat down, and as she turned around, she wiped away tears from both eyes. She sat down, and said, "That didn't turn out so well, did it?"

"No. Certainly not like either of us had hoped it would. Of course, he's upset about the amount too. He's talking about appealing."

"Can he do that? Seems like it should be us that's appealing. Can we appeal, or is it worth the time and energy?"

"To be honest, probably not. There were very few issues that might even remotely provide the possibility of a higher court overturning that verdict. Of course, the same is true of him and any appeal he might take."

"What went wrong?"

"I don't know. I'll talk to a juror or two, but I'm just thinking it was the nature of the case, and the fact that Jack sounded so remorseful. Hope, I'm sorry that we didn't end up with more. I'll certainly reduce my fee so you…"

"You're not doing any such thing. We had a deal. You'll take what we agreed on."

"I guess we can talk about that later. It's hard telling when we'll get our money. We'll have a judgement against him, but if he appeals…"

"I understand." She looked away. "Actually, I wasn't going to keep any of it anyway. I was going to set up a trust fund for kids to help pay their college expenses. None of it was for me."

She stood and walked toward the window, as she said, "I need to make some tough decisions, David. I just don't know if I can live here anymore—in Nashville. Now that everything is over, I need to figure out where to go from here—to figure out what's best for me, for the rest of my life."

He stood and walked up behind her, putting his arms around her waist. "I hope there's at least a little consideration in those plans that might involve you *and* me. I feel like we have something special and I don't really want it to end."

"I know. I feel the same way." She hesitated. "But I just don't know if I can live here anymore. Too many bad memories."

He took her home, and then drove back to the office to finish up the day. He still had a few late afternoon appointments to handle.

Gail was on the phone when he walked in. He waived at her, as he continued to walk back to his office. Just as he sat, Gail walked in and said, "How'd it turn out?"

"They awarded her a hundred grand."

"That's it? I'll bet that didn't go over well."

"Nobody was happy. Jack wasn't happy, she wasn't happy, I wasn't happy—on the other hand I take that back. Ted was smiling the whole time. He's the only one that really benefited from the whole process."

"Was Hope really upset?"

"Conflicted. Glad to get it all over with, but not happy with the result."

"She'll be fine. She's pretty good at swinging with the punches."

Once she had gone back to her desk, David took a moment to think about the past few months. He was really concerned about the possibility Hope might leave town. He absolutely couldn't even consider leaving with her. His mother, her health, Griff and all his issues—and then there were his own issues, including all that alimony he was paying, and a thriving office practice.

These were all matters that would preclude him from leaving with her. The last thing in the world he wanted was to lose her. But right now, the problem seemed impossible to resolve. Hopefully, something would change to the point where all of the factors worked in harmony, instead of in conflict. He sure as hell didn't want to lose her, but the way everything stood right now, there was a strong possibility that was exactly what was about to happen.

Chapter 52

Betty stood, coffee cup in hand, looking at the perennials that were just starting to pop up out of the ground. She had no doubt April showers of the past few days, would help all those that had not yet broken through the topsoil, do just that. As she thought of the many years she had enjoyed watching all the flowers bloom in early spring, she wondered how many future springs she might have left to enjoy. Her phone rang, and she picked it up off the arm of the chair she had just left.

"Morning, David." She sat down and set her coffee cup on the table as she continued. "I don't think I've talked to you since a week or so after Hope's verdict."

"Hi, Mom. I think you're right. I thought I'd stop over this Saturday and see both of you. It's so busy here it's difficult for me to walk out the front door during the week. I really got behind while I was trying Hope's case. You going to be home?"

"Saturday…Saturday. Oh sure, we'll be home, at least most of the day. We're to go out for supper with some friends that evening, but we'll be here until at least six. You gonna bring Hope with you? I haven't seen her for a while, and I really do enjoy spending time with her."

He hesitated, then said, "I haven't seen her much either. I can call her and ask her if she wants to come, but I doubt she will. She's a little lost right now. She's all wrapped up in trying to figure out what she wants, where she wants to live, or what she's going to do in the future. To be honest, I've only seen her twice since the trial."

"She's not thinking of leaving here, is she?"

"I think she is, but I'm just not sure. She won't open up to me about what she's considering. Of course, Jack's appeal didn't help matters either. That's all still in limbo. She really thought it would all end once the verdict was rendered."

"Her ex must be a bastard. Oops, excuse me. That's probably not quite the right term."

David laughed. "No, you pretty well nailed it, Mom."

"Let me ask you this. *If* she decides to leave here, you going with her?"

"You know, really, I haven't thought to much about it. I really don't *want* to think about it unless and until she comes to that conclusion. I'm just hoping she decides to stay. But she alone, knows how she can handle living in the same town with Jack along with all those bad memories that grew out of that relationship. I haven't contacted her lately. She needs to make her decision without my interference."

Betty said, "You have a lot on your mind."

He laughed. "Just another day. The only difference now is that Hope and the decision she must make, is also a part of my every-day life, even when I'm not with her. It's going to be a concern until she finally decides. I better get off. I got some people waiting for me. Love you, Mom. I'll stop over sometime during the day on Saturday."

"Love you. See you then."

Howard, who had been in the basement, walked in the room as she terminated the call. "Who was that?"

"David. He said he would stop over this Saturday sometime during the day."

Both heads turned toward the back door as Griff knocked, then walked in.

"Morning you two. Got any coffee?"

"Hey, Griff. Morning to you." Betty stood, and hugged him, before pouring another cup and both taking a chair at the table.

"Join us, Howard."

"No, no I have some things to do in the basement yet. You two enjoy your time together. I'll be up in a few minutes."

Once he had left the room, Griff said, "How's everything—I mean with you and Howard? Is it working out as you hoped it would?'

She smiled as she said, "He's without doubt one of the finest individuals I've ever met. He treats me like a queen. One of the best decisions I ever made. Yes, we're very, very happy."

"Good. I really never doubted that would be the case from day one. But you never know them until you're living with them, as I can certainly attest to."

"Nothing from Kristy?"

"Nope. I have no doubt she's gone for good."

"I'm so sorry, Griff."

"It's probably just as well. I'm unemployed, and living day to day, until I find something to do. Luckily, I pigeonholed a little money I didn't tell Kristy about. I was going to surprise her. That didn't work out so well—at least the part about surprising her. But because of that, I have a little money to live on while I regroup."

"Any prospects of employment?"

"Right now, I'm just waiting. I've got three possibilities that I should hear from about any time now."

"That sounds about like David and his situation with Hope. I just talked to him. There's no doubt in my mind he's in love with her, but she doesn't know what she wants right now. You talked to him lately?"

"No. I need to call him."

"That idiot ex-husband of hers appealed the decision in her case, so that's still hanging over both of them."

"You know, that guy must be something else. What's his name—is it Jack? Jack Whitmore I think maybe is his name."

"You're right. Too bad the bastard doesn't just disappear. It would certainly make your brother's life easier."

"I'm sure it would. Finding a job would make *mine* a lot easier too."

"What about that guy you owe—the one you were working for? You still hear from him?"

"Not lately, but I will. He got another crew to finish up the building so they're involved with moving everything out of the old one and into the new one. But I'll hear from him before long. I have no doubt about that."

"What's gonna happen with that situation?"

"I'm not really sure what'll happen."

"Both my boys have a few problems. I worry about both of you."

"We're fine, Mom, believe me we're fine. We've both weathered life's storms before and we both will again."

Griff left a few minutes later. As soon as the outer door closed, Howard walked through the basement door and into the kitchen.

Betty was cleaning up breakfast dishes, as he walked up behind her, and put his arms around her waist.

"How was your conversation with both the boys, Betty?"

"You know, you don't have to leave the room when they show up, or when they're on the phone. You know that don't you?"

"I know. I just thought it best this time that you talk to both without me around. Did you tell them?"

She continued washing dishes for a moment before she whispered, "No, I didn't."

"Don't you think you should."

She turned around, kissed him, smiled and said, "You know, this has happened before. This isn't the first time it's made an appearance. I get it, it goes away, I get it, it goes away. This time should be no different than any of the others. I have faith it will disappear just as quickly as it has the past few times."

Howard continued to hold her as he said , "You're right. You'll beat it this time like you have every other time. Now, you up for a ride? Let's go take a ride around the countryside. Maybe drive over to Shelby Bottoms and take a walk."

"But it's raining. Shouldn't we wait?"

"It's only a shower. We have an umbrella if it's still raining when we get there. Now, you in or not?"

"I'm in." she walked away and as she did, she muttered, "Now if I can just find that damn umbrella." She turned as she walked and yelled, "Howard, do you remember where I put that damn umbrella?"

Chapter 53

Hope needed to end her phone call with Ann, which had now extended beyond 20 minutes. She was to meet David for supper across town, and, in addition to the drive time, she needed at least a half hour to get ready.

The discussion between both women, had covered a myriad of subjects, but the subject of her date for tonight had not yet been broached. Hope didn't want to discuss him, or the relationship between the two of them, with anyone. She hadn't come to a conclusion concerning what her future might hold, and verbalizing the problem, at this point in time, only left her more confused.

Unfortunately, once Hope indicated she was leaving to meet David, and, as a result, needed to end the call, Ann said, "Now wait. What *about* David? Any plans for the future or is it over?"

"No, it's not over. It might be on hold, maybe, but it's not over. At least, I don't think it is. Maybe it is, I hope it isn't, but...In answer to your question I obviously have no idea where we are. I'll let you know when I know."

"Do you love him?"

"More than anything."

"Isn't that the answer? Isn't that what's most important? What am I missing here? Isn't that one of life's ultimate goals—to find someone you really love?"

"Maybe he's *not* the answer, or I wouldn't have so much doubt. On the other hand, he most likely is the one I want to spend the rest of my life with." She hesitated, before she said, "Hell, I don't know. There are so many factors at play I don't have time to go into all of them with you. I have to meet him in about 45 minutes and I think that issue— whether love, as the saying goes, 'conquers all',will probably be the one issue we cover over supper. I'm so afraid…so afraid…"

"What are you afraid of? Just tell him…"

"Wait, Ann. I really need to discuss this with *him* not you. I need to figure out *his* take on our lives and what his priorities are before I can begin to come to a conclusion of my own. I'll talk to you tomorrow."

"Well, okay then. Just let me know what you decide. And if you need to discuss it with me, just…"

"Sure will."

An hour later, Hope walked through the front door of a restaurant in east Nashville, where the two of them had met numerous times in the past. David was waiting for her at the table, and stood as she approached. He embraced her and kissed her on the check once she reached him. As he sat, he said, "Can I get you something—a glass of wine or something else?"

"Yes. Maybe a house pinot would be fine."

He ordered, then turned to her and said, "You look great. Seems like it's been months since we've been together."

"It's been quite a while I know that—and I know I've missed you."

"As I have missed you."

The waiter brought her wine and sat it down on the table. As quickly as he placed it on the table, she picked it up and took a long drink.

"Would you like to order?"

"David, let's just talk for a moment. Let's just visit about what's going on in each of our lives—what each of us have in mind concerning our relationship, if you don't mind."

"Okay, if that's what you wanna do. Go ahead. What are your thoughts now that we've come to basically the end of this mess with Jack?"

She took a drink, then said, "First of all, throughout this conversation, please keep in mind how much I love you. Don't ever doubt that. I love you more than I've ever loved anyone."

"I understand. Go on."

"I am so conflicted right now I honestly don't know what to do. I have you here, but I also have all these memories of such sad days in Nashville. I don't want to stay here, but I have you here, and I really am lacking enough funds to comfortably make a final move away from here. I've got two houses now, and the one here, if I sell it, will probably result in a loss because I've owned it for such a short time, and it hasn't had time to appreciate in value. And then…"

"Hold on. Let's approach this in a different fashion. In a perfect world, would you marry me today?"

"Are you asking?"

"No. There's no sense in asking you when we don't even know at this point, if we're going to be living in different states. I just want to know if that's how much you care for me—yes or no?"

She looked away for a moment, then turned toward him, and said, "Yes."

"Then there shouldn't be anything that keeps us apart."

"It's just not that simple."

"Why?"

"I can't live here, David. You ready to move with me—to Tahoe? You ready for that?"

"Can you financially afford the move? I thought that was a significant issue for you."

"It is. I'm going to check with a few realtors and see what I might be able to do with the house here. That will help me decide what to do."

"So you have definitely concluded you're moving?"

"That's the plan for now, unless it just becomes financially impossible. Right now, I can't leave with two house payments to make and little cash. But my ultimate plan is to leave Nashville. Do you understand my reasoning? Do you understand why?"

"Not really. It's a great city, it's a great…"

"Liston to me. Every time I leave the house, I drive by his school or I drive by a park where I used to take him. If I go another direction, I drove by the lake where we fed the ducks, or I walk in our regular grocery store, and I see Jack, or his secretary or one of his clients. I can't go anywhere to get away from the disaster of the marriage we had—or Billy."

"You know, no matter where you go, you're never going to forget Billy. He'll always be with you."

"I know that. I understand that. And I don't *want* to forget him. But I don't want to be reminded of our life together every hour of every day either. I want, at least some time in my day-to-day life, without *that t*ragedy, *and* the tragedy of a horrible relationship with Jack staring me in the face. I need to leave here, and if I had the money I would do it tomorrow."

"Without me?"

"Will you come with me?"

"You already know the answer to that question." He looked away and said, "By the way, my mother called last night. Her cancer has returned. She told me she was again experiencing some major problems." He looked at her, and said, "On top of that, I find myself trying to be both father and brother to Griff who just seems to be floating around out there with absolutely no purpose concerning any aspect of life. Then there's the office. No, I can't leave here. Not now. Not the way things are."

Hope looked at her half-empty glass of wine, and remained quiet. Finally, she wiped a tear away, as she said, "First of all, I'm sorry about your mother. I love her. She has always been so good to me. But…"

"Hope…Hope…look at me. Just lay it all on the table. What are you thinking?"

She looked up, cleared her throat and said. "I think we shouldn't see each other for a while, David—until we both resolve a few issues in our complicated lives and we can determine what's best for both of us. Maybe…maybe in a year or two, the answer will be much clearer than it is right now. We both have too much baggage to try and make this work right now."

"I don't agree. But, in any event, surely we can continue to see each other while we're both figuring out what's best. Surely, we don't have to go to that extreme just because we have a few problems complicating both our lives."

She stood. "I'm so confused right now, David I don't want to make a decision concerning my life with you, and both our lives in the balance, without cleaning up some of the drama from my past first. I don't think we should see each other for a while. Let me figure out what's best for me, and you do the same for you. Maybe it will all work out. I hope so. But I need to get a few things figured out before I can fully commit to anyone. I'm sorry David, but that's just the way I see it."

She turned and walked away. It took all the fortitude she had to keep walking, but until she knew what she was doing with her life, she couldn't ask him to make decisions based on an amorphous, ambiguous life-plan that could end up completely different from one day to the next.

She sat in her car, until she quit crying to the point it wouldn't affect her ability to drive. As she drove away, she knew it had to be this way. She hated it. She knew she might be making the biggest mistake of her life—even bigger than marrying Jack. But that was simply the way it had to be—at least for now.

Chapter 54

A month had passed since Betty informed both David and Griff, of the renewal of her battle with the disease. David could tell she was growing steadily weaker, so when Howard called a couple of weeks ago, and told him he had taken her to the hospital, it had not come as a surprise.

Since then, David had spent more time at the hospital than he had at the office. They all knew it was inevitable. This time, she had lost. She had played its game the best she could—the same game that, in months past, for a time, she had won. But in the end, she would be the loser. Howard had stopped the flow of visitors a week ago. Betty just wasn't up to it. She seldom spoke, and she ate nothing.

As David sat with Howard, while all those in white clothing just tried to make Betty comfortable, he thought of Hope. He hadn't seen her since their date for supper, when she had laid her cards on the table, and then walked away. He had ultimately concluded if she had her life all figured out, and if her plans involved their relationship, she would let him know. He would not contact her. The only exception would be to inform her of arrangements if his mother passed.

Griff had stopped by once, about a week ago. He was almost unrecognizable, both physically and mentally. It appeared he had been using, but David didn't have time to determine whether he was or wasn't. He would have to attend to Griff some other time. His mother demanded all his attention at the moment.

One aspect of the conversation with Griff was, however, a little strange, even for a user. He wanted to know about Hope—he wanted to know how she was doing, and whether "that idiot former husband of hers was still creating a problem". David explained the appeal process. Griff continued to press him, wanting to know if Jack was continuing to create issues in his relationship with Hope, to which David answered in the affirmative. He seemed much more interested in that problem, than the problem his mother had.

"Howard, can you come here?"

David was close enough to hear the whisper, and he stood.

Howard looked at David, and said, "Sit. I don't want you to leave."

David sat down, as Howard moved closer to Betty. "I'm here, Betty, I'm right beside you."He took her hand.

"Before I'm so weak…I can't tell you this, I want you to know how thankful I am you came into my life when you did."

"Don't talk, Betty. I know. I understand. Just conserve your energy right now."

"You need to know this, Howard. Just give me a second."

She took a couple of deep breaths before she continued. Her words came slowly.

"I had nothing to live for, until you came along. These past months have been the best of my life, and that was because of you."

Howard started to cry.

"You gave me strength, you… gave me drive, you gave me hope, even though… I had a pretty good idea how this was all going to end. You made my life, the time I had left, worth living." Again she paused to breathe deeply a couple of times. "My life was going along day-by-day without a reason for living. My boys were gone…grown men, and they no longer needed me…nor my motherly advice. My existence had absolutely no meaning, nor purpose, until you. You…gave…me…a reason to live. Thank you, Howard. Thank you for that."

She released his hand, and closed her eyes.

Her funeral was short and simple, just the way she wanted it.

David had attempted to locate Griff. He spent a day trying to find him. He went to all the locations where he knew Griff had frequented. He called the few friends Griff still had, asking each of them where his brother might be. None of them had any idea, and when pressed, painted an ugly picture of Griff's current life, as they knew it.

He checked Griff's prior residence, but he had not lived there for months. He apparently no longer had a phone. At least the number Griff had given him was not working. It was as if he had dropped off the face of the earth. David had to many other things to do, to continue his search. He would find time after the funeral to look for him. This wasn't the first time this had happened, and most likely wouldn't be the last.

He had called Hope, but only got her answering machine each time. He wanted to tell her about Betty, but wanted to tell her in person. He finally just left a message. He told her Betty had died and when her funeral would be held. He also told her to return his call, which she never did. David was surprised to see her sitting near the back of the church during the service. Once the service ended, as David walked through the church and out the door, Hope was waiting for him.

"David, can we talk for a moment."

"Sure, if you wish. Where do you wanna go?"

There was a small wooden bench located in a garden setting, a few steps from the door. Everyone in attendance at the funeral had found their way to their vehicles and were in the process of leaving. The area surrounding the bench was quiet, and they would be alone.

"How about the bench? Do you have time to sit for a few minutes?"

"Certainly."

As she sat, she said, "First of all, David, I just want you to know how much I cared for your mother. She was a wonderful woman. I wish I had met her earlier in life."

"Thank you. I know she thought a lot of you."

"By the way, where's Griff? Is he okay? I noticed he wasn't here."

David looked away, as he said, "I have no idea. I tried the best I could to contact him. I'm afraid he's using again, but I didn't have time to figure that out. That's my next project—to try to get him under control—again."

"I'm sorry you're having to go through that. It's not something that should be your responsibility."

"I'm his brother. I'm the only family he's got left. I'll do all I can do to help him, for as long as I can."

"I understand. Now, what's happening with the appeal?"

"It's moving along fine. I really don't think the court is going to alter anything that happened, but to be honest, I have no idea how long it's going to take for them to come to that conclusion. My best guess is between six months and a year."

"Okay. I guess there's nothing we can do about that."

"No, there isn't. Now, what about you? Have you ever come to any conclusions?"

She smiled. "Not really. My life is about as undecided as that appeal is. And it may take me as long to sort everything out, as it does for the court to rule."

He took her hand. "Are you leaving?"

"I don't know yet. I have a broker coming to look at the house this week. I just don't know if I can get out from under it without losing a lot of money. I'll know more the middle of the week."

"If you can just break even on the house, are you still planning on leaving?"

"Yes, I am. David, I just can't handle it here, and the last few weeks have made that even more apparent."

 "I understand."

"I hope so, I really do. I simply cannot live in an up and down world as I would be, if I stayed. I can't drive by his grave one morning, and then have you come home to me that night. The extreme in emotions of each day will not work for me. I'd rather be broke, and living away from here, than live that kind of life. Come with me. Please. If I do conclude, financially, that I can leave here, come with me. We'll figure it out, together."

He looked away, as he considered his response.

As he turned to face her, he said, "First of all, you know how much I love you. Don't ever question that, Hope. Maybe someday I can leave here, but not much has changed since we last discussed this. I really can't even consider it right now. The timing is just not right. My brother needs me. I have a practice I can't leave. I got alimony...I got..." He hesitated, then smiled and said, "Maybe, someday...but not now, not the way things are."

Hope looked down, released his hand, and said, "I understand."

She stood and wiped the tears from both eyes. "I'll let you know what's going on. I'll give you a call when I know what I'm doing."

He nodded, and watched as she walked away.

Chapter 55

Griff sat in a car a friend had loaned him, parked in an alley. It was now completely dark. If the present was any indication of the past, in about thirty minutes Jack Whitmore would be walking out the back door of an apartment building where his secretary lived, and into the ally where he sat waiting.

Jack had been so easy to figure out. The pattern was one he followed twice each week. Most of the time it was on Tuesdays and Fridays, but it was always twice a week. One of those nights he would leave by 6:30 or 7:00 p.m. But there was always the *other* night when he would stay just a little later. Griff assumed that was necessary to accommodate his secretary who most likely regularly complained about his speedy departure home—to his wife.

He had watched him for weeks now, and the pattern was always the same. Griff had concluded tonight should be the night he stayed later, since the visit earlier in the week was a short one. He really wasn't worried about anyone seeing what he was about to do—the alley between the two apartment buildings went from nowhere to nowhere. During the time he had been watching Whitmore's movements, not one vehicle, nor one individual, had passed between the buildings.

He knew he needed a bath. He could smell himself. It had been a while. But most likely after tonight it wouldn't matter.

Griff tried to get a better view of the door—the windshield on the driver's side was cracked and it was imperative that he know the exact moment Jack walked out that back door of the apartment building. Timing was critical.

Luckily, he had made a few friends at the shelter. He had no method of perpetuating the plan without his friend's vehicle. He no longer had a vehicle of his own.

As he waited, he thought about the last six months. His life had turned into a living hell. No money. No home. No vehicle. Recently he learned his mother had died. He never had heard from Kristy—smart woman. She could ascertain a loser when she saw one. Then there was Mr. Chase, who was looking all over town for him. On a couple of occasions, it had only been by luck he had avoided his men. Griff knew when he found him, he would punish him in ways that would involve unbearable pain, and then finish him off.

He had concluded there was no way in hell that would happen to him. Tonight, he would end his own life before he ever let Chase touch him.

Griff wore plastic gloves. He would need to enter Jack's car, and nothing in the vehicle could indicate it was him that had committed the murder. He would do this for David and for Hope, but it was absolutely imparitive his brother not be connected to what he was about to do, in any repect.

Griff had walked the alley on two prior occasions, once during the day and once during the night, looking for those pesky security cameras. There were none.

He was so ashamed—he never even saw his mother before she passed. He never had the opportunity to attend her funeral. As he approached the church that day, he saw Chase's men. They were everywhere. There was just no way he could take a chance. Luckily, he hadn't had to rely on Chase for his drugs—an old friend had provided him with enough drugs to keep his body satisfied, yet cognizant enough to formulate this plan.

As he watched, Jack walked out the back door of the apartment building right on time. Thankfully, he was a true creature of habit.

He watched as Jack walked to a small, empty parking lot near the end of the alley, and pulled out his car keys. He then quickly opened his car door, and quietly shut it, as he pulled the .22 caliber pistol from the pocket of the light weight jacket he was wearing. His victim never heard, nor noticed a thing until Griff was near and Jack's car door was open.

Griff shoved the pistol into his back, and said, "Get in. Move over to the passenger side, and do it right quick."

Jack started to turn, and Griff shoved the pistol further into his ribs, as he said, "Keep quiet. Get in or I'll shoot you right here."

"Okay, okay. I don't have much money on me. I…"

Griff pushed him down and into the seat, then followed him through the driver's door. Once Jack was situated in the passenger seat, Griff pulled the door shut.

Jack said, "What the hell's going on here? I'll give you all the money I have on me. I can even get you a little more if you'll take me to my office."

"Give me your wallet."

He only took it to appear to those investigating, that the confrontation was a robbery.

Once he had his wallet, he said, "I don't want your money. This is for Hope and David."

He shoved the pistol tight against Jack's body to muffle the sound and pulled the trigger. Jack let out a loud breath of air, and his head lunged sideways, toward Griff. Once that happened, Griff put his hand behind Jack's neck, and held him forward. He then placed the end of the barrel of the pistol against Jack's check and once again, pulled the trigger.

Jack's head lunged sideways against the passenger window, then slumped forward, now leaning against the dash. It was more than obvious he was dead.

Griff opened the driver's door, closed it quietly, and walked back to his own vehicle. He got behind the steering wheel, and slowly drove out of the alley, and down the street towards the entrance to I-40 east.

Griff continued to watch his rear-view mirror, just to be certain. He knew there was absolutely no way anyone had seen what occurred. He knew it, but he also wanted to continue to reassure himself that he hadn't been seen.

As he drove towards the east, he thought of all the good times he had had with his family—with his brother. He remembered the joy when both he and Kristy had finally decided the construction business was the way out of all of their problems—and the resulting desperation he had felt when it had all come to an unsuccessful conclusion.

He had nothing left. He had no plan for the future. He had no hope for a life that was any different than what he had endured in the last few months. That wasn't enough. He concluded his best option was the one he was pursuing tonight.

On the way to his final destination, he momentarily left the Interstate and drove to the shores of Piercy Priest Lake just east of Nashville. He exited his car, walked down to the edge of the water, and threw the pistol he used to kill Jack, as far out into the lake as he could. Griff knew there was one chance in a million anyone would ever find it.

Even if they did, it would be virtually impossible to then connect it to the murder of Jack Whitmore.

He disposed of Jack's wallet in a large trash container, filled near capacity, that was situated near a picnic area close to the lake. Back in his vehicle, and on the Interstate, once he had driven by the exit to Mount Juliet, he found the exit he was waiting for. He left the roadway, driving north into the hills. Not far from the exit, he found a farm lane which led to a small clearing in the trees.

It was dark, but he had been here before—he knew the way. About a mile down the lane, he stopped the car. Before he exited, he pulled a small folded piece of paper out of his shirt pocket and left it in the seat of the car. Hopefully, the note would help explain his suicide to David.

He exited the vehicle, and with the aid of a small flashlight, walked into a small clearing. There, using his light jacket as a pillow, he lay down in the grass, and looked up into a sky filled with a million points of light. He had pulled the needle out of his jacket pocket, right before he wadded it up into a pillow. Griff knew from experience, once he pushed the plunger as far as it would go, he wouldn't need to worry about waking up.

Griff took one last look around. He took a deep breath and once more thought about the complete mess he had made of his life. He inserted the needle and shoved the plunger forward, until it could go no further. Tears filled his eyes, and he felt them roll down his checks. Not long after, he closed his eyes, and finally, for the first time in his life, left all his worries behind.

Chapter 56

"So have you learned anymore about Jack's death?"

It had been a couple of weeks since Jack Whitmore had met his untimely demise. Both Ann and Hope sat in a small coffee shop located within a mall not far from Ann's home. Hope had called her while Ann was shopping and said she needed to talk. Ann told her they could meet at the same coffee shop where they had met many times before.

"No, I've heard nothing."

"What a horrible thing to have happened. I can't imagine how his wife must feel, finding out he had been murdered *and* was having an affair. Apparently, there were no eye witnesses and not a clue as to whom might have done it."

"That's also what I understand to be the case."

Ann hesitated before she said, "By the way, how are you and David doing?"

"I haven't seen him since his mother's funeral. I did talk to him briefly on the phone. I needed to find out how Jack's death impacts our case."

"What'd he tell you?'

"He was concerned the money Jack had, would pass to his wife, since both most likely had their names on all of their accounts. There might not be anything left in Jack's name alone, to pay off the judgement if we do win the appeal. I've given up ever collecting anything from it."

"At least the jury found him responsible."

"Yes, I guess we did get that done."

"How's the house situation? Any potential buyers, or have you forgotten about it, and just decided to stay here?"

"I wish I could, Ann. But that's just not possible. Yesterday, I signed a contract selling it. I need to be out within the next few weeks. I'm in the process of lining up a moving van and getting everything ready to ship."

"Good, I guess. I know it's what you want. I just hate to see you go. I hope you know what you're doing. Are you still going to be in a bind financially?"

Hope hesitated for a moment, then reached for her purse, and pulled out a couple of folded papers. She handed them to Ann, and said, "I got this in the mail this morning."

Ann took the papers, unfolded them and started to read.

Dear Hope

I know you don't know me, but I know you. We have a lot in common. We were both married to Jack. I have no doubt your marriage had to have been as unstable as mine. He was not a nice man, and I'm sure you paid a price for being married to him, as did I.

I finally know for certain what was going on. He was murdered outside his secretary's apartment house. I confronted her, and found out she had been having an affair with him for years.

I knew he hid money when the two of you were going through the divorce. He cheated you out of hundreds of thousands of dollars. Even though I knew what was going on, I said nothing, ignoring my conscience, just assuming he knew what he was doing and concluding it was his business, not mine. But I have found that conclusion impossible to live with, especially now, when I know at least half of all the money I have because of his death, should belong to you.

I have enclosed a cashier's check for what I feel is your share. I have made certain there are no taxes of any nature due from you concerning the amount you are receiving.

Don't contact me to discuss this gift. I believe it is the right thing to do. I knew that as soon as I came up with the idea. Jack had few redeeming qualities. I'm truly sorry either of us had to go through the hell that resulted from a marriage to such a horrible man. Hopefully the money will help heal the pain.

Best of luck,
Beth

Ann looked at Hope, eyes wide open, and said, "How much was the check for?"

Hope pulled the check out of her purse and handed it to Ann.

Ann took the check, looked at it, and then at Hope. "Three hundred forty-two thousand dollars! *Are you kidding me?* Is this legit?"

"Yes."

"What are you going to do?"

"Exactly what she told me to do—keep the money, and leave her alone."

"Why aren't you excited? You act like this is just another day."

She looked down at her cup of coffee, and said, "Because I have no excuse not to go. I now have everything that stopped me from leaving. But, I'm still leaving him behind."

"Jack's gone now, Hope. You don't have to worry about him anymore. You could stay. You don't have to leave him behind."

"I can't. It wasn't just Jack. There were and *are* many issues here, and it's just time for me to get out. I really thought I might be able to get David to go with me. I'm going to try and convince him one more time. I have an appointment with him in a half hour."

Gail escorted Hope into David's office.

She walked in, and as she did, he said, "Morning Hope, nice to see you."

She sat down looked at him and said, "Don't do that. Don't be angry with me. I know you're upset I'm leaving. So am I. But let's don't leave it this way.

He starred at her for a moment, then said, "You're right. It's just so damn hard to let you go. I wanna go with you." He hesitated. "But we've discussed all this before. I know where you stand, and I'll not ask you to change your mind again."

"You have no idea how hard this is for me. It's killing me. I so badly want you to come with me, to start a new life with each other, together."

"I know you do, as do I. Maybe, in the near future…maybe we…"

"Tell me about the appeal. Is it all basically over?"

"I don't know. What worries me the most is whether there's any money left in Jack's name to collect the amount, if the court *does* rule in our favor."

"There probably isn't."

"Whatta you mean? Why would you say that?"

"Here, look this over."

He read the letter from Beth, looked at the check, smiled and said, "Well, I guess that takes care of your money issues."

"Is there anything I need to do—or to be aware of?"

"Not really. Deposit the check. You want me to contact Ted and arrange to end the suit?"

"You might as well. Do I owe you? I don't wanna leave town owing you anything for what you did for me concerning the suit."

"You owe me nothing. What about the house?"

"It's sold. I signed the contract the other day. You'll be getting copies of everything. I want you to do whatever you need to do to finish up the sale for me."

"I'll take care of it. Are you ready to leave?"

"Yes. I need to line up a moving van, but that's about it." She looked down, and said softly, "One more time before I walk out your door—is there any way I can convince you to come with me?"

"Not really. Certainly, not now. I guess you haven't heard about Griff. He's missing. No one has seen or heard from him in weeks. I need to find him. I have no idea where to look, or what to do. I can't leave here now, Hope. I have all this business to handle, and …"

She started to cry.

He stood and walked around his desk. He took her hand, pulled her up, put his arms around her, and whispered, "Is this it? Is this the last time I'll see you?"

She wiped away the tears and looked away as she whispered, "I guess."

"I love you, Hope. You need to understand that and understand why I just can't leave here—at least at the present."

She looked at him and said, "Does that mean you might leave here in the near future—that there might be a chance for us?"

"Maybe. That's all I can tell you. Maybe."

She kissed him on the cheek, then backed away, turned and walked out of his office.

Chapter 57

It had been 13 days, 23 hours, and ten minutes, since she had walked out of his office. David had to check his watch to make sure of the exact number of minutes.

As he looked out his window, he wondered what she was doing—where she was.

He had a long day ahead, with a number of appointments. He wondered how his schedule would look if he were with her—would they hike, would he work until late in the day, then meet for supper, or would they sit by the fire most of the day and ...

"Morning. Your schedule looks pretty involved. It appears as though the conflict between husbands and wives is growing increasingly popular. I don't think you've ever been busier."

David swiveled around and said, "Morning, Gail. How was your evening?"

"Fine. Whatta ya thinkin' about? You seemed deep in thought. Maybe Hope? Was she part of your thought process?"

He smiled. "Probably was, Gail. Yes, she probably was."

"You heard from her?"

"A couple of times. She's doing fine. She still wants me out there, but I've told her it's just not possible, not now."

"Probably need to rethink that. Now, that's just my opinion, but I know you—and I've seen you without her the last couple of weeks. You need her. At least that's my opinion, for what it's worth."

"I miss her, I know that."

"By the way, have you heard any more about Griff's death? Have they come up with any other information or are they even looking?"

"No. They gave me the note, and it appears that's the end of it. They have no doubt he committed suicide, and they led me to believe they're finished with their investigation."

"Again, I'm so sorry. What a way to end it all."

"Looking back, I think it was just plain inevitable. I did everything I could do to help him as did mom, but in the end, he was his own worst enemy." He paused for a moment, thinking about the morning law enforcement contacted him. "His death wasn't really a surprise, but it's still darn hard to accept. By the way, I did get some good news last night."

"Oh, really. What was that?"

"My ex-wife called. She's getting remarried. That's going to end my alimony payments. In addition to that, she's getting married in a *couple of weeks*, so I don't have to wait another six or eight months—basically I'm done making payments *now*."

"Great. That should help take a financial load off you."

"You're right. You ready to go to work? I think my first appointment is in about 15 minutes."

"Yes, it is." She hesitated.

"Okay, what's going on? Why the hesitation?"

"Got some bad news."

"What is it?"

"I'm quitting."

"Excuse me. What the hell's going on? Why? What'd I do?"

She smiled, as she said, "You did nothing, nothing at all. It's just time for me to move on. I'm tired of all this divorce stuff. I got a job with a firm that does everything *but* divorce. I'm just burned out. I'm sick of all the turmoil and all the negative vibe that goes with the job. Believe me, it has nothing to do with you. I'm just sick of the work."

He thought for a moment. "What if I increased your pay? I could…"

"No, no, no, I don't want more *money,* I want a different *job*. You've been so good to me, and I love working for you, but I need to move on."

"How long are you giving me?"

"Would four weeks be enough? I was going to just go with two, but I asked my new employer if I could have four weeks, and he said that was fine."

"Well, I'm sorry to see you go. I'm really going to miss you. I hate the prospect of training someone new, but I understand. This line of work does get a little old now and then."

He waived at the judge as he walked through the front door of a small bar located not far from the courthouse.

David had already had one drink and had ordered another. He knew Henry was on his way. He had already ordered what he knew the judge would drink so it would be there when he arrived.

As his friend took his seat, the waiter delivered both their drinks.

Once David had described all the events that had happened to him during the last couple of days, Henry leaned back and said, "What are you gonna do?"

"Whatta ya mean? I'm gonna find myself a new secretary and move on. What else can I do?"

"You know, I remember so many times within the past few months, when you talked about Hope, and how much she meant to you. Then there were all those discussions about moving with her, and why you couldn't go—you just had so many things to do, so many things keeping you tied in to Nashville. Well, it seems to me, buddy, like most of those things have gone by the wayside. Don't you think you need to take a hard look at how you want the rest of your life to develop?"

"No, I…no." He studied his drink for a moment, then looked at the judge, took a deep breath and said, "Maybe I do. I've been wrapped up in so many issues for so long, I haven't stopped long enough since most of those problems have been resolved, to realize…*most of those problems have been resolved.*"

Henry smiled, and said, "You need to stop and take a deep breath, David. You need to take a look at where you've been, and where you're going. It's time to adjust to your new life and take a few moments to figure out which direction you're headed. This particular moment may not come around again. The slate is pretty well wiped clean. You got a lotta years left. You better figure out, right now, at this *very moment*, how you want to eventually look back and remember these years."

Chapter 58

She had just sat down for a cup of coffee with her neighbors. It was a beautiful morning. The sun was rising over the mountains east of the lake, and had only begun to take the chill out of the air. It was still light jacket weather, and you could see the steam rise up off the three cups of coffee sitting on the small table in front of them.

Earlier, Hope had watched as both Sam and his wife walked out on their porch. She then, with coffee cup in hand, walked over to ask if she could join them. She knew the answer before she left her porch. The three-membered coffee-club had met in this same manner on numerous occasions.

After they had discussed the weather and all their neighbors, which was standard conversation at each coffee-club meeting, Sam said, "So Hope what's your plans for the day?"

"You know, I'm really not sure. I need to stock up on groceries, and I need to call a friend of mine in Nashville."

"Is the friend that gentlemen you brought with you that one time?"

"Yes."

"He seemed like a nice guy."

She looked away. She found it hard to talk about him— to think about him. Maybe a little more time would finally end the pain, but she missed him every minute of every day.

Upon reengaging in conversation, she said, "Yes, he was...*is* a nice guy."

Sam looked past Hope, and said, "Looks like you got company."

She turned and noticed a car parked in her driveway. She didn't recognize the car and the driver hadn't exited the vehicle yet.

"Oh, god, I hope it's not a salesman. If it is, I'm just staying here. I'm not going to tell him 'no' for the next hour."

All three watched as the car door opened slowly.

Hope tried to see the driver through the trees, but it was difficult. She just quit trying—not important enough to strain her eyes.

Sam said, "You know, I could be mistaken, but that looks a little like that guy that you brought with you that one time."

Hope sat up, situating herself in her chair so she could see. There were two trees directly in her line of sight. She stood and walked to the end of the porch to get a better view.

All of a sudden, she backed up, turned and said, "Gotta go. Be back... sometime..."

She took the steps two at a time, then ran down the pathway connecting the two cabins, finally reaching her driveway just as David started to turn around after shutting his car door.

She reached him as he turned, threw her arms around him, then kissed him, as he embraced her.

"Tell me you're here to stay, please, please tell me you're here to stay," she whispered.

He leaned back, looked in her eyes, smiled and said, "I'm here to stay."

She kissed him again and again, until he smiled and said, "Should we take this reunion inside. The neighbors are watching."

They walked up the steps, and once inside the door, she kissed him, then held him, refusing to let go. Finally she said, "Apparently everything worked out. Have you got any more of those loose ends to tie down?"

"No. I have a little office work to clean up, but very little. It won't take me but a couple of days to handle that. Even though all of those many issues are cleaned up, it was still…it was still hard to leave my home. To leave everything I knew. It was hard."

She whispered, "Not long ago, someone I really admire, provided me with a little insight about love and about life. I've concluded it's pretty darn accurate, too."

"Okay. Fill me in. What was it?"

"He once told me, 'A committed heart can be hard to control'. And you know, I've found that to be pretty darn accurate."

He smiled, pulled her close, and never let her go.

ABOUT THE AUTHOR

J.B. Millhollin has written a number of mystery/legal thrillers. Whisper of Hope is, however, a slight departure from prior novels, in that this story centers around the relationship between both the major characters, more than it does their legal issues.

He continues to reside near Nashville and has written a number of new stories using Nashville and the surrounding area as a backdrop. If you enjoy his novels, stay in contact through his Facebook author page, Twitter, and his website at www.jbmillhollin.com. Leave your email address at his

website, and he will contact you concerning the release of
future novels.